HER BILLIONAIRE SUNRISE

BILLIONAIRE COWBOYS SECOND CHANCE
ROMANCE AT SUNSET RIDGE BOOK 1

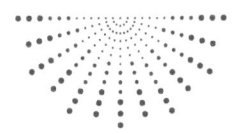

BRENDA CLEMMONS
KATIE WYATT

Copyright © 2022, 2025 by Brenda Clemmons

Copyright © 2022, 2025 by Katie Wyatt

Copyright © 2022, 2025 by Royce Cardiff Publishing House

All rights reserved.

No part of this book may be reproduced in any form or by any electronic or mechanical means, including information storage and retrieval systems, without written permission from the author, except for the use of brief quotations in a book review.

RoyceCardiff
Publishing House
WHOLESOME INSPIRATIONAL ROMANCE

Dear Reader,

It is our utmost pleasure and privilege to bring these wonderful stories to you. I am so very proud of our amazing team of writers and the delight they continually bring us all with their beautiful clean and wholesome tales of, faith, courage, and love.

What is a book's lone purpose if not to be read and enjoyed? Therefore, you, dear reader, are the key to fulfilling that purpose and unlocking the treasures that lie within the pages of this book.

THANK YOU FOR CHOOSING A INSPIRATIONAL READS BY ROYCE CARDIFF PUBLISHING HOUSE.

Welcome and Enjoy!

CONTENTS

Reader Note	1
Would you like a weekly FREE book?	4
A Personal Word From Brenda	6
1. Lee Evans	9
2. Jenna Miles	35
3. Lee	59
4. Jenna	97
5. Lee	127
6. Jenna	151
7. Lee	180
8. Jenna	210
9. Lee	237
10. Jenna	265
11. Lee	293
12. Jenna	318
13. Lee	346
Epilogue	376
Sneak Peek! Book 2	385
Did you Know?	414
Discover the Bestsellers by Brenda & Katie	416
About The Authors	419

READER NOTE

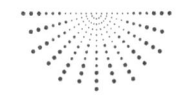

Welcome to Sunset Ridge: Where Faith, Love, and Second Chances Ride High

If you're looking for clean Christian Western romance packed with heart, adventure, and second chances, the *Billionaire Cowboys of Sunset Ridge* series is the perfect escape.

The cowboys of Sunset Ridge may have wealth now, but their lives have been anything but easy. Each of these six rugged, faith-driven men has faced life's toughest challenges—loss, betrayal, illness, and even the shadow of murder. Their trials have taught them to lean on their faith, work hard, and always show kindness, even when life feels impossible.

But the storms of life keep coming, and the stakes are higher than ever. When strong, courageous women arrive in their lives, bringing hope, love, and a renewed sense of purpose, these cowboys realize they've been given a second chance—not only at love but at life itself.

Each book in the series is packed with suspense, heart-pounding drama, and the beauty of redemption. From overcoming sabotage to navigating illness and even solving mysteries, every story will keep you turning the pages, rooting for these couples to find their happily-ever-afters.

Will faith and love be enough to see them through the storm?

Or will the darkness that follows them threaten to tear them apart before they can ride off into the sunset together?

Join us at Sunset Ridge, where faith lights the way, love is worth fighting for, and second chances are always possible.

This six-book series will leave you inspired, uplifted, and longing for your own slice of cowboy romance.

Thank You for Reading! 😃📖

Brenda

WOULD YOU LIKE A WEEKLY FREE BOOK?

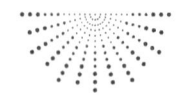

Join our Preferred Reader Club, and we'll send you exclusive free reads—straight to your inbox! As a VIP reader, you'll also get early access to new releases, Exclusive updates, Special discounts, and limited-time offers so you'll be the first to dive into our latest stories, filled with adventure, faith, and romance.

Just sign up with the links below & Start Reading for Free!

Katie Wyatt

Clean and Wholesome Historical American Mail Order Bride Christian Western Romance

Signup today!

Brenda Clemmons

Clean and Wholesome Contemporary Christian Western Romance

Signup today!

A PERSONAL WORD FROM BRENDA

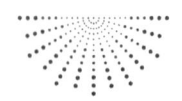

Dear Readers,

First, let me say how grateful I am that you've chosen to spend your time with Her Billionaire Sunrise: Billionaire Cowboys Second Chance Romance at Sunset Ridge. This story holds a very special place in my heart, and I poured so much love, hope, and faith into every word.

Writing Lee and Jenna's journey was an emotional experience for me. As I brought these characters to life, I found myself walking alongside them—feeling Lee's longing to make things right, Jenna's guarded pain, and the quiet strength that grows when two hearts learn to trust again. I laughed, cried, and prayed with them through every twist and turn of their story.

This book isn't just about romance; it's about redemption, forgiveness, and the kind of love that reflects God's grace even in life's most uncertain moments. I hope as you read, you'll feel the small-town charm of Sunset Ridge, the depth of the characters' faith, and the beauty of a second chance at love.

I truly hope this story resonates with you, warms your heart, and reminds you that even in the darkest times, there is always light waiting to shine through.

Thank you for being part of this journey—I'm so excited to hear what this book means to you!

Read all the books in Billionaire Cowboys Second Chance Romance at Sunset Ridge by bestselling authors Brenda Clemmons and Katie Wyatt!

Book 1 Her Billionaire Sunrise

Book 2 Her Billionaire Love on Fire

Book 3 Her Billionaire Learning the Ropes

Book 4 Her Billionaire in Hawaii

Book 5 Her Billionaire No Place Like Home

Book 6 Her Billionaire Thief of Hearts

With love and blessings, 😊📖

Brenda

1
LEE EVANS

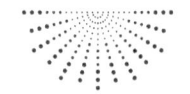

It was raining when Lee Evans passed the sign, which read "Welcome to Sunset Ridge."

Torrential rainfall wasn't unusual during July, and Lee slowed his car, not wanting to get in an accident on his first day back in town.

How long had it been since he had stepped foot in the town he had once been so desperate to get away from?

Well, desperate was a harsh word. He had simply wanted more. Running a ranch had not been in his blood, even if he had descended from a family of proud land owners.

No, Lee had other interests.

Interests that had paid off in the long run, leaving him a wealthy man with billions to his name. He had God to thank for bringing him this far in life.

As he entered the town, his eyes immediately went in search of the gas station, which he knew was around here. He drove the car under the shade of the station and got out to put in some fuel. Hands in the pockets of his expensive suit trousers, he looked around. He had barely entered the town, and already he could see that everything was the same. The faded building of Sunset Ridge High School stood tall and proud, bearing the lashing rain as it had for decades, the paint having peeled years ago.

Next to it was the town hospital, along with a car rental agency. The town businesses were arranged in parallel streets in the center of the town, ranging from major establishments to necessities to eateries. The residential areas followed a similar pattern on the outskirts. Behind the town was a thickly wooded area locals enjoyed hiking and hunting in.

He was about to get in his car when his eyes fell on the gas station, and his stomach rumbled. He hadn't eaten since he got on the plane, and the flight to Rock Springs from New York was a long one.

Lee made his way inside and saw a teenager sitting behind the counter, chewing gum and looking at something on his phone.

Lee grabbed a bucket of chips and a cold bottle of water and brought them to the counter. When the boy lifted his head, he looked oddly familiar for some reason, but then Lee had been away from this town for ten years. There was little doubt to him that he would seek familiarity in everyone he saw.

"You a tourist?" the boy asked bluntly, peering at him as Lee opened his wallet.

"No."

"You're definitely not from around here," the teenager scoffed. "You look too rich."

Lee would've felt flattered if there had been an ounce of awe in the boy's voice. However, he was just sneering at him, and Lee just picked up the bag and water. "Well, you're wrong. Have a good one."

He could've taken the back road as he drove toward the ranches, but Lee chose to drive through the town, taking in the local eateries. The old diner was still there, and even in the pouring rain, he could see that the parking lot was not vacant. A block down, a coffee shop caught his attention and he scowled.

He could have just gotten coffee and a sandwich instead of the chips. However, a quick glance at his watch made him decide to just stick to what he had. He was pretty sure that there would be something to eat once he reached his destination.

He passed by the large town hall and shot it a quick look.

It hadn't lost any of its magnificence.

The further he drove into town, the more people he began to see. Everyone was just going about their day, not bothered by the rain. Lee recognized a few people, but he didn't stop his car. A lot of these people were those he had abandoned and just walked away from.

He pushed his car along the dirt road, which led outside of town toward the ranches. Surrounded on both sides by open fields, Lee found himself gradually relaxing.

It was surprising to him that even ten years away from this place had not taken away the feeling of home. Those feelings just expanded into something nostalgic when he turned left into an extension of the road, which led to a large house.

Lee stopped in the driveway and stared up.

Home.

He didn't get too much time to reminisce because just then a tall man with a beard white as snow and wrinkles that gave away his age pushed open the door, walking out slowly, perhaps to see who it was. He stared in the direction of the car, and Lee felt his heart almost stop as he looked at the man who had raised him.

Benjamin Evans looked old and tired, and the fact made Lee's chest tighten as guilt wormed its way into his heart.

"Who is it?" his grandfather growled, his normally thunderous voice filled with weariness.

Lee got out of the car, not even caring to grab his umbrella.

He saw his grandfather freeze when he saw him. "L-Lee?"

Seeing the giant of a man stammer his name in shock made Lee cover the ground between them even faster, leaping up the steps to come and stand in front of his grandfather.

"I'm home."

His grandfather just stared at him, not saying a word.

Lee glanced in the glass of the house's window to check if he had really changed all that much. His brown hair was a little longer, and his eyes were just as brown as they had been when he had been a ten-year-old, stepping into this house for the first time. He realized that he looked more like his grandfather now than he did when he had stormed out of the house a decade ago, throwing harsh words over his shoulder.

"You finally remembered me?" Benjamin Evans growled.

Lee scowled. "You're making it sound as if I forgot you. I invited you multiple times to come visit me. I even sent you plane tickets!"

"And I told you that I don't like big cities!"

Lee just sighed. "You could've still come and visited me. It wouldn't have killed you."

"You could have come home for a visit!" his grandfather rumbled.

And once again, like always, the two were at a standstill, so Lee just decided to be honest. "I got a call from Midge. You're sick."

His grandfather turned around and started walking inside. "I'm old. I'm supposed to get sick."

Lee followed after him, looking around. Nothing had changed. The flowery wallpaper that had probably been his grandmother's idea was still there, along with the furniture in dark shades of brown and a few family photos in the living room.

Lee decided to retrieve his suitcase later and followed his grandfather into the kitchen. "Why didn't you tell me?"

His grandfather took out a pot from the fridge and placed it on the table before turning to glare at him. "So, now every time I sneeze, I have to report it to you?"

"Gramps," Lee scowled. "You know that's not what I'm talking about. You've had two heart attacks!"

"Blah." His grandfather shuffled around the room, grabbing a plate from the cupboard and a spoon before setting them down on the table. "Those darned doctors will call anything a heart attack now. Sit. Eat."

Lee glared down at the mac and cheese in the pot and ignored his rumbling stomach. "I have the doctors' reports, Gramps! I'm not ten anymore where you can just say anything you like and I'll just nod my head along like a fool."

"Hah!" Benjamin snorted, sitting down heavily into a chair. "You were never that obedient to begin with! You always had a bit of your father in you. Rebellious to the core."

Lee gaped at his grandfather. "Rebellious? Me? You've lost your memory too? Is that it?"

"Sit down and eat, boy!" Benjamin roared, and Lee's body reacted almost instinctively and sat down before he realized what had happened.

He frowned. "I came here to look after you."

"I don't need looking after."

Lee put a few spoonfuls of the pasta on his plate. "Well, that's not up to you, is it?"

"This is my house and—eurk!"

His grandfather began coughing, one hand grabbing the table for support as his body violently spasmed in terrifying-sounding coughs.

Lee's spoon clattered to the floor as he rushed toward his grandfather. The older man was wheezing now, his lips stained with blood.

"This isn't just a simple heart attack, is it?" Lee stared at him as he crouched down to Benjamin's level, horror gripping him. "What else is going on that Midge didn't tell me?"

His grandfather shook off his hand. "Nothing. She just—"

He wheezed again, clearly struggling to draw in air, and Lee felt his stomach sink. "Gramps, why didn't you tell me things were this bad?"

Benjamin wiped the blood off his mouth with a paper napkin and balled it up. "It's not as bad as it looks."

"It looks like you're dying!" Lee exclaimed, frustrated. "We're going to the hospital!"

He tried to grab his grandfather's arm but was shaken off.

"I'm not going anywhere!" the older man growled. "Just because you showed up here doesn't mean you can tell me how to live my life now!"

"I'm trying to save your life!" Lee snarled. "I don't want you to die!"

"How is it going to affect you?" his grandfather retorted. "Did anything that happened to me in these ten years affect you? You didn't even come back for a visit! When I broke my arm, it had no effect on you or your life. So, how will my death impact you? You'll shed a few tears and then go back to your life."

Lee froze at his words. His strong, larger-than-life grandfather sounded hurt.

"You know that's not true," Lee looked up at him, his heart clenching. "If I cared so little, I wouldn't have put my whole life on hold just to come look after you. And this is the first I'm hearing about your arm. You never said a word."

Benjamin refused to look at him and Lee added, "I was just trying to build a life for myself."

"Well, I needed you here!"

His grandfather was not a selfish man by nature, but now, when Lee actually looked at him and noticed how old he had become, he realized that he should've visited sooner and stopped putting it off for so long.

"I'm sorry, Gramps." He sighed. "You know how I am. I get lost in my work. But you're right. I should have been here. I should've visited you more."

He saw his grandfather sneak an annoyed look at him. "You still have that way about. Can't you just let me stew in my anger?"

Lee gave him a small grin. "If I let you stay angry at me, you'll be adding more of my transgressions to the list. I can't afford that."

His smile broadened when his grandfather hit him upside the head. "You always were a smooth talker."

With a fierce temper that blazed like a forest fire, his grandfather was just as quick to fizzle down as he was to light up in flames.

The fight hadn't even begun yet, but for now, Lee knew that he was partially forgiven.

"Thanks, Midge." Lee leaned down and kissed the elderly woman's cheek

Midge had been with them since Lee could remember. Small, with bright blue eyes and prominent dimples when she smiled, the loving housekeeper had always been a crucial fixture in both his and his grandfather's lives. She was family.

"Make sure you drink plenty of water, Lee," Midge scolded him. "This isn't New York. It's very hot here. You have to stay hydrated. And give me your suit so that I can press it for the Sunday church service. My boy looks so fine. You'll have girls tripping over themselves when they look at you."

"Yes, yes," Lee grinned.

He saw her uneven gait and he frowned. "Why aren't you wearing the heel I sent you? It'll help you walk easier."

"I do wear it," Midge told him, stirring the pot and throwing in some diced carrots. "I just forget sometimes."

When Lee made a face at her, she looked over her shoulder at him, offering him her sweetest smile. "You're a good boy, Lee."

Lee wouldn't have minded spending the rest of the afternoon with the woman who was almost like a mother to him, but he had things to get done and people to meet.

"Does Gramps ever leave the house now?" he asked.

Midge sighed. "His condition has just been getting worse over the months. It kills him that he can't even work on the ranch. He has to settle for supervising."

Lee's heart sank. From everything that Midge had told him, he was looking at a pattern, and he didn't like it. His grandfather was on a serious decline, and while there were bouts of recovery, he was still growing weaker and weaker.

He should have come home earlier. He should have known.

It was almost as if Midge could read his thoughts because she said quietly, "You can't control everything, Lee. You don't know how happy your grandfather is that you're back. The fact that you're spending all this time with him is the best gift you can give him."

Lee disagreed. He could always have done more, but he didn't want to upset the older woman.

"You're right. I should get going now."

Kissing her cheek, he departed for the neighboring Fairweather Ranch that belonged to the Miles family.

As a child, he would traipse through the patch of woods that separated his grandfather's ranch and the one that belonged to his best friend's parents. But it had been years since he had seen Cole Miles.

Or his sister.

It would be better to drive up there.

The ground was still wet and muddy from yesterday's rain, and the air was so humid that it was difficult to breathe. Lee parked his car in the driveway of the Miles family house, and he was making his way up to the front door when he saw a slender brunette with long hair in a thick braid. She was wearing fitted jeans and a red-checked button-up with the sleeves rolled up.

He must've been staring at her because she clearly noticed somebody watching her, and she lifted her head. Her eyes were a light hazel color, and when he saw her face, it wasn't difficult to recognize her.

"Jenna?" Lee mumbled, stunned by her transformation. The last time he had seen her, she had had braces on her teeth, chopped hair, and had looked every bit a tomboy.

But even if everything else had changed, her face hadn't.

"Can I help you?"

There was no recognition in her friendly voice, and Lee tried to say something, but his mouth was too dry.

Fortunately, however, the front door opened, and a man stepped out who shared a remarkable resemblance to Jenna.

"Hey, I'm heading out to the diner. I'll head off for my shift at the firehouse from there."

Cole's voice was deeper than he remembered, and Lee realized that the friends he had left behind had changed. Of course, it was silly to expect them to have remained the same way as they were in his memories, but Lee had to wonder what else had changed in the decade he had been gone.

Cole Miles saw his twin looking at Lee, and he turned to follow her gaze.

Lee mentally prepared himself not to be recognized, but to his pleasant surprise, Cole gaped at him before grinning. "Well, I'll be! If it isn't Lee Evans!"

From the corner of his eye, Lee saw Jenna flinch, but Cole was bounding down the steps. "When did you get back, man?"

Lee grinned. "Yesterday. How's it going?"

His friend's easygoing nature had not changed, and Lee accepted the one-armed hug.

"Why didn't you call me and tell me you were coming? I would've picked you up at the airport!" Cole looked over his shoulder. "Jenna, it's Lee! You remember him, right?!"

Lee shot a hopeful look toward the woman, who had once been among his closest friends, and he saw the disgusted look on her face. "Sorry. I don't remember every rat-faced scoundrel that I've encountered."

With that, she stormed up the steps of the porch into the house.

Lee stared after her. "Is she angry with me?"

His friend shrugged casually. "Well, you never said goodbye to her. And rat-faced scoundrel isn't the worst insult you could get from her. She's developed quite a creative vocabulary."

Lee found his gaze lingering on the closed door before he turned his attention back to his friend when Cole asked, "What brought you back? Last I remember, you swore you wouldn't return to this small town."

Lee's expression darkened. "Gramps. I heard he was sick, so I came back to look after him."

He saw Cole close his eyes briefly, his smile disappearing. "Yeah. I was actually thinking of contacting you. I don't even know how he got sick. He was the picture of health, and then a few months ago, he just collapsed. The doctor said it was a heart attack, and Mom decided to oversee his meals to make sure he was following the doctor's orders. But he had another one last month."

"I was actually on my way to the hospital." Lee stuck his hands in his pockets. "Wanted to talk to his doctor. I tried to talk to the old man, and he just blew up at me. Took me down a wonderful guilt-trip lane."

Cole's lips twitched. "He was so angry when you left. Broke things all over the house until Midge stepped in and gave him a piece of her mind. She lectured his ear off until he calmed down."

"I sent him tickets multiple times to fly down and stay at my penthouse for a few weeks," Lee groused.

"I don't know what you're complaining about," Cole studied him. "The problem that I see is that both of you are far too prideful. If you had come down here, he would have won in your head. And the same went for him." His friend sighed. "Come on. Have lunch with me, and we'll drive down to the hospital. I'll introduce you to Ben's doctor. You might even be surprised when you see who it is."

Lee decided that was a good idea.

They drove down to the diner, which was a half hour drive.

It wasn't very crowded since the lunch rush hadn't really started. As they entered, Lee looked around and noted that the place had changed. The decor was different, as was the furniture. His eyes fell on a woman behind the counter who was talking to a customer. Her hair had pink highlights, and her eyes were a light blue, the familiar dimple in her cheek leading him to recognize her.

"Lily runs the place now?" he asked.

Cole grinned. "Her father decided to retire, and she took over the whole place. Changed the entire look and everything. She's quite a businesswoman."

Lee wasn't surprised.

Even when they were young, Lily Shawn had had the smartest brain of them all.

She looked up at them when they entered, and it took her a minute to recognize him before she blinked. "Lee?" Before Lee could say anything, she was quick to dart out from behind the counter and wrap him in a warm hug. "You're back!"

He hadn't expected a warm reception from his friends, but they kept surprising him. Jenna's cold brushoff was what he had been prepared for, if he was completely honest.

"How was New York?" Lily beamed at him. "Tell me everything!"

As Lee found himself dragged to a stool on the counter, he realized that he was beginning to feel as if he had never left at all.

"New York is exciting. My company is doing well."

"Just well?" Cole rolled his eyes, slapping a hand on his back. "My boy here is worth billions. That software you designed really took off!"

It was true.

Lee's interest had always been in technology, and he had created cybersecurity software, which had become so successful on its launch that he had ended up getting a patent for it and starting his own company. He hadn't expected his friends to follow his work, and it felt surprisingly pleasant that they did.

"So, how long are you here for?" Lily asked, returning behind the counter and holding out two menus to them.

Lee shrugged. "As long as Gramps needs me. I can work remotely for as long as necessary."

The menu had also changed, he noted, but there were a few things on it that Lily hadn't removed.

"You still have Yetty's shepherd pie on here?" he said, pleased. "Can I have a slice of it? And one for Gramps."

Cole also placed his order, and after informing the cooks, Lily returned to them. "So, how is Ben? I haven't seen him in a long time."

"He doesn't leave the ranch much," Lee told her. "At least, that's what I've heard from the men working for him."

He didn't mention how they had told him that Ben tired easily lately and had begun to eat less.

Lee had a lot of regrets, but he wasn't a man who focused on his mistakes. He would rather do something about them. And right now, that meant making sure that his stubborn old grandfather received the care that he needed.

"So where are you two off to after this?" Lily asked.

Cole jerked his thumb in Lee's direction. "I'm taking this one to the hospital, and then I'm going to go to work."

Lee took a sip of the lemonade that Lily had just put in front of him, glancing at his friend. "I never took you for a firefighter. I thought you wanted to inherit the ranch."

Cole grinned. "Firefighters get more women. And besides, Jenna is way more equipped to handle the ranch than I am. I still work part time there, but Jenna's the foreman."

"Your parents are fine with that?"

"Are you kidding? Dad's over the moon! She's reduced his workload by half, and the men listen to her. He gets to sit back now and relax. I mean, he still works, but not as much as he used to. I heard both my parents are thinking of retiring in another few years, so this works out."

Lee blinked. "So, who takes over the ranch then?"

Cole shrugged. "We'll cross that bridge when we get there. Besides, Jenna loves that ranch way more than I do. And it's not like I don't have a full-time job."

"You working in the fire department here?"

Cole shook his head. "Nah. The staff here is full. I've been with the Rock Springs one for a couple of years now. I recently became lieutenant."

Lee studied him before smiling. "Good for you."

Just then, the food arrived and both men dug in.

Lee didn't waste any time after his lunch because he knew that his friend had to get to work. Taking his grandfather's share with him, he made his way to the hospital.

Lee saw a few familiar faces as he followed Cole to the first floor. His friend was checking his watch before he stopped in front of the door, which read, *Sharon Westfield, Head of Cardiology*.

Lee frowned. "Sharon?" He turned to look at Cole. "The same Sharon?"

Cole smirked. "You'd best believe it." He gave a sharp rap on the door. "Hey, Sharon! It's Cole. I got somebody here who wants to meet you."

There was a clicking sound as the lock was disengaged and the door opened, revealing a blonde woman with a short haircut, wearing a doctor's coat. She was clearly having lunch because a spoon was sticking out of her mouth.

"Darn it, Cole. I've told you multiple times not to disturb me during lunchtime! Whatever you did to yourself, I'll look at it later."

Disregarding her complaint, Cole pushed the door open. "See who I have with me?"

Lee smiled at her. "It's been a long time, Sharon."

He saw Sharon go slack-jawed at the sight of him and then she scowled, glancing at Cole. "You're pulling my leg."

Cole made a face. "He's right in front of you! How can I—Lee, tell her!"

Lee glanced between the two of them. "I don't really know what to say. How did you end up a doctor?"

Sharon scratched her head. "Well, going to the doctor every two days was starting to become expensive. So, I just decided to become one."

To any other person, the excuse would've sounded weird, but Lee remembered Sharon as one of the most reckless people he had ever met. Sharon used to be the king of bad ideas. If there was any activity that could possibly endanger your life, Sharon would be at the forefront of it.

No wonder Cole had sounded so confident that Lee would be shocked by who his grandfather's doctor was.

"So, you're treating Gramps?" Lee asked.

Sharon stared at him for a moment longer before returning to her seat. "Well, the two times he was brought in after the heart attack, I took a look at him, so I guess you could say that. He's missed two appointments, so I'd appreciate if you bring him in tomorrow."

Cole put a heavy hand on Lee's shoulder. "I'm going to leave now. I'll be late for my shift. If you're free, let's meet up for dinner tomorrow. I have a day off."

Lee agreed, and once his friend left, he turned his attention back to Sharon, his expression serious now. "So, what is happening to Gramps?"

2
JENNA MILES

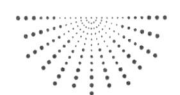

"How is the harvest coming along?" Jenna climbed down off Thunder, who nuzzled at her hand lovingly. She let the horse lip at her hair as she waited for the man walking toward her to reach her.

Paul's face was red, and he took off his hat and fanned himself. "We're meeting our daily goals, so it's good. One of the men had heatstroke, so I sent him to lie down."

Jenna frowned. "If we are a man down, I'll pitch —"

"Nah," Paul shook his head. "You've been working since morning. You should probably take a breather. Besides, I already called the

Dawson boys to help out. They're nearly done with the repairs of the shed, so they'll be along in another few minutes."

Jenna gave him a look. "Fine. Let me know the progress at the end of the day."

She decided to walk back to the stables with Thunder, and once she had the beautiful black horse settled in for the evening by giving him a good rubdown, she made her way back to the main house.

The long walk allowed her to sort out her thoughts. Jenna had never imagined that she'd run into Lee Evans again. She also never thought that the gangly teenager that had once been her partner in crime would become so handsome. There was a confidence with which he carried himself now.

Maybe that's what happens when you become a billionaire overnight, she mused.

She'd waited months for a letter, a phone call, anything, but Lee had decided to cut all contact with her.

Sticking her hands in her pocket, Jenna stomped on the ground as she walked, irritated. She knew that a decade was a long time to hold a grudge, but the child in her, who had waited for so long and had been so badly hurt by her close friend, had not forgiven him.

"Not like it matters," she muttered to herself as she began to climb the steps up the porch. "I'm hardly going to see him again."

"See who?" came her mother's voice as Jenna entered the kitchen.

"Nobody, Ma," Jenna grumbled. "What's cooking? I'm starving!"

"Don't you have food at the cottage?"

"I don't cook as well as you do," Jenna replied lazily.

She saw the lasagna resting on the kitchen counter and immediately grabbed a plate, only for Glenda Miles to scold, "That's not for you."

Jenna gave her an incredulous look. "Not for me?" She glanced down at the golden crust of the lasagna before giving her mother a betrayed look. "But, Ma!"

"It's for Benjamin." Her mother shooed her

away. "His boy's back, so I thought it would be nice to send something up there."

"Why are you cooking for Lee?" Jenna complained as she sank into one of the chairs. "I've been working all day! You know I missed lunch, don't you?"

Her mother wandered over and pressed a kiss on top of her head before depositing an apple in her hand. "Here. Eat this."

Jenna had never felt more insulted in her life. "I don't want an apple! I want your lasagna!"

"Now, sweetheart." Her mother proceeded to layer the lasagna with a transparent wrap to protect it. "I've got another one in the oven. Just go drop this one off, and by the time you get back, it'll be ready."

Jenna was about to protest when the last part of her mother's statement registered on her, and she was immediately on her feet. "No. Oh *no!*" She waggled a finger in her mother's direction. "I'm not going there. You can't make me!"

Her mother gave her an easy smile. "Of course you're going. It will be a nice reason for you to see Lee again. You two were such good friends."

"*Were*, Ma," Jenna snapped. "Past tense. I can't stand his stupid face now."

Her mother gave her a disapproving look. "I would hardly call his face stupid, sweetheart. It's been three days since he came back to town, and all the women are gushing about how good-looking he's become."

"So?" Jenna glowered at him. "Just because he's good-looking, he gets your lasagna? *Dad! Are you hearing this? Ma's got designs on Ben's grandson!*" Jenna yelled toward the study, and her mother slapped her upside the head, scolding,

"Shush! Your dad's taking a well-deserved nap. Now, stop complaining and go."

Her mother was using her stern voice, and even if Jenna was an adult woman in her late twenties, she was still terrified of her mother when she used that voice.

"Fine!" she hissed, grabbing the dish and reaching for her keys. However, she still wanted the last word, so she pointed at the oven before leaving. "When I get back, that lasagna had better be ready!"

Her mother just rolled her eyes and waved her off.

Jenna stormed over to her truck, carefully placing the lasagna on the passenger seat before sliding in and starting the truck.

She really didn't want to see Lee.

Even if it was childish behavior, she didn't care. He had turned his back on her and had not even afforded her a goodbye before leaving on his eighteenth birthday. He hadn't even sent her a card on her own birthday.

She couldn't even just drop the lasagna off and walk away. If she ran into Benjamin, he would ask her to stay for a cup of coffee, and since she liked the old man, she'd always end up saying yes.

The drive was shorter than she had hoped, and Jenna rang the front doorbell, praying silently that Midge, the housekeeper, would answer.

But luck was not on her side, it seemed, because the door opened to reveal a freshly showered Lee, standing there in gym shorts and nothing else.

So, he works out, was the first thought that popped into Jenna's head before she growled at herself and fixed her eyes on his confused face.

"Here." She thrust the dish into his startled hands. "Ma sent this. You can choke on it for all I care."

Satisfied, she was about to climb down the steps when she felt a firm hand curling around her wrist. "Wait!"

Jenna's eyes widened as she turned her head slowly to look down at the hand holding her wrist, her gaze incredulous. She lifted her eyes to his and said after a long second, "If you don't let go of my hand in three seconds, I will shoot you. Don't think I won't."

She saw the alarm on Lee's face as he quickly released her hand. "Sorry. I just—" He scratched the back of his head sheepishly. "I just wanted to ask how you are."

"I'm fantastic," Jenna said coolly. "You got something else to say?"

When Lee just blinked in that familiar awkward way of his, Jenna started walking down the steps again.

"Wait," He tried again, and Jenna closed her eyes, her back to him, wishing that she could just turn around and deck him. "Why don't— Why don't you come in for a bit?"

Jenna turned to face him. "I got better things to do with my time."

"Jenna," Lee's face fell. "Are you still angry with me?"

Now, she could play it one of two ways. Either she could get angry and beat him up as she used to do when they were children, or she could play it cool and act unaffected and just insult him and walk off.

Jenna had never been a "lady" lady. Unlike her cheerful brother, she was quick to use her fists rather than her words. She had just about balled her hand into a fist when she heard a gruff voice. "Jenna, is that you? Get in here, girl!"

Jenna's jaw tightened, and she forced her hand to relax before pushing her way past Lee.

"Ben," She greeted the old man. "Ma sent over a dish of lasagna. *For you.*"

She enunciated the last part, and she saw Ben's eyes go toward his grandson and then back to her before he smirked and said, "Come on. Have a cup of coffee with me."

Jenna shuffled her feet reluctantly. "I really have to go—"

"Have you eaten?" Ben demanded, and she pursed her lips.

"I mean, I've got food at home—"

"Lee, make the girl some coffee—"

"I'll have juice."

"Pour the girl some juice, and for God's sake, go put a shirt on!"

Hearing Lee get scolded gave Jenna enough satisfaction to follow Ben into the kitchen. She poured both of them a cup of juice and returned to the foyer to pick up the lasagna that had been left there.

"Go get me a plate, too, and one for yourself," Ben ordered. "You look like you haven't eaten in days. Why do you look like you've lost weight every time I see you?"

Jenna, who had been reaching for the plates in the cupboard, froze.

She had to force her voice to remain calm as she replied, "Maybe you're finally losing your sight."

When she turned around, she saw Ben watching her with a sharp look in his eyes. His voice was steady. "When did you get so good at lying?"

Jenna just stood there, holding his gaze, and her smile was tight. "When I learned that certain white lies do more good than harm."

She set down the plates and grabbed some utensils.

"Jenna—"

"Did you go to the doctor, or do I have to drive you there myself?" she asked, baring her teeth in a fierce smile.

She didn't like the color on Ben's face. His cheeks were sunken, and his hands were not quite steady. He had been slightly better last time she had seen him. All that energy seemed to have faded.

Ben blanched, growling, "Lee forced me to go. They took a look at me, but I'm fine. Just old age."

"Two heart attacks in quick succession isn't a sign of old age, Ben," Jenna scowled. "I know plenty of old people. Nobody's having heart attacks every other day."

"You talk too much!"

"Because I'm worried about you!"

"Bah," Ben burst out. "I'm fine. The doctor said my heart looked fine."

"He said you were growing weaker every day." Lee's cool voice came from the doorway as he walked in, now wearing a black button-up shirt. "You're supposed to be resting. Not working."

"Somebody has to run this ranch!"

"You can sit and delegate!"

Jenna watched the argument unfold as she put a piece of lasagna on Ben's plate and then hers. Her voice was slightly calmer now. "You want me to help out? You know I'm good for it."

Both men shut up at her words and then Ben glanced at her, grumbling, "You've already got too much on your plate."

"I can spare some time here," Jenna said firmly. "You really don't look that good."

"I'm fine!" Ben snarled, and Jenna scowled.

"You don't look fine, old man!"

Ben glowered at her and she glared right back, not in the least intimidated.

Finally, she saw him look away, muttering, "Do what you want. You always were a stubborn one."

Jenna grinned. "I'll talk to your foreman before leaving."

She heard the scrape of a chair and saw Lee sit down. Immediately, Jenna started eating the lasagna, determined to leave as quickly as possible.

"Slow down. What's your hurry?"

Jenna chose to ignore him, and it was only when Ben said gruffly, "Slow it down, Jenna," that she stopped.

"I have to get back," she told the older man, who just lifted a brow and glanced between her and Lee, his voice sarcastic.

"Oh, is that all?"

Jenna finished her juice and got to her feet. "Well, I gotta go. I'll drop by tomorrow in the afternoon, Ben."

She saw the narrow-eyed look the old man shot her, but she ignored it and grabbed her keys.

She was almost out the door when Lee called, "Jenna!"

She was beginning to get really annoyed with him. Couldn't the man just catch a hint?

"What?" she snapped, immediately rounding on him. "What do you want?!"

Her harsh tone clearly took him aback, and he stared at her. "I just want to have a civil conversation."

Jenna gave him a long look. "You can't be serious. Listen, I don't want anything to do with you. There are ten thousand people in this town. You're welcome to go find one of them to have a friendly chat with."

As she turned around and walked away, he shouted after her, "You're acting childish!"

Jenna tossed a look over his shoulder, "Then don't talk to me!"

Once in the car, she slammed on the accelerator and left in a flurry of dust.

"An iced coffee, please," Jenna called out, sinking into the large couch in the center of the coffee shop.

The other occupant of the couch didn't so much as budge when she sat down, and Jenna nudged him with her foot. "Hey, Dean."

"It's Pastor Dean," the brown-eyed blond glared over his book at her. "And will you stop kicking me?"

Jenna frowned. "Sorry. Fine. Listen. I heard you're selling your old truck."

The pastor immediately blinked. "You interested in buying?"

"What're you asking for it?"

When the man named a price, Jenna narrowed her eyes. "You're supposed to be a man of God. What're you scamming people for?!"

Pastor Dean put down his book, glowering at

her. "I had work done on that truck! I got new tires and installed a CD player."

"It breaks down once a year!"

"Once in eighteen months!" he corrected her. "And it's vintage!"

"Just because something is old doesn't make it vintage," Jenna sneered. "Kathy, tell him he's being ridiculous! I'm not paying that much for an old broken-down truck!"

Kathy Middleton was Pastor Dean's older sister by a year, and they shared the same gentle brown eyes and blonde hair. That was where their resemblance ended.

Kathy was sweet tempered, with a soothing nature, which was probably why her coffee shop was so popular.

"Stop it, Dean," she scolded, handing Jenna her cup of coffee. "We both know that you're not good at haggling."

Dean scowled. "I'm not haggling. I tuned up the car." He turned to Jenna. "Why do you even want it? You just bought a truck last month."

Jenna glanced around before lowering her voice. "I wanted to get it for Laurel. She was talking about how a car was out of her budget, so I thought I'd buy yours and fix it up myself."

Kathy's eyes widened, and she covered her mouth in a soft gasp. "Oh, that's just so darned sweet of you!" she nudged her brother. "Come on, Dean. Don't be a miser."

Dean gave both of them a begrudging look. "I mean, if it's for Laurel, then I can probably fix it up myself."

His sister didn't give him a chance to continue, adding, "Why don't we split it, Jenna? Her birthday is coming up in a few months. We can go fifty-fifty."

The offer wasn't all that bad, and Jenna tapped her finger against her knee. "I don't see why not. It's just still really overpriced…"

The pastor scowled at them. "Fine. I'll lower the price."

Jenna beamed at Kathy. "Thanks."

Her friend patted her on the shoulder before sitting on the arm of the couch next to her. "So, have you run into Lee yet?"

Jenna frowned. "Yeah."

Pastor Dean, who had been trying to return his attention to the book, looked up. "I heard you called him names. That's unchristian, Jenna."

"I didn't call him names," Jenna gave him a baleful look. "I just have better things to do with my time than catching up with him. And he's a stinking weasel."

"Jenna," Kath murmured her name in a knowing voice, and Jenna narrowed her eyes.

"I don't know why you're so hostile toward him," Pastor Dean commented, studying her. "The Bible says to forgive and let go of your anger. It's like poison."

Jenna gave him a long look. "Didn't you not talk to me for a week because I stole your blueberry muffin last month?"

Pastor Dean huffed. "That was different. Stealing is a sin. And I do mean it about forgiving him for whatever he's done. You'll feel better about it." He picked up his book and opened it on the bookmark. "Just like how I felt better about forgiving you for stealing my muffin."

Jenna just threw her cushion at him, which he deftly warded off with his arm.

Kathy left to tend to another customer, and Jenna picked up a magazine as she sipped her coffee. She hadn't run into Lee yesterday when she had gone to help out Benjamin. She had mentally prepared herself to run into her childhood friend, but he hadn't been there.

It wasn't like she was disappointed.

She had been just shy of eighteen when they had parted ways. Seeing him reminded her of a time that she just wanted to forget. Initially, she had thought that Lee leaving without so much as a goodbye had been painful. It was only later that she realized that it hurt more that he had never once looked over his shoulder, as if she had never mattered to begin with.

Lee Evans had broken her heart and stomped on it, and now that he was back, he suddenly wanted to have a *civil conversation?*

She didn't think so!

As she looked through the magazine, she saw something splash in her coffee, and she blinked in surprise.

It was then that she felt the wetness on her upper lip.

Wiping it off, Jenna saw the deep red color and her heart went still. Setting aside the coffee quickly, she lowered her head and rushed toward the bathroom, trying not to catch anyone's attention. Once inside, she locked the door and looked in the mirror.

She saw the blood coming out of her nose, and she turned on the tap and tried to wash it off. The coughing that started almost immediately was a terrible sound, although not an unfamiliar one, and Jenna held onto the marble counter as she coughed, the white sink turning red.

Her knees gave way and she sank to the floor, unable to stay vertical. Grabbing toilet paper, she tried to cover her mouth with it as the violent coughs refused to stop. Curled up, she discarded blood-soaked tissue after tissue until her system had finally had enough.

Feeling weak, she looked around at the mess and closed her eyes wearily, the tough, smart-mouthed shell disappearing to reveal the exhausted, frightened woman inside.

She knew she should get up and clean the area before someone suspected anything, but she felt so tired, and her chest hurt.

Her eyes still closed, a silent prayer left her heart. *Lord, give me strength.*

Just then, there was a knock on the door and Kathy's voice sounded, her voice quiet. "Jenna, let me in."

"I'm fine," Jenna croaked.

There was a heavy silence, and then she heard a key being inserted into the lock and the doorknob turned.

Kathy entered the bathroom, and her expression grew tight as she saw the scene. She quickly turned and closed the door behind her, locking it once again.

"It's nothing—"

"Shut up," her friend said harshly, so different from her usual sweet tone. Her voice shook as her eyes glittered with tears. "Just stop talking." She leaned down next to Jenna and checked her pulse before asking. "Where is your medication?"

"I have to get the prescription filled again," Jenna muttered, her voice hoarse.

"How could you get so careless?"

"It's not working, Kathy." She looked up at her best friend and closed her eyes to avoid seeing the pain in Kathy's eyes. "Don't cry. Please. I can't stand it."

She heard a soft sound, and then her friend muttered, "I wasn't crying. Come on. Sit on the seat. I'll clean you up."

Jenna struggled to help her, but Kathy just brushed away her hands, saying sternly, "Once we are done here, go rest in my office. I'll bring you something that's easy to eat."

Despite her friend's attempts to make her rest, Jenna insisted on helping clean up her mess. Her hands were shaking as she rolled up her sleeves after wiping the floor, and she saw the large bruise on her arm from where she had hit it against the counter.

She quickly rolled her sleeve back down.

After her diagnosis, bruises had become commonplace to her. Her body was filled with them.

She threw the last piece of toilet paper away and stood up, determined not to ask for assistance. She murmured another silent prayer for strength as she grabbed the edge of the counter and propelled herself into a standing position.

"Go to my—"

"I'll go home," Jenna muttered. "I just want to go home right now."

"Fine," Kathy gave her a long look before holding out her hand. "Give me the prescription. I'll get it filled for you and drop it off after work."

"I can—"

"Jenna!"

"Fine!" Jenna gave in. "It's in my bag."

As they walked out, Jenna refused to let Kathy help her. Her face was pale, but she just smiled at her friend as if to reassure her that everything was fine.

However, when they got back to the sitting area, Jenna froze at the sight of the person who was now sitting in her spot.

Lee was talking to Pastor Dean, who was grinning.

He hadn't seen her yet, so Jenna took a good long look at him. She could no longer see the lanky, shy teenage boy anywhere inside him. He had become a man in these past ten years.

Her heart throbbed in pain, and she looked away. "Just grab my purse, Kathy."

She wasn't up to facing Lee.

However, he had just spotted her, and he quickly got to his feet. "Jenna?"

Jenna just gave him an indifferent look. She didn't know how effective it was because she could feel how clammy her skin was and how pale she looked.

Lee approached her, his face concerned. "You don't look so good. Are you okay?"

Out of all people, Jenna could not bear to have Lee look at her with any sort of pity in his eyes, so she instantly lied. "I'm fine. I'm just on my way out." Her panic was so instant about being discovered that she was actually civil to him.

"You look like you're about to pass out," Lee said insistently, his tone hard as he grabbed her arm. "You're definitely not fine!"

"Will you let go of me?!" Jenna tried to shake off his hold, but he was far stronger than he had once been.

She saw Kathy look at her, and when she saw the sudden gleam in her friend's eyes, Jenna had a very bad feeling. But before she could do anything, her friend immediately said, "Why don't you drive her home, Lee? I think she's a little overworked."

Jenna glared daggers at her traitorous friend, who just smiled at her. "I'll come by in the evening with the things you asked for. I'll bring your car."

And just like that, Kathy picked up Jenna's keys and pocketed them, along with the prescription that she deftly plucked from Jenna's bag. Kathy winked at Jenna and waved. "Have a safe drive!"

Her body aching, Jenna had no choice but to let Lee drive her back to the ranch as she silently prayed that she didn't end up murdering him on the drive there.

3
LEE

JENNA LOOKED WEAK AS SHE HUDDLED AGAINST the car in an attempt to stay as far away from him as possible.

Lee glanced at her every now and then.

She looked angry.

The girl that he remembered was nowhere to be found in Jenna. While his friend had used to be bossy, she had never been one to hold a grudge like this. Jenna had always been a smart-mouthed girl who never failed to make him laugh, even at his worst moments.

He didn't know how to fix this.

He wanted to be back on good terms with her and to see her smile. But all he got was death glares and snippy comments. He knew she was angry, but aside from an apology, there was not much he could do.

"Wait, where are you going?" Jenna sat up immediately when she saw him take a right turn. "That's not the way to the ranches."

"I'm taking you to the hospital," Lee said firmly.

Jenna's head whipped around to face him. "Have you lost your mind?"

Lee ground his jaw. "Have you taken a look at yourself in the mirror? You look like death warmed over."

He saw a flare of what looked like panic on Jenna's face before she snapped, "I don't want a knight in shining armor, Evans. If you can't even do the simple task of taking me home, I'll just jump out of the car and find my own way back."

Lee was beginning to get frustrated with her, and he scowled. "Can't you see I'm worried about you?"

"And can't you see that I don't want your concern?" she retorted. "If I needed to go to the hospital, I would go to the hospital. But I just need to get home. Now, if you feel you're not up to that task, tell me right now. Don't go making decisions for me. You're not my keeper."

Lee flinched at her harsh words. She wasn't wrong. But she also couldn't see what he was seeing on her face.

It might have been a long time since they had crossed paths, but Lee knew that she really meant it. She wouldn't hesitate to jump out of the truck.

That reckless streak that Jenna had always had had clearly never faded away.

"Fine," he growled. "Fine!"

He swerved the car around.

He stewed in his own anger at her stubbornness as he drove toward the dirt road that led in the direction of the ranches. He glanced toward her, and she was looking out the window, refusing to even face him.

"You know," he gritted out. "I thought you would have changed when I got back. But you're the same stubborn, selfish person you've always been."

His words were meant to draw a reaction, and he saw her flinch, but she didn't say anything, just kept looking out the window.

"I've tried to be nice to you and reach out, and you're just acting like a child," he spat out, his feelings hurt over how she was treating him. "You keep acting this way, and you'll lose everyone around you."

This time, Jenna let out a bitter laugh that made the hair on the back of Lee's neck rise at how unnatural it sounded.

"Good," she said coolly. "Now, if you're done with your attempts to get under my skin, either drop me by the side of the road or drop me home. Either way, I don't care."

Her unaffected tone drove him mad.

It was only once Lee had entered the business world that he realized he was good at negotiating and getting his way. It was a skill he had never realized he had. As a child, he had been quiet, reserved, patient, and just a little bit stubborn, and it was those qualities that had eventually made him so successful at the negotiation tables.

This was why Lee had assumed that all he had to do was wait out Jenna's apparent anger, and once she calmed down and figured out that he wasn't going to retaliate, things would go back to normal.

But he hadn't expected how easily she would get under *his* skin and cause him to lose his own composure. He wanted to shake her and get her to stop sniping at him like an angry cat.

"You're just angry with me because I didn't say goodbye to you when I left!" he retorted. "I can't believe you're acting like a child over something so small and so long ago."

He heard her snort, and she turned her head and gave him an amused look, which was tainted with disgust. "You can try and gaslight me all you want, but I'm not eighteen. I am a woman running an entire ranch. All my employees are men. I didn't get them to respect me by being so easily manipulated. You should do us both a favor and just stay out of my way."

Lee winced at her words and he muttered guiltily, "I'm not trying to gaslight you."

"Sure you're not," Jenna sneered. She was about to add something when her phone rang and she dug it out of her bag.

Lee saw the way her face brightened when she saw the caller ID, and then she put the phone to her ear. "Nick!"

Nick?

Who is Nick?

Lee didn't know what this Nick fellow said, but Jenna's lips curved in a smile so beautiful that his heart nearly stopped. She had always been pretty, even as a tomboy, but right now, after all these years, she had become even more gorgeous.

Not that he cared.

But it irritated him when he heard her say softly, in a tone so unlike the one she had been using with him, "Sure. I'll pick you up tomorrow. You can just stay at my place. We'll pick up a pizza and some movies."

Lee's hands clenched on the wheel, and he scowled.

Who in the heck was Nick? And why was he staying with Jenna?

He saw Jenna glance toward him and heard her lower her voice. "I'll call you when I get back home. Yeah. I missed you too. Love you!"

The last part made Lee freeze, and when she ended the call, he saw that some of the color had returned to her face, and she looked happy.

It annoyed him.

"So, you've got a boyfriend now?"

"Can you go ten minutes without talking, or is that just too difficult for you?"

Lee muttered something under his breath. Back in New York, he had women throwing themselves at him. It wasn't that he expected Jenna to do the same, but she could at least not treat him like he was a leech or something equally disgusting.

"I just asked a question," he scowled. "Who's Nick?"

Jenna just shrugged.

"How old is he? What does he do?"

However, Jenna had apparently decided to hold her tongue for the rest of the drive. And at some point, Lee just gave up. He had barely reached the main house when she told him to stop.

"The house is another ten minutes away," he frowned.

"I don't live at the main house," she responded.

Her voice was almost faint, and he saw that her color was gray once more.

"Jenna." His anger faded, replaced by alarm.

"I'll get out here," she muttered, and when she started fiddling with the door handle, he was forced to stop the car.

"Listen—" Lee tried to talk to her, but she just got out.

"Thanks, I guess," she muttered and then closed the door after her, making her way to a small cottage in the distance.

Her gait was slow, almost as if she was using every ounce of her strength to just move. She had taken just a few steps when Lee could not bear it any longer.

He parked the car alongside the road and got out, striding over to her and grabbing her bag.

He saw Jenna's eyes widen, and when she was about to say something, he snapped, "Oh, just save it. You look like you're dying."

"I'm—"

From the looks of her, she clearly wasn't in any state to put up a fight, and he defiantly scooped her up, ignoring her squirming and shouting, and began to carry her toward the cottage in the distance.

"I don't need your help!" she shouted at him, her struggles weak.

"Shut up, Jenna," he retorted. "Either accept my help, or I will go over to your parents and tell them what's going on. And if they look at what I'm looking at, they will drag you to the hospital. It's either me or them."

He hadn't expected her to fall for his bluff. She went still, her cheeks flushing slightly in anger, and she turned her head away stubbornly.

Lee didn't say anything further, but he was definitely suspicious. This was not somebody who was just overworked. Something else was wrong. But she wasn't going to tell him, clearly.

When they reached the cottage, Lee was surprised to see how well it was maintained. Jenna had built an entire garden around the cottage with a single pathway leading to the front door. Since it was the middle of summer, the flowers were blooming, and the place looked straight out of a fairy tale. She hadn't just planted one type of flower. There were different flowers planted in a deliberately haphazard manner to create a stunning sight.

For a moment, Lee stood still, mesmerized. "It's beautiful."

"Thanks," Jenna muttered, not ungraciously. "Now, will you let me down, *please.*"

The "please" was progress in Lee's book, and he lowered her to the ground. She gripped the wooden fence that surrounded the house and dug into her bag for the keys.

Her breathing was a little uneven, and she walked slowly but steadily toward the door.

He waited at the fence, and when she looked

toward him, he lifted his hands. "I'm not asking to be invited in."

"Good," she retorted, and he felt a hint of hurt at her clear dismissal. But when he turned around to leave, he heard her mutter, "Thanks."

He paused and looked over his shoulder, wondering if he had imagined it, but she had already closed the door behind her.

"Here," Lee put down a bowl of soup in front of his grandfather. "Eat this."

His grandfather looked down at the murky-looking liquid and then gave him a suspicious look. "Are you going to poison me? What is this?"

"I contacted a dietitian in New York and shared your results with him. He gave me a nutrition plan for you to follow."

However, his grandfather was not willing to play along. "Sharon told you that there's nothing wrong with my arteries. They're not blocked or anything."

"Gramps, you've had two heart attacks," Lee glared at him. "She's still trying to figure out what's going on, but even she agrees that this is a good diet for you to be on."

"So now you're calling me fat?"

Lee closed his eyes and whispered a loud prayer for patience before saying, "Gramps, this is good for you. It's even got beef in it. I asked Midge to prepare it. I know you like her cooking."

On hearing that the housekeeper prepared it, Benjamin gave the soup a reluctant look.

However, Lee knew that his grandfather would not touch the dish if he was around, so he said, "I have a call to make, so I'll step outside."

He did have a call to make to his assistant, Natalie.

"How's the progress going on the new patch?" Lee sat down on the porch stairs, his back to the door.

Natalie had been with him for a couple of years now, and he could hear her clicking on something on her laptop before she replied, "I forwarded you the progress reports. When do you think you'll get back?"

"I don't know," Lee said honestly. "My grandfather isn't in good shape. I'll be here for at least two months for now, and then we'll see. I'll fly in if there's anything urgent. You'll let me know?"

"Of course," Natalie replied, and then she hesitated before saying, "I know it's not my place, but don't you think your grandfather would be better off in a hospital here rather than a small-town hospital?"

Lee ran his fingers through his hair. "I did think of that, but the doctor treating him right now is a specialist. She's an old friend, but I still had her checked out. Her credentials are solid. I've also sent his reports to a specialist in London. She should get back to me in a few days."

"I see. Let me know if I can help."

After Lee ended the call, he lingered around the porch steps, watching the men work in the distance. It was lunchtime, so a few of them were leaving to the mess hall.

Hillside Ranch had been in his family for three generations, but when Lee had initially been raised in a one-room apartment in Denver. He hadn't even known about his grandfather until he was ten, and the old man had shown up at Lee's parents' funeral when they'd both died in an accident.

Lee's lips curved slightly at the memory, which was still clear as water in his head, even after all this time.

His grandfather had approached him as he had sat there alone in the rain, no relatives, no friends to take him home. He had been soaked to the bone and had dimly been wondering if he should try and catch the bus.

And then he had looked up in surprise to see a dark umbrella over his head and a tall man with a white beard, studying him.

His grandfather hadn't had the best bedside manner, but he had raised him, and after a while, Lee had begun to appreciate and care for the old man who made sure he was fed three times a day. He no longer had to figure out a way to get to school every day. His grandfather drove him.

He didn't have to wonder what the best way was to sneak something to eat out of the fridge. Midge would call him for mealtimes, and all three of them would eat together.

Unlike Lee's parents, who had been uninterested in worrying much about their child, Benjamin had looked after all his needs.

Lee settled his chin on his folded arms, his knees pulled to his chest as he stared idly out into the night. There was no way he could have just left his grandfather to his own devices when he had heard about the heart attacks.

But he hadn't imagined how bad things would be when he arrived. His grandfather was getting worse as the days went by. He seemed weaker, almost listless at times. Those large hands that had once shielded him from the world were now frail and weak. They could barely hold a spoon without dropping it.

Lee felt his heart tighten in pain and he swallowed, refusing to think of the inevitable.

Benjamin Evans still had years in him. There was no way his grandfather would—

He shook his head, discarding the thought that was too agonizing to even consider.

He had time.

Hearing a scrape inside the kitchen, he stood up and walked inside.

"What're you doing?" Lee arched a brow at the old man, who had clearly been in the midst of getting seconds from the pot on the stove.

Benjamin glowered at him. "I need food. You think that meagerly bowl is going to fill me up?"

Lee tried not to grin. "Pour me one, too, will you?"

His grandfather acquiesced and brought over two bowls to the table before digging into the second helping. "So what's going on with you and that Miles girl?"

Lee's good mood instantly evaporated. "Nothing. She hates the sight of me."

His grandfather gave him a long look. "I wonder why."

Lee narrowed his eyes at him. "What's that supposed to mean?"

Benjamin shrugged. "I didn't raise you to be a coward. You should've said goodbye to her. You two had been thick as thieves. After you left, she used to show up every day, asking if you had sent a letter. She did that for six months before she realized that you had thrown her away."

Lee's spoon clattered in his bowl. "I didn't throw her away! I just had to get out of this town!"

"You broke that girl's heart," his grandfather said, watching him. "You said goodbye to everybody but her."

Lee opened his mouth and then snapped it shut. It was true.

"It's complicated," he muttered.

"What's so complicated about saying goodbye to a friend or reaching out to her?" his grandfather demanded. "I know you kept in touch with Cole."

"I emailed him two years later and called him on his birthday," Lee protested.

"But you did that, at least," his grandfather said gruffly. "So what did that girl do to not even deserve that much?"

Once again, Lee had no response. He just looked down at his soup.

His grandfather shrugged. "Not my problem. She's a good girl. Hard worker too. She and you would've made a good pair if you hadn't gone and acted like a fool."

Lee's face turned bright red as he looked up. "We weren't dating!"

His grandfather scooped a spoonful of the soup, looking unbothered. "Never said you were. But maybe down the line, you could have. She's loyal, that one, to the bone. She'll make a good wife to some lucky man."

Lee stabbed his bowl with his spoon, muttering, "That's not as far off as you think."

Benjamin looked at him in surprise, "You saying she's got a man?"

"Some Nick. I heard her on the phone with him."

When his grandfather didn't respond, Lee looked up to see the old man wearing a strange expression. "Nick, you say?"

Lee frowned. "Do you know who he is? Is he a ranch hand?"

He saw amusement flare in his grandfather's eyes. "Well, not exactly. But he's special."

"Do I know him?" Lee demanded, but his grandfather just snickered.

"You haven't met him."

Lee stared at him, but he was clearly not going to get a proper answer out of the old man.

"Well, what kind of person is he?"

Benjamin grinned. "He's a good kid. Sweet, friendly. Usually attached at the hip to Jenna."

"How has she not eaten him up with that temper of hers?" Lee muttered, and when his grandfather burst into laughter, he scowled.

"Enough about Jenna," Ben said. "I have a more serious matter to discuss."

"What?"

"You should really learn a thing or two while you're here." His grandfather ate another spoonful of soup. "After I'm gone, you'll have to look after this place."

Lee froze. "I can't take care of the ranch. I don't know the first thing about running this place."

"That's why I'm saying that you need to learn."

"Gramps," Lee frowned. "I don't want to inherit the ranch. Besides, nothing is going to happen to you. You said so yourself."

His grandfather snorted. "I'm in my eighties. I'm going to die sooner or later."

"Gramps!"

"What?" Benjamin retorted. "It's true. I can't live forever. After this, you come with me. I'll show you a few things."

"I don't want to run this place. I have my own company in New York."

Benjamin set down his spoon and lifted his head to study Lee, his expression severe. "So, what are you going to do when I die? Just leave this place to rot? I spent my entire life running this ranch. I raised you on this ranch. You can't just turn your back on your home because it's inconvenient."

Lee was silent. He knew his grandfather had a point, but his heart wasn't in ranching.

"I can hire somebody—"

"Over my dead body!" Benjamin was on his feet with a roar, his face flushed. "You're not going to throw away my home to a stranger to look after!"

Lee's eyes widened. "Gramps, calm down!" His grandfather's face was an unhealthy shade of purple. "Look, let's talk about it. Gramps—"

"Ben?" came an alarmed voice from the kitchen door, and Lee found himself pushed aside as Jenna wrapped her arm around the old man's shoulders and lowered him into his chair.

"What's wrong with you?" she scowled, grabbing the glass of water and handing it to Ben. "Stop getting worked up over every small thing! You want to have a stroke or something?"

Lee watched helplessly as his grandfather allowed Jenna to care for him.

Then Jenna shot him a ferocious look that would have quelled a less brave man. "What did you say to him?"

Lee shook his head. "We were talking about the ranch. I didn't think he'd overreact like this."

"Overreact?!" his grandfather snarled, getting red in the face again. "You want to give the land I put my sweat and blood into to a random stranger because you can't be bothered to look after your home!"

"That's not what I meant, Gramps!" Lee tried to calm him down, feeling like a terrible person. However, surprisingly, it was Jenna who came to his rescue.

"Look, Ben, before you fly off your rocker again, Lee doesn't know a single thing about running this place. Would you rather he destroy the ranch or let someone manage it who'll keep this place afloat?"

Her voice was calm and steady, and Lee could see his grandfather studying her.

"Besides," Jenna continued. "I doubt he's going to hire a complete stranger. And if you're so concerned, I can look up some managers for you. You know I have contacts. And I'll always be right around the corner to keep an eye on your place. Do you think anybody will dare to run this place into the ground while I'm around?"

Benjamin wrapped his hand around hers, as if seeking support, something that terrified Lee. In this moment, his larger-than-life grandfather looked so frail that Lee felt his chest tighten. He got up, and without a word, walked out, needing some air.

I don't know how to fix this, he prayed as he walked along the dusty path, his mind in shambles. *Lord, help me know how to communicate with him.*

The brisk five-minute walk did nothing to calm him down, but when he returned, he saw Jenna standing on the porch, waiting for him. It was obvious that she had something to say.

So, Lee waited.

"Don't bring up what will happen to the ranch after he's gone," Jenna said, her eyes meeting his. "His heart can't take topics like that."

"I have my company in New York—"

"You have nothing here," Jenna cut him off. "I understand that you don't want to throw away your life and your friends there. I'll introduce some managers to you, and I would recommend that you let Ben train you while you're here."

"Jenna—"

"Don't give him another shock like that," Jenna said. Her voice was a little kinder this time. "The ranch is a touchy topic for him, and I know you didn't mean to upset him. I'll be honest with you. Things aren't really looking good for your grandfather. So whatever time he does get with you, just keep him happy."

As she walked down the steps past him, Lee reached out to grab her wrist. "He's not going to die anytime soon."

The look that Jenna gave him this time when she turned her head was a dull one, her eyes blank. "We're all going to die. Be happy that Benjamin lived a full life, and for whatever time he does have, let's make sure that he's happy."

At the time, Lee didn't really understand the gravity of her words, but he went inside and made up with his grandfather, assuring him that he would do what he wanted.

His grandfather was quick to anger and also quick to forgive.

It was two hours later that Lee, tired after trailing after the older man as he showed him the workings of the ranch, complained, "Gramps, I already know all this. Stop treating me like a newbie. I'm better with the business aspect of the ranch."

His grandfather was a little out of breath. "There's more than just the business side to this place," Benjamin groused. But he paused, probably not wanting to scare him off. "We'll get to the rest tomorrow. Come on. Let's go back."

As they returned to the ranch, Lee could see his grandfather's breathing worsen. He was struggling to draw in air, and his face was pale.

"Gramps—" he murmured in alarm as they reached the main house, but his grandfather lifted his hand.

"I'm fine. Happens from time to time."

Lee was doubtful. "Let me take you to the hospital."

"I don't need to go. I'm fine." Benjamin pushed his way into the house, and Lee rushed forward when he saw the older man nearly topple forward.

Fear began to fill Lee and once he got his grandfather settled in one of the more comfortable armchairs in the living room, he stepped out to make a call to the doctor.

Sharon picked up after two rings.

"Gramps is having trouble breathing," Lee said in a tense voice. "We were walking around the ranch, and he began wheezing. He says it's normal, but I've never seen him like this."

Sharon was quiet for a moment and then she said, "I'm in the area. I'll drop by."

Lee had barely managed to get his grandfather settled when he heard the front door open ten minutes later.

Sharon looked dressed up, and Lee wondered if she had been out on a date. She took a stethoscope out of a small black bag and conducted a brief examination even as Benjamin complained.

When she was done, she pressed her lips into a thin line. "His condition isn't great, but it's nothing that warrants a hospital stay. I mean, if you want him under observation, I can make arrange—"

"No," Benjamin shook his head, his voice weak. "No hospitals. I'm fine. I want my own bed."

Lee wanted to argue, but he knew how stubborn the old man could be.

"I'll keep an eye on him during the night," he told Sharon. "Thanks for stopping by on such short notice."

Sharon packed her medical bag. "Don't worry about it. If things get bad at night, let me know. I'll come by immediately."

Once she left, Lee noticed that his grandfather was in a pensive mood. He didn't speak much, but as evening turned into night, Benjamin was becoming visibly weaker.

Lee felt his heart sink at the sight.

"It'll be fine, Gramps," he whispered. "You'll get better. I'll make sure you do."

However, Benjamin's health deteriorated that evening, and finally, late in the night, Lee called for an ambulance.

Sharon was already waiting for them when they arrived, as were Cole and Jenna.

"What happened?" Jenna demanded.

"He couldn't breathe." Lee watched from outside the room as the team of doctors and nurses checked his grandfather. "I think his chest was hurting. He kept clutching it."

"His medicines—"

"He took them all. I made sure of it," Lee said, sinking into the waiting chair, trying to calm himself down.

"I'm going to go talk to Sharon—"

"No, you're not," Cole grabbed his twin, forcing her into the chair next to Lee, his voice stern. "Let the doctors do their job. Either of you interfering is not going to be helpful. I'm going to go get all of us some coffee."

Lee watched him go and then heard Jenna sigh.

"Every time I feel that he's going to get better, he gets worse." Her voice was unsteady, and Lee could tell how much she loved his grandfather.

His own heart was aching so much that he couldn't think straight. "Ever since I arrived, I have not seen a single good sign that he's recovering. I keep telling myself that tomorrow will be better. But he's always worse. His breathing has gotten worse, and he sleeps all the time. When he's awake, sometimes he's lucid, but lately he's a bit hazy."

He was about to go on when Jenna's smaller hand curled around his, her voice heavy. "Just pray for the best and for his recovery. All the money and all the resources in the world can't do a thing if we don't ask God for help."

Sharon walked into the room a few seconds before Cole returned. "Well, it's not good. I'm sorry, Lee. He's not doing better. I think you need to leave him here so that we can observe him and provide treatment."

Lee's knees felt weak as he got to his feet. "What do you mean he's not getting better?"

Sharon's face was grim. "His heart is failing. We can do surgery, but his chances of survival are slim."

Lee found himself reaching automatically for Jenna, who grabbed his hand.

His face was pale. "What does that mean for him?"

"It means that if he keeps deteriorating at this rate, he's only going to have a few months at best."

"But I've been doing everything you told me to do. I'm monitoring his diet and his medicines!"

Sharon shook her head, and Lee felt a sinking sensation in the pit of his stomach. "I wish I could give you an answer you would like to hear. We are still trying to figure out why his condition is getting so bad this fast. But I want to prepare you for the worst-case scenario."

"So, do I leave him here?" he finally asked, trying to steady himself.

"That would be best for at least a week," Sharon said. "I need to monitor him. I'm not going to give up just yet."

When she walked away, Lee sank into the chair behind him. Cole sat next to him, his hand on his shoulder. "I'm so sorry, Lee."

Lee just sat there silently, prayer after prayer leaving his heart, his mind blank.

"Here you go, Lee." Lily put a cup of coffee in front of him. "How's Benjamin doing?"

The diner was nearly empty since the lunch rush had just ended.

Lee had his laptop on the table, and he felt exhausted. It had been two weeks since his grandfather was hospitalized.

"He's doing better," he told Lily, who sat down across from him. "Better enough to shout at me and kick me out of his room."

Lily smiled softly. "That's got to count for something, right?"

"Sharon said I could take him home today." Lee stared down at the cup of coffee before him. "He seems to be more stable."

"Which is good," his friend said firmly. "So, why do you look so lost?"

Lee slowly looked in her direction. "I just don't know what to do. From the moment I came back to town, I could see that he was doing poorly. I guess a part of me knew what was coming, but I just kept hoping and praying that I'd get more time with him. "

"You do have more time with him," Lily murmured. "You came back. You're taking care of him. It's never too late, Lee. You can't blame yourself for leaving."

Lee flinched, and she reached out to cover his hand with hers. "It's all over your face. You went away, and you achieved something. We all have to leave the nest sometime. At times, we fly to another nearby tree, and other times to a field farther away from our loved ones. We all know how much you love and respect Benjamin. And he knows it too."

The words soothed some of the hot grief that was stuck inside of Lee's throat.

"You're right," he murmured. "I know you are. But I just look at how old he's gotten in these past years, and I keep wondering if things would have been better if I had stuck around. I know I'm crying over spilled milk, but—"

"Of course you would think that. But you were always meant to leave and forge your own path. That's what God willed for you. And you were meant to come back now."

Lee let out a heavy sigh. "I know." He did know, but it didn't help ease his guilt. However, he chugged down the coffee and got up. "Thanks, Lily."

She just smiled at him.

Tucking his laptop under his arm, Lee made his way out of the diner toward his car. Maybe his grandfather would be in a better mood now.

As he drove into the hospital parking lot a few minutes later, he saw Jenna get into her truck, and he wondered if she had come to see his grandfather again. She was coming by quite frequently, and he could tell that Benjamin enjoyed her visits. They argued half the time, and when they were not arguing over sports or ranch business, they were fighting over what to watch on TV.

But Jenna would leave with a grin and a spring in her step, and Lee's grandfather would be less fussy for a few hours after her visits.

His grandfather was sitting up in the bed when he walked in. "Where were you?"

"You told me to get lost," Lee said casually. "So, I got lost and bought you a muffin." He put the bag next to Benjamin's pillow. "How're you feeling?"

"Fit as a horse. I told you, all these doctors are quacks."

Lee rolled his eyes. "Do you want to get going then? I can start the discharge process."

When his grandfather looked pleased, Lee went to find a nurse.

THE DRIVE HOME WAS ODDLY PLEASANT. Benjamin was in good spirits, and he seemed to be doing well. When they arrived home, Midge was waiting at the entrance, and she nearly burst into tears at the sight of Benjamin.

"About time you came home."

"He's doing much better, Midge," Lee told her. "Why don't the two of you go inside? I'll bring in the bags."

When he walked in, Midge was settling Benjamin into his favorite armchair, handing him a cup of tea.

"Here," Lee turned on the air conditioner. "Gramps, don't overexert yourself. You have to take it easy."

"I know," his grandfather groused, and then he looked toward Midge. "The boy is too fussy."

"He's worried about you, Ben!" Midge scolded, putting a throw over his legs. "You be nice to him now. Drink your tea. I'll bring you some cookies to go with it."

Lee just grinned.

They spent the evening like that, sitting together in the living room. Lee worked on his laptop while Midge knitted a hat for her friend's grandchild. Benjamin sat in the armchair, reading the newspaper. His color was better, and he seemed to be in much higher spirits.

It was only when the sky turned dark that Lee told Benjamin to go to bed.

"I know you feel better, but you still have to rest."

His grandfather huffed and puffed. Finally, he gave up and just sighed as he shuffled into the bedroom, and Lee helped him get comfortable in bed.

Lee commented, "You're being oddly quiet."

His grandfather sighed again, a quiet sound so unlike him, as he stared at the ceiling. "I want you around me today for some reason, even if I also want to kick your behind."

Lee's chest tightened at the words, and he wanted to make a light joke or something, but there was a lump in his throat.

Settling in a chair, he picked up a book but barely read a few words, his eyes straying toward the old man lying so still in his bed. All his vigor from earlier in the evening had vanished, and he looked weary. There was an air of finality around his grandfather, and Lee didn't know how to shake off the ominous feeling.

It was when he thought his grandfather was asleep that he heard Ben ask, "I raised you right, didn't I?"

Lee glanced in his direction, frowning. "Gramps?"

Benjamin turned to look in his direction. "I was a little hard on you, but I gave you strong values. I was never a good father, but I hope I was a good grandfather to you."

Lee's voice was unsteady. "You were a great one. Everything I am is because of you. Everything I achieved in life is because you were standing beside me. I don't think I ever thanked you for it."

His grandfather smiled. "I'm proud of the man you've become. You did well for yourself."

Lee felt his chest turn so tight that it became hard to breathe. "Thanks, Gramps."

His grandfather didn't speak after that, closing his eyes.

A desperate prayer left Lee's heart.

For a while, there was silence, and he thought his grandfather had gone to sleep.

It was around midnight, however, that he saw Benjamin's breathing worsen.

Lee reached for the phone and called 911. "I need an ambulance!" He rattled off the address, his voice harsh, his hands shaking.

But his grandfather just watched him, struggling to breathe.

"It's going to be okay, Lee," he told him, but Lee shook his head, tears in his eyes.

"No. Don't you dare give up."

He could see the truth in his grandfather's dimming gaze.

"You were fine!" he growled, trying to keep himself together. "You still have months! Don't take him from me, God," he prayed desperately, his voice choking as he held onto the withered old hand. "I still need him."

But everyone who comes into this life has to go home at some point, and it seemed like Benjamin's time had come to return to the arms of the good Lord.

Lee watched, his heart breaking as his grandfather's eyes slipped shut.

The ambulance didn't arrive until it was too late.

And for the second time, Lee became an orphan.

4
JENNA

IT WAS RAINING WHEN THEY BURIED BENJAMIN.

It seemed like the sky was also mourning the loss of the man who was so well-liked in the town of Sunset Ridge. Lee stood apart from everyone, his face a blank mask.

Jenna watched him throughout the funeral and later, at the wake.

His responses were almost mechanical, and she knew what he was doing. He might have changed in these ten years, but he was still the same boy who had been her close childhood friend. The same boy who internalized his deepest feelings.

So, Jenna waited and watched.

People spoke sweet words, remembered happy memories, laughed at memories of Benjamin's antics. The wake was lovely, but not for Lee, who stood there like a statue.

As the sun began to set, people began to leave one by one. There were casseroles and lasagnas and cakes that Jenna put away, her own heart badly bruised at the loss of someone she had loved so dearly. She finally sat alone in the kitchen chair, tired, and leaned her head against the wall, closing her eyes.

The tears fell, hot and heavy, the grief in her heart almost unbearable.

She didn't make a single sound, just cried silently, her eyes closed.

Help me deal with his loss, she prayed, struggling with her grief.

It was when she heard the door of the kitchen open that she saw Lee enter. He looked surprised to see her and said, "I thought you left with the others."

Jenna stared at him. "I was putting away the food."

"Oh." He hesitated. "You can go now. Everybody's gone."

She held his gaze for a second longer before looking away. "I think I'll stay." She stood up. "I'll make some tea. Sit down."

Jenna heard a soft chuckle, and she looked over her shoulder to see him laughing, his eyes sad.

"What's so funny?"

"You being nice to me," Lee replied. "It's been two weeks since I got here, and you've been nothing but mean. I got so used to it that I almost forgot that you have this nice side to you as well."

Jenna didn't respond for a moment, pouring water into the electric kettle and turning it on.

"When you left, I came here every day," she looked outside at the pouring rain. "At first it was because I thought you might've left me a letter or something. Or maybe that you would send one, and I didn't want to miss it. But after a while, I noticed how lonely Ben was and how he would look forward to my visits. I made it a point to come here every day after classes ended. I would help him out with the housework and the ranch for a few hours before I went home. I did that for quite a few years until I became busy with my own ranch."

Her heart was heavy as she recalled how eagerly Ben would wait for her. "I stopped coming by every day eventually, but I would still drop by two three times a week."

The electric kettle began to beep, and Jenna poured hot water over the tea bags, murmuring, "I'm not a complete monster."

"I know that."

She handed Lee the cup and sat across from him, with her own cup in her hands. "I'm sorry, Lee. About Ben."

Lee stared down at his cup and his voice was hoarse. "I don't want to hear any more condolences, please."

"Okay."

They sat in silence as the sun set and the kitchen grew dark.

Finally, at some point, Lee stood up and flipped the light switch, flooding the room with bright light. Jenna closed her eyes.

She could see the cracks forming in the mask that he had maintained the whole day. Lee, while very calm and patient, had always had a habit of holding in his emotions to the point that they eventually burst out explosively.

Jenna sipped her tea, waiting, and then she heard a loud crash in the adjoining room.

When it continued, she finally stood up, setting down her cup and making her way toward where the sounds were coming from.

The door to the study was closed, and she heard another loud, smashing sound. She opened the door.

The whole room was a mess, things broken, glass shattered. Lee had his back to her, his hands on Ben's big desk as his whole body shook.

Not with rage, Jenna realized. With sobs.

He lifted his arm, and he was about to sweep something else off the table when Jenna crossed the room toward him and wrapped her arms around him from behind, whispering, "That's enough."

She expected him to fight back or to push her away from him, but he just crumpled into her arms. "How could he just leave me like this? He was all I had. He was supposed to get better. He was getting better. He just went and left me all alone. Again."

Jenna let out a deep breath. "He didn't leave you alone. You have more friends here than you know."

Lee let out a hoarse laugh. "You can barely tolerate me as it is. I bet you can't wait until I get lost. You've made your feelings about me pretty clear."

Jenna had to resist the urge to knock some sense into him, but she knew he was grieving and that she couldn't hold his words against him.

"Don't be ridiculous," she muttered. "Nobody wants you gone. But you have your whole life in New York. And you're not alone." She was still holding onto Lee, and she felt his shudders subside. "I knew this would happen, which was why I stayed."

Even as he tried, he couldn't hold back the hitch of the sob in his voice. "Yeah, you always did know me better than I knew myself."

The question was on Jenna's tongue, but she held back. This wasn't the time and place for her to get answers. But it seemed that Lee had something to say.

"That's why I never said goodbye to you. I said goodbye to everybody, but I made sure to avoid you because I knew that if I saw you, I would want to stay. You were the only one who could convince me to stay. Even if you didn't say it. One look at you would have had me doubting my own decision. So, I chose to be a coward and leave you behind."

Jenna's heart ached with a different sort of pain now. Knowing what she did now, maybe it was for the best.

"It's fine," she muttered. "You were never meant to stay."

But Lee wasn't aware of the turmoil in her heart. He asked, his words a broken whisper, "What am I going to do now, Jenna?"

Jenna released him, and he took a staggering step forward before sinking onto the ground, his knees bent as he rested his arms on them, watching her through red, grief-stricken eyes.

She sat down in front of him, crossing her legs. "You're going to grieve for a few days, and then reality will hit you. When you're ready to talk about what to do with the ranch, we'll do that. If you want to go back to New York for a while to sort yourself out, you do that. I'll look after the ranch for you in the meantime."

"You're doing it again," Lee muttered. "You're being nice to me again. It feels so out of place."

"Well, I'm hardly going to pick on you today. Ben would haunt me in my dreams if I did."

Lee let out a sudden laugh at that. "He would, wouldn't he? That would be just like him."

His smile disappeared. "It feels like I've suddenly become an orphan all over again. Only this time it's so much worse."

Jenna's heart throbbed painfully at his broken words, and she scooted over the floor until she was next to him, both their backs against the desk. "I know it seems impossible right now, but things will get better. Life will move on. You'll go back, and the pain will become this hard ball inside of you that will just grow smaller and smaller over the years."

She froze when Lee shifted and rested his head on her shoulder. "Look at us. It's like I never left. I used to sit like this and complain to you all the time."

Jenna's eyes filled with tears for a different reason now, and she turned her head slightly so he wouldn't see the yearning and grief. "Yeah. But everything comes to an end. So did we. So did our friendship."

Lee was silent and then he said, "Things will never go back to the way they were before, will they?"

Jenna pursed her lips and swallowed. "Not for us."

She felt Lee straighten up and sigh. "Yeah. You have a boyfriend now. Guess he wouldn't like me sitting so close to you."

Jenna blinked. *Boyfriend?*

"Huh?"

He gave her an annoyed look. "Nick. Even Ben approved of him. Said he was a sweet guy."

Jenna's eyes widened. "*Nick?*"

Lee gave her a confused look. "Yeah."

Jenna closed her eyes, trying not to laugh. "I see. And Ben liked him?"

"Yeah."

Lee didn't seem very pleased about it. "Although, knowing you, I can't imagine any guy who could be so sweet and still survive your sharp tongue."

Jenna shot him a dark look. "Maybe I should make arrangements for you to meet up with Ben again sooner rather than later."

Lee grinned suddenly, and her heart stilled at the sight of his tired smile.

He scooted away from her, still chuckling. "Well, I'm right. You chew people up and spit them out in minutes nowadays. You were never this mean before."

Jenna shook her head at him.

Things had been different before. Her life had been different.

Jenna saw the hint of a bruise on her exposed arm, and she casually lowered the sleeve. "I was always mean. Just never to you."

Lee just sighed and leaned against the front of the desk. "I have so many regrets. I should have come back earlier."

"You came back when you were meant to come back," Jenna said, standing up and brushing off her jeans. "God has a plan for everyone, and He brought you back so that you could spend time with Ben. He went home happy."

Lee just let out a shuddering breath, his eyes fixed on the ceiling. "Maybe you're right."

"I am right," Jenna offered him her hand to help him stand up. "Go take a shower. I'll heat up some food. We'll have it together, and then you should go to bed."

Lee stared at her for a few long seconds until she frowned, feeling awkward. "What?"

He shook his head, a little smile on his lips. "You always act tough, but you're still soft on the inside."

Jenna scowled at him. "You're really asking for it, Evans."

He laughed, taking her hand. "Fine. I'll stop."

Jenna pulled him to his feet and he stumbled forward, clearly not having expected her grip, until he was inches away from her. It was then that she really realized that he had grown much taller. He towered over her by a head, and it was difficult to breathe with him so close to her.

But he didn't move either, staring down at her, his expression shifting.

Jenna didn't wait to find out what was going on in his head. Forcing her own feelings down, she took a step back and cleared her throat. "Go. I'll clean up down here."

"I can—"

"No," she gave him a dismissive look. "I've got this."

He was reluctant, but he walked away, and Jenna started clearing up the mess. Fortunately, he had just broken small things. It seemed that even in his grief and anger, he had been careful not to destroy his grandfather's most valued possessions.

Jenna was almost done when she coughed.

She felt something wet on her lips and when she glanced down at her white shirt, she saw the blood. Panic filled her, and she immediately grabbed a few napkins and started wiping it. Rushing to the bathroom, she locked herself in and kept coughing.

Turning on the water to hide the sound, she kept wiping at her shirt at the same time to wash out the red stain. It took her ten minutes to stop coughing violently, and by the time she was done, she was exhausted.

There was still a brownish stain on her shirt, but she could easily explain it away. Sitting on the closed toilet seat, Jenna leaned her head against the cool marble of the sink.

The doctors said she still had two to three years before her liver completely shut down.

She no longer felt grief at her situation. Five years ago when she had found out, she had been heartbroken, and her first instinct had been to hide the news from her family. But it was getting harder and harder to hide her deteriorating body. Jenna knew that she had to tell them sometime, but she just couldn't bring herself to tell her parents that their only daughter was dying. She couldn't tell her twin that she would soon be leaving him forever.

Lately, it had seemed to her that Ben had suspected that something was wrong. But he had never brought it up, and she had held onto her secret.

Jenna heard footsteps, and she quickly washed her face again and stepped out of the bathroom.

She saw Lee coming down the steps and wondered if he was dating. Once upon a time, she had wanted to be the woman beside him. But perhaps God knew that Lee had already suffered a lot of loss in his life, and He had chosen to separate them, knowing Jenna's fate.

Lee reached the bottom of the stairs when he stopped and stared at her. "What is it?"

Jenna blinked, breaking out of a daze. "What?"

Lee frowned and said slowly, "Nothing." He then asked, "What did you drop on your shirt?"

"I was a little careless. Ignore it," Jenna said. "Come on. I'll heat up the food."

They ate quietly, and Jenna could tell that Lee was tired. But when she was about to leave, he stopped her. "I'll drive you back."

"I have my car," she told him. "You just go to bed. You need to rest."

She saw his stubborn nature shine through, but she was more stubborn than him, and she ultimately got into her car and drove away, leaving Lee alone in an empty house.

"So, what are you saying?"

Jenna stared at the doctor, who was looking at her bloodwork.

"I'm going to try and push you up on the list, Ms. Miles," Dr. Ralph said, his face grim. "But you have to keep in mind that no matter how much I try, there's always going to be somebody who needs that liver more than you do. I'm surprised your twin isn't a match."

Jenna let out a long sigh. "If he was, I would have talked to him. It was fortunate that he had that small surgery here last year so I could give you his bloodwork."

Illegal as that was.

"And are you sure that your parents…"

"My aunt had a similar condition, and my mother was a living donor for her," Jenna explained. "The doctor told her not to donate anymore. And my father is a diabetic, so that's going to be a problem."

The doctor closed the file with a heavy sigh and studied her. "If that's the case, then I'll do my best to put you at the top of the list, but I can't make any promises. Also, even if you do manage to get on the list, the procedure is going to be very expensive."

"Money isn't a problem," Jenna told him.

Her family had an oil well on the ranch. She wasn't worried about being able to afford the surgery.

But as she left the hospital, she knew deep inside that there was no possible way for her to transfer that kind of money without letting her parents get a hint of what she was doing. Plus, that money belonged to her parents. And her salary as a ranch foreman wasn't anywhere near what she needed to cover the surgery, even with health insurance.

Jenna got herself an iced coffee on the drive back from Rock Springs.

Her gut was twisting throughout the ride and at some point, she forced herself to stop before she had a panic attack. Parking the car on the side of the road, she leaned her head against the steering wheel and struggled to regulate her breathing.

Her eyes went to the small bracelet that hung around her wrist. It was a simple bracelet with multicolored threads of wool. To anyone else, it was just a normal bracelet, but to Jenna, it was a reminder of every month that she had survived. At the first of every month, she added another thread to it, a silent victory.

Jenna was no victim, and she refused to be one now.

A few days after her diagnosis, she had come across a small handmade charm at the church dinner. One of the members of the women's sewing circle had made a few of them and was selling them to raise donations for the church.

That crocheted angel now hung from her rearview mirror, reading, *Heal me, Lord, and I will be healed; save me and I will be saved, for you are the one I praise.*

It was Jeremiah 17:14, and it gave Jenna a sense of peace. The angel had resonated with her when she had seen it, and she had been unable to prevent herself from purchasing it.

Jenna let out breath after breath, trying to stop the fear from rising of what the future held.

She was terrified, and she had no one to turn to. Aside from Kathy, who had found out by pure accident, Jenna had no one. She tried her best to shield her friend from the grim realities of her situation because there was nothing Kathy could do.

Deep inside, Jenna was scared.

She was scared of dying. She was scared of the pain she would experience alone. She had decided to leave town when things became too much for her. She couldn't make her family live through this sort of trauma, watching their loved one wither away and die in front of their eyes.

"Don't let them suffer," she whispered a desperate prayer.

Jenna closed her eyes and tried to calm down.

She needed to stop thinking about it, close her mind to this matter, and focus on the day's tasks.

There was a sharp rap on the window.

Startled, Jenna nearly jumped when she saw who it was.

Lee was staring at her, wearing a concerned look on his handsome face. She cursed under her breath when he motioned for her to lower her window.

She did so, complaining, "I can't even take a nap without you barging in, can I?"

He didn't retort, instead staring at her. "You okay?"

"I was just tired," Jenna responded. "So I was resting my eyes."

"In the middle of a deserted road?"

"It's hardly deserted," Jenna said in an unconvincing manner. "You're here."

And then, to her surprise, Lee lifted his hand and touched her forehead and her cheeks, making her turn bright red. "W-What are you doing?"

"Checking your temperature," he said tightly. "Well, you don't have a fever."

"Take your hand off me before I bite it off," Jenna scowled.

Instead of getting annoyed as he usually did when she bared her fangs at him, he gave her a quick grin. "No need to get so testy. I just wanted to be sure that you were fine. Is this a normal thing for you? Taking a nap on the side of the road?"

Jenna glared at him. "You'd better not be stalking me, Evans."

He laughed, that familiar sound that she suddenly realized that she'd never stopped missing. "I don't have a death wish."

She tried rolling up the window, but he stopped her. "Let me take you home if you're tired."

She gave him an incredulous look. "I'm not leaving my truck in the middle of nowhere!"

Lee glanced toward his rental car. "I'll drive you in yours then—"

"So somebody can just steal your vehicle?"

Jenna glowered at him. "Look, I'll be fine. Just keep driving. I'll be along in a bit."

But Lee was persistent. "I wanted to talk to you anyway. Why don't I drive behind you, and we can get coffee?"

"I just had coffee—"

"Lunch, then," he insisted. "I'll buy."

Jenna hesitated. Beef stew would do her a world of good right now.

"Fine. I'll meet you at the diner."

"I'll be right behind you then," Lee said pleasantly, and Jenna cursed once again.

"You're a real pain in the behind, you know," she muttered, and he just smiled.

"I know."

Jenna had no choice but to start the truck.

Lee was a man of his word. He followed her all the way to the diner, which had quite a few cars in the parking lot, and walked over to her door.

Not used to such gentlemanly behavior, Jenna just shot him a suspicious look before getting out.

"What were you doing in the city?" Lee asked as he trailed alongside her.

"Some personal stuff," Jenna replied. "What were you doing there?"

"I had a meeting with Gramps's lawyer," Lee told her.

Jenna stuffed her hands in her pockets, glancing at him. "How've you've been dealing?"

It had been two weeks since the funeral. Jenna knew that Cole had been checking in on Lee every day. Jenna had dropped by and made sure that the ranch was running smoothly.

Lee was quiet. "It's strange, but I've kept myself busy. There's a lot to get done. The transfer of the property, going through Gramps's logs. Keeping track of the business dealings he had."

"I see," Jenna murmured.

She lifted a hand to wave at Lily, and the diner owner smiled at her in response before her eyes widened at the sight of her companion.

"That's kind of why I wanted to meet you," Lee said as they managed to find an empty booth. He steepled his fingers together and said seriously, "I want you to help me find a person to manage the ranch on my behalf. You said you knew some people."

Jenna picked up the menu. "I'll send you their contact information."

"I'd rather you be there next to me when I interview them," Lee said, watching her. "You're more knowledgeable about running the ranch, so I trust your opinion."

"So you want my help in hiring a manager to oversee the ranch?" Jenna asked slowly.

"Yes."

She tapped her finger against her knee. "Well—"

"You said you'd help!" Lee said quickly, as if sensing her reluctance.

Jenna scowled internally. *Me and my big mouth.*

"I'll help you choose a manager, but you should keep in mind that just hiring a manager to oversee the ranch isn't going to fix your problems. No matter how reliable the person I recommend is, at the end of the day, you need to be on top of all the expenses and the clients and suppliers. If you're not physically involved, then at least you need to be aware of everything. Otherwise, don't come crying to me when you get cheated."

Her words were harsh, but she meant well.

Lee gave her a steady look. "I know. I've been going through Gramps's books. It's not like I'm completely clueless when it comes to running the place. After all, I grew up there. I just need to catch up with everything."

"Well, hello you two," Lily beamed. "Look at the two of you being friends again."

Jenna gave her friend a dirty look. "I know what you're doing."

Lily blinked innocently. "I have no idea what you're talking about. What do you guys want to eat? We have beef stew and cordon bleu burger. Our specials of the day."

"I'll have the beef stew with garlic bread, please." Jenna put the menu back in the stand. Lee chose to go with the burger.

Lily just winked at her, and Jenna knew that she would be assaulted with questions the minute her friend tracked her down.

She didn't get a chance to say anything further because two other people slid into the booth alongside them.

"Cole," Jenna complained when he shoved her aside. "You stink."

"I just got off my shift," her brother shrugged. "Ran into Dean outside, so we decided to have lunch."

"*Pastor* Dean," Dean corrected.

Cole just rolled his eyes. "What're you two up to?"

Jenna said, "Lee wanted to discuss the ranch and how to manage it."

Cole's expression turned somber. "How're you doing, man?"

Lee shrugged. "I'm managing."

Jenna saw her brother turn to her. "So you two are friends again now?"

"No, we're not," Jenna narrowed her eyes at him. "I'm just helping him out."

"Isn't that the same thing?" Her brother stared at her.

"Was it my lecture on forgiveness?" Pastor Dean beamed. "It worked, didn't it?"

"No, it didn't!" Jenna retorted. "And what's the update on the truck, Dean? I thought you said you'd fix it up."

"What truck?" Lee looked between the two.

"I'm painting it," Pastor Dean frowned. "She's buying my old truck."

"But you already have—"

Just then, a pretty blonde with tight curls walked over. "Lee? *Lee Evans?*"

The shock in her voice was so fake that Jenna had to resist the urge to cringe.

Lee looked up with a hint of puzzlement in his eyes. "Hi. Do I know you?"

Before the woman could answer, Jenna took massive satisfaction in replying, "Don't you remember Vicky? She used to bully you when we were in high school."

Vicky Torres flushed an ugly shade of red. "That's not true! And nobody asked you, Jenna!"

Jenna shrugged with a grin. "No harm in jogging his memory."

What she didn't add was how Lee used to have a massive crush on the girl, despite her behavior.

"Vicky," Lee murmured. "How are you?"

Vicky beamed at the lack of hostility and fluttered her lashes. "I'm so sorry about your grandfather. How are you doing now?"

"Thanks. I'm doing fine."

Jenna watched Vicky move closer as she smiled. "I'm so happy to hear that. You know it's been so long since we last saw each other. Do you want to catch up over dinner tonight?"

Jenna saw Lee glance in her direction. He seemed to be contemplating something before he turned his attention back to Vicky. "I'm a little busy tonight, but Friday would be great."

Jenna tucked her tongue in her cheek, her brows arching. He was going to go on a date with the girl who used to get her jock boyfriend to scribble cruel nicknames on his textbooks?

For the first time since Lee had returned, Jenna felt acute disappointment in him.

Her hand curled into a fist in her lap, although her expression didn't change. She saw Vicky touch Lee's shoulder in a flirtatious manner before shooting her a triumphant look.

Jenna's lips curved when Vicky walked away, her smile sharp enough to slice skin. "You two make a lovely couple."

She saw Lee frown, but she didn't care. "Move, Cole."

Her brother scooted out of the booth to make way for her. "Where're you going?"

"I just lost all my appetite," Jenna muttered, clambering out of the booth before calling out, "Lily, pack that up for me, will you? Oh. And Lee," she turned to look at Lee, who was wearing a strange expression on his face. "I'll send you the list of potential candidates, and you can tell me who you want to interview."

"Wait, Jenna—"

"Jenna!"

A second later a little human-shaped cannonball hit her straight in the stomach, wrapping his arms around her waist.

Jenna smiled. "What're you doing here?"

The six-year-old boy looked up at her, the gap in his teeth prominent as he smiled. "Mom's meeting a client. She told me to tell you to look after me!"

He pointed toward a red-haired woman with frizzy curls and a soft smile, walking toward her. "Sorry, Jenna. You're going to have to babysit this one today. I have a few pitch meetings, and he got his hands on the cookie jar at home. He's your problem for today."

Jenna didn't have nephews or nieces, but when her friend's son had been born, she had been right there with Laurel in the hospital room. Jenna had been the second one to hold the little boy, and she had fallen in love in a heartbeat.

Jenna grinned at the boy. "Let's convince your mother to let you have a sleepover. We'll watch movies and eat ice cream until the sun comes up."

Laurel had reached them at this point and overheard the last part because she lifted a brow. "If he's not in bed by eight, I'll never let you babysit again. Come on, Nick. Take your bag."

"*Nick?*" Jenna heard Lee say in shock. "*That's* Nick?!"

5
LEE

"So, Jenna is his godmother?" Lee asked in an astounded voice.

Cole nodded. "I don't know why you look so surprised."

"I thought Nick was her boyfriend," Lee muttered, but Cole overheard him because his friend's eyes widened before he snorted.

"Where'd you get an idea like that?"

Lee kept his mouth closed because now that he thought about it, his grandfather's reaction had been dumbfounded. But then again, he hadn't exactly clarified the matter for him. And neither had Jenna.

Which brought about the question. Why did she want him to think she was in a relationship?

He blinked and then turned to look at his friend. "Wait, so Jenna isn't seeing anyone?"

Cole shrugged. "She gets asked out every now and then. It's not like she doesn't date. It's just that she isn't seeing anybody actively."

"So, she's single?"

Cole was about to say something when an odd look appeared on his face. "You're not thinking of asking her out, are you?"

Lee didn't get a chance to say anything because Pastor Dean began to choke on his iced tea as he spluttered, "Jenna hates you." He coughed, trying to clear his airway, and continued, his eyes watering, "That woman eats puppies for breakfast."

"Hey!" Lily gave the pastor a baleful look. "Jenna is an absolute sweetheart. Don't listen to them, Lee. I always thought you two would have made an amazing couple. You balance each other out. Jenna is the most helpful person you can find in this town. Even if she's busy, she takes time out. When my electricity short-circuited last month, she drove up in the middle of the night and spent hours fixing it without charging me a penny. That woman is a gem!"

If Lily hadn't sounded so resolute, Lee would not have believed that she was talking about Cole's twin sister.

"I mean, she's not awful," Pastor Dean muttered in a guilty voice now. "She's getting Laurel that truck to help her out."

"My sister's tough," Cole reiterated. "But she's got a good heart."

"She's had to be tough," Lily said sternly. "She's the foreman of a massive ranch. She can't get those men to respect her if she smiles at them all the time."

Lee recalled Jenna saying something similar to him.

"I'm not going to ask her out," he corrected, but his eyes went toward the door Jenna had just walked out of. "I don't like her like that."

However, the last part felt insincere. When he found out that she had a boyfriend, he felt a little uncomfortable. He didn't know why he felt so much more at ease now. He didn't have feelings for Jenna. All the woman did was pick on him or snipe at him whenever she got the chance.

As he sat there, half listening to Lily lecture both Pastor Dean and Cole, Lee recalled the way Jenna had sat with him the day of the funeral. She had been so uncharacteristically gentle with him that it had taken him aback.

He glanced out the floor-to-ceiling windows of the diner, lost in thought. So who was Jenna really? The tough, no-nonsense woman or the sweet woman who offered him the comfort he had needed at his lowest point?

She confused him.

And yet he sought her out every opportunity he got.

Lee shook his head, scoffing at himself. No. He didn't have feelings for Jenna. That would be ridiculous.

She was just an old friend.

But as he drove home after lunch, he found himself wondering why he was so insistent on mending fences with his childhood friend.

It was a few days later that Lee ran into Jenna again, and this time it was at his own ranch.

He was on his way back from a meeting when he saw a familiar figure atop a horse, talking to somebody. Lee nearly ran into the large oak tree on the edge of his property because he was so busy staring at her. He watched her climb off the horse, holding onto the reins, as she talked to the foreman. It struck him suddenly that Jenna looked weary.

Now that he thought about it, Jenna was often tired. The other day at the coffee shop and then when she had parked the car in the middle of the road to rest. Nobody had ever brought it up around him, and he had to wonder if even Cole knew whatever it was his sister was going through.

Did the woman ever rest?

Just as he was thinking this, he saw her turn her head and look straight at him.

His lips curved when he saw that familiar look of disdain on her face. He couldn't help but be amused every time she gave him that look. Tucking his phone in his pocket, he strode over to where she stood.

He watched her end her conversation with the man she was talking to and turn to face him, waiting.

Lee had become accustomed to women fawning over him. After he had returned to town a wealthy billionaire, there had been no shortage of women trying to get with him. But Jenna had never been in that crowd.

It wasn't that Lee wanted this particular woman to fawn over him, but it irked him to see her turn her back on him so easily.

"You're back early," Jenna commented when he reached her.

"What're you doing here?"

She reached into her pocket and brought out a folded piece of paper. "This is a list of names of the potential managers. I've included their résumés and contact information as well."

Lee took the paper from her, commenting, "That was fast."

She didn't smile. "Well, you asked me for them."

There was a warm breeze blowing, and Lee saw a few strands of dark hair escape her braid. Without thinking, Lee reached forward to tuck the strands behind her ear.

It was when he saw Jenna's eyes widen that he realized what he had just done.

Her cheeks turned red, and she immediately moved back. "What're you doing?"

"Why are you blushing?"

She spluttered. "I'm not blushing. It's hot! And don't touch me!"

Lee stared at her, fascinated by the soft color in her cheeks. "I—Sorry. It was just—I was trying to fix your hair."

Jenna gave him a disbelieving look and quickly took off her hat to pat down her hair, muttering, "Unbelievable."

Lee frowned. "What?"

"Nothing," she glowered at him, taking another step back, her expression wary. "You have the list. Just call me when you want to set up the interviews."

He saw her turn around, about to climb back on the horse, when he said, without thinking, "Come inside. There's some iced tea in the fridge."

"I don't—"

"Jenna," Lee said in a disapproving tone. "You've probably been working since morning. Having something to drink won't kill you."

She stared at him and then suddenly let out a morbid-sounding laugh. He didn't know why the sound sent chills down his spine, but he shuddered.

"Don't you have your date with Vicky today?"

Lee's brows knit together. "It's not a date."

"Could've fooled me."

He didn't know why he felt so frustrated as he repeated, "It's not a date, Jenna."

She lifted a brow. "She says it is. She's been going around town telling everybody it is. And I have to get back to wo—"

She had just turned around again when he said in a quiet voice, rocking back on his heels, "Does it bother you?"

Jenna froze and looked over her shoulder at him. "Excuse me?"

He didn't know why he was egging her on, but he couldn't help himself. "Does it bother you that I'm taking Vicky out on a date?"

"You just said it wasn't a date," she said, narrowing her eyes at him.

Lee shrugged. "I mean if she thinks it's a date, I can always make it into a date."

He saw Jenna turn around, her jaw tight. She seemed to be on the verge of saying something, and Lee's blood hummed in anticipation, but then she snapped her mouth shut.

"If you want to go out on a date with your childhood crush who used to get her boyfriend to dunk your head in the toilet, that says more about you than her," Jenna said coldly. "I just regret standing up for you back then and getting my behind kicked to keep you safe."

The last part made Lee go still. "Wait, what?"

He grabbed Jenna's arm. "What do you mean? Did Vicky hit you?"

She snorted, pulling away from him. "Vicky? Precious, I-have-to-protect-my-nails Vicky? No. I would've buried her in the ground. She used to sic her boyfriend Dylan and his buddies on me."

Lee's blood ran cold as he recalled a sudden childhood memory of bruises on Jenna, which she had claimed were from falling off a horse.

"When?" His voice was icy now, his blood boiling. It was a long time ago, but he couldn't control his surge of anger.

Jenna shrugged. "Why does it even matter? It's in the past, and I gave back as good as I got."

Lee clenched his hands into fists, unreasonably furious. "Why didn't you ever say anything?"

Jenna lifted a brow, her hand reaching out to pet the dark horse nibbling on her hair. "And what exactly were you going to do, Lee? You could barely defend yourself."

Jenna's words were harsh, but they held a grain of truth. But what she didn't know was that his refusal to fight back hadn't been because he couldn't, scrawny as he had been. It had been because Lee hated violence. He had seen enough of it in the first decade of his life to want to stay away from it. But his grandfather had taught him to fight, and he had been more than capable of defending himself. And her!

"Why didn't you ever—"

Jenna let out a heavy sigh. "I wasn't going to go to the principal and complain because it would have made things worse. And like I said, I fought back. I didn't tell you this so that you would feel bad. It's just kind of funny to see you go out with the girl who used to harass us both. But then again." She turned her back to him and climbed onto the horse. "Life's funny that way. Do what you wa—"

Lee grabbed the horse's bridle, making Jenna frown. "You should have said something back then. I would have protected you."

Jenna gave him a long look and then said, "I didn't tell you this to upset you."

"I'm not upset," Lee bared his teeth. "I want to get even."

This time he saw her grin. "Well, sweet as that may be, God has a funny way of dealing with such people. Dylan now works at the mechanic shop with his father. And his father has a contract with us, so he has to be respectful every time he sees me."

Even so, Lee found himself burning with anger.

"Boy, you're really upset," Jenna studied him. She shrugged. "Go for a walk and cool off. It was a long time ago, and while I still dislike the sight of Vicky, it doesn't mean I was trying to sabotage your date. Besides," she smacked his hand away from the bridle and smirked. "I have my own date tonight. See ya!"

Without waiting for a response from Lee, Jemma galloped off.

He stared after her, stunned by this new development.

Jenna had a date?

With whom?

Suddenly his desire to punch something intensified.

Sunset Ridge didn't have many high-class restaurants. Those who wanted to go on a fancy date would usually go into the city. However, a little birdie who ran a popular coffee shop had told Lee that Jenna's date was going to be in the lone Italian restaurant in town.

So that was where he had taken Vicky.

Lee wasn't going to think too hard about why he had chosen the same place Jenna was going. He had fully intended to take Vicky to a French restaurant in Rock Springs, but on his way to pick her up, he had changed his mind. He'd only decided to still take her to dinner to avoid a tantrum.

His poor planning led them to wait for five minutes for a table.

Vicky looked around with a forced smile. "I was expecting something fancier."

Lee gave her a cool look. "Why?"

She looked startled at his visible hostility. "I mean, it's not like you can't afford it."

Lee asked one of the waiters to hand them a menu. "Well, you didn't specify where you wanted to go."

Vicky giggled. "Well, next time, I want to go to a proper restaurant and not some hole in the wall."

Give me patience, he prayed silently.

Lee studied the menu, saying idly, "Next time? I thought we were just catching up today."

He lifted his gaze to see her smile slipping, and then she fixed it back up. "I mean, yeah, but you never know what could happen."

"True." Lee cast a sweeping glance around the restaurant.

Vicky clearly took that as encouragement, and she babbled on. "You're single, and I know you must want a good woman in your life. I mean, I'm just about ready to find a man who can take care of me. And when two single people meet—"

"I prefer my women to be independent and tough. If I wanted to take care of someone, I'd get a pet."

Vicky's face flushed at the insulting words, and Lee had to give her credit for not storming off.

The vibes Vicky was giving off made him feel disgusted. She was clearly looking to be a trophy wife, and she had zoned in on him as a potential target.

"Oh good heavens," He heard Vicky whisper in an appalled tone. "I can't believe she's wearing something so tacky."

Unconsciously, Lee's eyes went toward the person Vicky was referring to, and his breath caught.

Jenna was smiling at a tall man with bronzed skin and a sharp smile. Lee didn't recognize him, but he wasn't really looking at the man to begin with. His eyes were on Jenna.

She wore a red, figure-hugging dress. Her hair, which was usually braided, had been twisted into luscious curls. She was wearing some light makeup, and her lipstick was a deep, slashing red.

It wasn't just Lee who was staring. Almost half the male patrons were eyeing her.

Gorgeous.

She looked breathtaking.

And she was on some other man's arm.

Lee glowered at the man, who hadn't noticed him. The maitre'd seated the couple a few tables away from Lee and Vicky.

Vicky must have interpreted his shock as disgust because she sneered, "She looks like a tramp."

"I would be careful about what you say next," Lee said in an icy tone. He saw Vicky's face turn white, and he continued. "Jenna is a dear friend."

He could see her jaw work, and while it satisfied him, he couldn't be cruel to a woman. It wasn't in his nature, so he just sealed his lips. However, that didn't mean that he would allow her to sully Jenna's name.

But when Vicky's hand covered his, his eyes grew wide. She was looking at him with a smile that looked almost sly. "Listen. Lee, I know you haven't been in town for long, but things have changed. You and Jenna used to be friends, but you should know the things she says behind your back."

She let out an exaggerated sigh of disappointment. "I never thought she would turn out this way, but lately I've heard her say how she just knows she's going to snag you because you're the richest bachelor in town right now."

Lee stared at her, stunned by her audacity, but Vicky clearly misinterpreted his look for shock, and she continued, sinking her teeth into her lower lip. "She's not the same girl that you knew back then. She just wants you for your money. I didn't want to tell you this, but Jenna has quite a reputation in town. She's seen with a different man every night. And the minute you came into town, she started telling everyone who would listen that she would have you eating out of the palm of her hand in weeks." She put on a pitiful expression. "I didn't want to tell you this, but I don't want people to use you just because you're doing well for yourself. It's just not fair."

She sniffled, and Lee gave her an incredulous look, stunned at how shameless she was acting.

Vicky curled her hand around his. "I'm just looking out for you. Jenna is nothing more than a bully, and I can't bear to see you being mistreated like that. She's already—" She let out a shaky breath. "She's already stolen away every man I was ever interested in. It's just so hard. I can't confront her because conflict isn't my style, so I just have to tolerate it."

No matter how hard Lee tried, he just couldn't imagine Jenna going around town claiming she'd snag him because of his money.

He glanced in Jenna's direction again and saw her smiling at the man across from her. He was telling her what seemed to be a story, and she had an amused look as she sipped from a glass in her hand.

Lee's hand clenched around his own glass of water.

She never smiled at him like that.

Vicky must have seen him look annoyed and assumed it was because her story really got to him because she was quick to clasp his hand, saying in a reassuring voice, batting her lashes, "You don't have to get angry on my behalf, Lee. I'm just sorry you had to find out this way. Please don't hold her behavior against her. You know how she is—"

"Do you ever stop talking?" Lee snapped, and he didn't care when she froze in shock at his harsh tone.

His eyes were on Jenna's hand, which had a pair of lips pressed to the back of it. Suddenly it felt like he couldn't think clearly as he abandoned his seat and strode over to her.

He saw both Jenna and her date look up as his shadow fell over them. There was surprise in Jenna's eyes before Lee announced, "We need to talk."

"Talk?" Jenna looked so surprised on seeing him that she didn't have her usual snarky comeback.

"Come with me." Lee grabbed her wrist, pulling her out of her seat. When her date tried to intervene, Lee shot him a dangerous look. "Sit down. This has got nothing to do with you!"

It was Jenna who said, "It's fine. I'll be back."

Her voice was tense, and if Lee had been in his right mind, he would've picked up on the dangerous edge to her tone. She yanked her hand back from him, her voice icy. "Let's step outside."

Lee didn't care. As long as he got her away from this person who was kissing her hand and making her smile, he was fine with everything else.

It was only when they were outside and reached his car that Jenna broke the silence.

"What on God's earth has gotten into you, Evans? Didn't you see that I was in the middle of a date?"

Lee didn't care about any of that. Instead, he whirled around to face her. "Who was that man?"

"What?" Jenna gave him a baffled look. "Derek? He's my date, you buffoon! I can't believe you dragged me out of there like that! Have you finally lost it?"

"He was harassing you!"

"Harassing me?" Jenna echoed, visibly confused.

Lee felt his ears heat. "I saw him kissing your hand!"

Jenna paused before her eyes turned into slits. "You have ten seconds to explain yourself, Evans, or I'm going to stab you with my heel."

"Do it then," Lee growled.

He saw her eyes widen in surprise and then she said angrily, "Who do you think you ar—"

Unable to bear for her to finish her sentence, Lee grabbed her by her arms, pulling her onto her toes. "Enough."

Once again, his actions seemed to stun her into silence.

"W-What are you doing?" she muttered, trying to get her bearings.

He didn't know himself. All Lee knew was that seeing that guy touch her had made his blood boil.

"Lee," Jenna finally said in a tight voice. "Let me go, or I'm—"

"What?" Lee demanded. "What are you going to do? Threaten me with bodily harm? You do that at least once a day. You've never gone through with it—"

"Don't tempt me," she bared her teeth at him. "You're doing a fine job of getting on every last nerve of mine."

There was a spark of delight within him when he saw that she wasn't backing down. She shouldn't look this beautiful when she was angry.

But somehow she managed it.

Seeing her up close like this, with inches between them, Lee felt his chest tighten. The air between them was electrifying, and his heart was racing. How had he never noticed his attraction to Jenna?

He could see that she felt it, too, but unlike him, she was determined to fight it.

It was only when he tightened his hands that she stopped, the awareness in her beautiful eyes growing.

"Cat got your tongue now?" he breathed.

She watched him warily. "I don't know what your problem is. But whatever you're after, you're not going to get it here. Keep pushing me, and you'll find out that I'm not the only one who can cut ties without breaking a sweat."

Something stilled inside of Lee at that threat. He could see that she really meant it.

"You wouldn't," he said slowly.

The smile she gave him was wicked, even as it stole his breath away.

"Fine," he snapped. "If you want to be that way, then I'll walk away with a consolation prize at least."

Saying that, he lowered his mouth to hers.

He expected Jenna to kick him or bite him.

He didn't expect her to kiss him back.

All the anger inside of him muted at the tenderness of the kiss. It seemed she was just as taken aback by the sweetness.

It felt good.

It felt like coming home, like this was what he had been searching for, for a long time.

The moment was interrupted, however, at a loud gasp and a scream. "Jenna, you tramp!"

Lee felt Jenna pull away from him. Her eyes were clouded, and he saw the apprehension form in her eyes as she realized what they had just done. And then she looked over his shoulder, toward Vicky.

Lee saw the irritation in her eyes as Jenna glared at him. "Good job, Evans. You've really done it now."

Lee couldn't bring himself to feel even slightly guilty, the taste of Jenna still lingering on his mouth.

6
JENNA

"So," Kathy sat down next to Jenna on the couch. "How are you doing?"

Jenna poked at the muffin on her plate. "Apparently I'm the town's new tramp. Didn't you hear?"

Her friend made a sympathetic sound. "Yeah, well, we all have bad days."

Jenna's eyes widened as the fork slipped from her grip and clattered onto the plate. "It's not a bad day. That little hussy is going around telling everyone who will listen some warped version of events!"

Kathy picked up the fork and stabbed a piece of the crumbled muffin. "How bad can it be?"

"Lee kissed me, Kathy!" Jenna fumed. "He interrupted my date during his own date, which he said wasn't a date, and then he dragged me outside and kissed me! That conniving—"

"I knew he had a thing for you," Kathy chuckled. "When he came in here asking ab—"

Her words cut off, and Jenna saw the flash of guilt on her friend's face. "*It was you!* You told him where I was going!"

"He just asked!" Kathy defended herself. "And you started it by telling him you were going on a date! Don't act like you didn't do that to step on his toes!"

Jenna scowled at her. "Because he thought I was jealous of him and Vicky!"

"You *were* jealous!" Kathy rebutted. "You kept talking about it!"

"There's a difference between disgusted and jealous. I was the former," Jenna said angrily.

"Really?" her friend replied dryly.

"Yes!" Jenna snarled.

When Kathy just stared at her, Jenna looked away, her voice lower. "Look. Even if there was something—and I'm not saying there is—you know my situation. I may be foul-tempered, but even I'm not cruel enough to get involved with somebody when I know what the future holds."

The grief in her friend's eyes was heartbreaking, but Jenna couldn't do anything about it.

"You go out on dates all the time."

"Just to have a good time," Jenna shrugged. "I don't want to miss out on life. I'm not going to spend my last years crying in a corner. And everyone I go out with knows I'm not looking for anything. We just get a chance to dress up to go out, have a good time, go dancing. And at the end of the evening, we part good friends."

"So why can't you do that with Lee?"

Jenna's lips curved in a hard smile. "It's different with him. It's never just going to be a good time with him. There's too much history there, and you never really forget your first love. I'm reckless, but not with my heart."

"Jenna," Kathy murmured.

Jenna lowered her voice. "The doctor gave me three more years while I can still function. And then I plan to leave. I'm not going to make anyone watch me suffer. I've been saving."

"No," her best friend whispered, her eyes filling.

"This is what I want, Kathy. I don't want anybody to see me at my worst."

"How do you think your family will feel when they realize that you suffered all by yourself?"

Jenna chuckled. "They won't. I'll make sure they think I died in a car crash or something like that."

It wasn't something to smile about, but Jenna preferred smiling rather than crying.

"You can't be this cold-hearted," Kathy whispered.

Jenna's eyes grew icy. "I'm not going to be upset over you judging me for my decision. But at least I expect you to respect it."

She was about to get up when Kathy grabbed her arm. "Wait. I'm not judging you."

"You are. I can see it in your eyes. But you'd do the same if you were in my position. You wouldn't be able to bear having your family see your struggle."

"Isn't there anything we can do?" her friend begged. It was a question she asked often, and Jenna always had the same answer.

"You know there isn't."

Seeing the pain in Kathy's eyes, Jenna smiled, patting her hand. "Come on. Let's change the subject. Otherwise you're going to cry all over me."

Kathy's smile was watery as she looked around the half-empty coffee shop. There were a few students in the corner, studying with earbuds in, lost in their own worlds. But since it was afternoon, not many people wanted to have coffee, especially at this time of the day and in this heat.

Jenna knew that it was difficult for her friend. "I know you don't like this whole thing, Kathy, but I have faith in God. Come what may, He'll get me through this."

Her friend sighed. "I know. But every time I see you in pain, it feels like my heart will burst. I wish I could take away some of your suffering."

Jenna squeezed her hand, grateful to God for giving her such a dear friend.

"So, did Lee come looking for you after you left?"

Jenna's mood instantly turned dark. "I don't know. I've been going out of my way to avoid him. I mean, the nerve—"

"He likes you."

"Does he realize how mean I am to him?" Jenna scowled. "I haven't said one nice word to the man since he got here. How does that make him want to kiss me?"

"Same reason he probably stuck around your bossy self when you two were kids," Kathy smiled.

Before Jenna could respond, the door of the coffee shop opened, and they both looked up to see a familiar face.

Laurel grinned at Jenna. "Good afternoon, tramp."

"Not you too!" Jenna groaned, sinking even deeper into the couch.

However, Laurel snickered, tossing her purse into the armchair next to the couch and sinking into it. "You should hear the things Vicky is saying. I overheard her in the bakery this morning, telling another version of the same story. I swear if you don't start selling poison apples at this point and cackling into mirrors, what are you even doing with your life?"

"Very funny," Jenna muttered, but her lips curved a little.

Laurel kicked off her heels and tucked her legs under her. "So, get this. Apparently, you were making eyes at Lee ever since you got to the restaurant and poor, sweet, harmless Vicky was so terrified that she couldn't utter a word when you strode over and just about had your way with Lee right there in the middle of the restaurant. Oh, the scandal! The audacity!"

"I like that version better," Kathy grinned. "So much drama."

"Are you two quite done?" Jenna asked dryly. "It was one kiss—"

"Did you kiss him back?"

Laurel's question had Jenna turning red, and she spluttered. "Why is that important?"

Both Lauren and Kathy looked at each other in shock, and Laurel smacked the armrest. "You did! You did, and you never told us?"

"Jenna!" Kathy looked just as betrayed.

Jenna jumped to her feet, flustered. "It was just a kiss! There's no need to make a big deal out of it. It was a normal reaction."

Laurel scoffed. "If you really didn't want him to kiss you, a normal reaction would have been to knee him. Not kiss him back. Any guy who puts the moves on an unwilling lady knows what he's probably got coming."

Kathy made a sound of agreement.

"It's been four days!" Jenna grumbled. "Why are you guys still so invested in this?"

"Because the whole town is buzzing with the news."

"Everyone in that restaurant, including my date, saw him drag me out. And Derek, that coward didn't do a single thing! And I'm pretty sure there must've been a few witnesses when Lee tried to manhandle me," Jenna complained in an exasperated tone.

"Like anybody could manhandle you," Laurel made a sound of disbelief.

"Well, he did!" Jenna sulked. "And he wasn't very nice about it."

She saw the humor fade out of her friends' eyes, and Laurel's gaze was serious. "Did he make you uncomfortable in any way?"

"I may look sweet, but I took a lot of self-defense classes," Kathy added, her voice dark. "I'm pretty sure I can knock him on his cute little behind in minutes."

As much as Jenna would have loved to say yes, she couldn't lie, and she muttered, sitting back down, "It wasn't completely awful."

"So, you liked it?"

"Can we please just stop talking about this?"

Her friends grinned and then leaned forward. "Give us the details first."

Jenna whispered a silent prayer for patience.

It was bad enough that townspeople were talking behind her back, but to have her own mother confront her made the entire situation so much worse.

"Why didn't you tell me something was going on between you and Lee?"

"Because there isn't, Ma!" Jenna said loudly, hurrying down the porch steps to get away from her own mother.

This was why she had avoided going home for these past few days.

However, Glenda Miles wasn't ready to quit as she jogged after her daughter. "Then what is it that I'm hearing around town?"

"Gossip!" Jenna shot back, desperate to get away.

She began running at this point, and her mother finally gave up, shouting after her, "Has that boy come to see you since that day?"

"I'll shoot him if he does!" Jenna retorted with a heavy scowl.

She would love it if Lee gave her an opportunity to use her rifle.

To her annoyance, when she reached her cottage, she saw a familiar figure standing at the edge of the gate.

"You!" she snarled, pointing her finger toward a startled Lee. "This is all *your* doing!"

Lee raised his hands. "Give me a chance."

"For what?" Jenna growled. "To give you another opportunity to make people whisper behind my back and point fingers at me? Do you know how difficult it is to step into town right now? They don't dare say anything to my face, but I'm not deaf. I swear, if one more person calls me a hussy, I will commit murder!"

"What?" Lee froze. "Who called you a hussy? Why?"

"Because you dragged me out during your date and my date and then proceeded to kiss me in front of anybody who had eyes. In fact, you did so in front of Vicky. Look, if you have a problem with me, I have no issue staying out of your way—"

"I don't want that!" Lee bit out. "Has Vicky been spreading rumors about you? I'll set the record straight."

Jenna laughed angrily. "You think you setting the record straight is going to do anything? People are treating me as if I wrecked somebody's home! Do you know how humiliating that is? My own men are giving me strange looks!"

It was something Kathy and Laurel couldn't understand.

Jenna had had to fight for every inch of respect when she decided to work in a male-dominated field. Now, she had to struggle to get it all back over one man's impulsive move.

"Then I will talk to everybody if I have to," Lee said, his voice harsh.

"Why do you even care? I'll fix it myself."

"I do care," he said firmly when she turned her back toward him. He grabbed her by the arm, whirling her around to face him. "Don't walk away from me. I came here to say something."

"I'm not interested. And quit manhandling me!" She glared at him, hating how his touch was making her heart race.

"*You kissed me back!*" Lee said loudly and forcefully. "You kissed me back, and you liked it, so I don't see why we can't have a conversation like two adults instead of you pushing me away every time I try to approach you!"

Jenna stared at him, stunned by his outburst, and she struggled to say something. Lee, however, apparently didn't plan on letting her have a say.

"I've put up with your attitude for far too long!" he growled. "If you want to act like a stubborn child, I have no problem treating you like one!"

"Don't even think about it," Jenna warned, her eyes sharp as she yanked her hand away from him.

He left bruises every time he grabbed her so recklessly, even though he was definitely never violent. Lee would die, Jenna knew, if he realized how fragile she actually was and how the lightest touch could leave a mark.

"Then talk to me!" Lee growled. "Invite me in and have a proper conversation with me instead of acting like I've brought the plague to town!"

Jenna wanted to toss him out on his behind, but the look in his eyes made her wary. She had a choice, and she wasn't up to fighting with him, so she said coldly, "You clearly have no intentions of respecting my say in anything, so just do what you want."

"Jenna."

Lee's murmur of her name was soft, and Jenna felt an intense feeling of guilt at her harsh words. He actually looked hurt.

Guilt and regret were never a good combination, and she shoved her hands in her pockets, kicking a patch of dirt and grumbling. "I didn't mean it that way. Just come in. I'll even open the door for you. See?"

She pulled open the latch and held the small gate open for him.

She saw him watching her doubtfully, and she scowled. "Get in while I'm still being nice about it."

He moved quickly, and she followed him.

"I'll make you something to drink," she muttered, the hurt look on his face etched in her brain.

However, he followed her inside the cottage.

It hadn't exactly been an invitation, but she was trying to be nice, so she couldn't exactly tell him to wait outside.

There was a jug of lemonade in her fridge, and as she took it out and poured out two glasses, she was very much aware of Lee exploring her small home.

"Are you done snooping? Would you like me to leave so you can look around to your heart's content?"

He gave her a quick grin. "If you don't mind."

Glaring at him, she watched him move about. It wasn't as if the cottage was very big. It was a two-bedroom building with a living room, a bathroom, and a kitchen.

The most that Jenna did was keep it clean, but the way Lee was looking around made her feel like he was checking out the inside of a five-star hotel room.

"How long have you been living here?"

"Five or six years," she shrugged. "I had it designed myself, and Laurel built me the furniture."

"Does she run the store now?"

"No, her father runs the place."

Laurel's family was in the business of making furniture. It was a very old family business with an excellent reputation.

"I see." He glanced at her. "What about the garden?"

"What about it?"

"Who maintains it?"

"I do. Why?"

Lee paused and studied her, an odd look in his eyes, and then he murmured, "You don't remember, do you?"

Jenna frowned. "Remem—"

And then she suddenly did remember. She remembered a warm summer day, years before Lee had left. They had been talking about the perfect house and had vowed to always live together once they were grown up. Lee had promised to build the biggest house in the whole world, and she had told him that she would plant the prettiest flowers she could find so that everyone would always envy their home.

"Ah." A small sound escaped her as a heavy sadness filled Jenna.

It had been a childish dream.

She put the lemonade jug back in the fridge, trying to blink away the sudden stinging sensation in her eyes. There was a wistful yearning in her heart at the childlike dreams that the younger version of her had had. *How naive.*

"You planted the flowers." Lee approached her, his expression strange.

Jenna ordered herself to hold her ground as she avoided his gaze and picked up the two glasses of lemonade to carry them outside.

But Lee blocked her path. "Why'd you plant them?"

He was studying her intently, and she hated that he had a few inches on her, forcing her to look up at him.

"I like flowers," she forced her voice to remain calm. "Is that a crime now?"

He studied her and then gave a quick smile. "Depends on your reason."

"I wanted to have a garden. Not everything I do has to have some link with you."

When she saw the satisfied look in his eyes, she cursed herself for her slip of the tongue.

Thrusting a glass toward him, she scowled. "Stop annoying me and just go outside."

Lee had clearly figured out which buttons to press at what time and so he obediently carried his glass outside. They sat down on the porch steps, and Jenna had to make a physical effort not to roll up her sleeves because of the heat.

"Say what you had to say," she ordered.

"You kissed me back." His voice was quiet and meaningful.

"So? I'm sorry, but if that's your only argument—"

"Why'd you kiss me back?" he asked, not at all deterred by her tone.

"It was either that or headbutt you," Jenna replied.

"So why'd you choose the kiss?"

"You're like a dog with a bone!" she scowled, turning to face him, and she saw him smirking.

"That's the only way to get anything out of you," he responded. "I've started to figure you out."

Jenna wondered if he would react violently if she emptied her glass of lemonade on top of his head. But a small voice told her that he might just kiss her in revenge.

"No reason," she finally said.

"But you're attracted to me?"

Jenna snorted now. "Listen, Lee. You're an attractive man. So was my date—"

This time when Lee grabbed her jaw and leaned forward, she froze.

His hold was gentle but firm, and his eyes were burning as his lips hovered over hers. "If you mention that man again, I'll kiss you senseless right here on your porch. I don't care if you shoot me afterward."

Jenna was still as a mouse, her body fighting her own instinct to lean in and close the distance between them. She already knew what it would be like.

Addicting.

She saw a gleam in Lee's eyes, and she blinked. "Fine. Get away from me now." He moved back, and she inched away from him. "You're like an animal. I'm going to start carrying around bear spray from now on."

He threw his head back and roared with laughter at her unsettled comment, his eyes dancing in amusement.

"This is not funny!" she said, annoyed.

"I just figured out how to get what I want," he chortled. "I just have to threaten to kiss you."

"That's harassment and, potentially, blackmail," Jenna pointed out indignantly.

"I don't think it is," Lee replied, studying her.

"Get to the point already, Lee," she snapped, feeling beyond flustered now and trying her best to hide it. "Don't think I won't kick you out."

"Fine." He stretched his legs. "I'll deal with Vicky."

Jenna's brow furrowed. "I don't need you to protect me."

"She said some things to me, which I was quite offended by," was Lee's response. "I plan to have a word with her."

Jenna knew that the Lee before her was different from the quiet, timid teenager in her memories, but she couldn't keep her hackles from rising. "What did she say? I'll break her face, I swear."

Lee grinned. "You really can't make up your mind when it comes to me, can you? Do you want to kill me or stab someone who's mean to me?"

Jenna's jaw worked, and she fell silent with a huff.

"Fine," she muttered. "It's not like I was going to say anything to her anyway. She's not going to come at me until she's sure I can't touch her. And it's not like we see each other a lot. So do whatever you want."

Lee nodded. "I also wanted to say that I'll make sure that all these rumors are dealt with."

"I don't need you looking out for me," Jenna frowned. "I can fight my own battles."

"But this one was my fault, so I'll fix it," Lee insisted. "I had already told Vicky I was not out on a date with her, but she kept treating it like it was."

"She always was deluded," Jenna grunted, kicked a stone in front of her. "I thought it was a date though. Just so you know. Can't blame her for misunderstanding."

"Speaking of dates," Lee said in a casual manner. "How serious are you about that guy you were with?"

Startled, Jenna looked at him. "Who? Derek? We're just frie—Why do you care?"

"I'd like to know who my competition is," Lee said smoothly, draining the glass of lemonade and standing up.

"Your *what?*" Jenna stammered, taken aback. "I'm not dating you, Evans!"

"I never said you were." Lee stuck his hands, watching her coolly. "But I've decided I want you."

"I'm not a prize pig at the fair," Jenna spit out.

"Once again, I never said that," he pointed out. "But you can't stop me from courting you."

Jenna didn't know why her blood was thrumming with excitement and anger, but she got to her feet. "I'm not interested in you, Evans! Get it through your head!"

Lee shrugged. "I don't believe you."

"If you—" Jenna had a hard time getting her words out. "If you try to court me, I'm going to go out on a different date every night! Don't think I won't!"

"Fine," Lee's eyes flashed. "Every man who touches you, I'll break his hands and drive his business into the ground. You're not the only one who can get your way, Miles. Try and push me. Go ahead. You won't like the results."

Jenna glared at him. "I should've just dumped the entire lemonade jug on your head!"

"Well, you didn't," Lee said in a taunting manner. "And now you're stuck with me." He began to walk toward the small gate. "Just remember my words. If anyone tries to get with you, I'll make him suffer!"

"That's not courting; that's blackmail!" Jenna shouted after him. "And that's illegal!"

"Go on, report me then," was Lee's unbothered reply as he left.

Jenna glowered at his disappearing figure before storming inside.

"Did you report him then?"

Jenna just glared at Laurel. "What do you think?"

Laurel snickered, waggling her brows toward Kathy. "I think love is in the air."

"This is not helping, ladies!"

Her friends laughed while Jenna sulked.

Finally, Laurel tried to comfort her. "Look, he has his entire business in New York. I don't know why you're so upset. Just have a small fling. Go out with him, flirt with him, have a good time. I know you're attracted to him. In a few more weeks or another two months, he'll leave. You said so yourself; he doesn't plan to stay here. And he certainly cannot expect you to go with him."

Even as Jenna brightened on hearing this, there was a small pang in her chest. She forcibly smothered it.

"That's true," she began to smile. "He can't stay here. And I can't go with him. So, it's just pointless. He just hasn't thought this through."

Laurel cheered her on. "Exactly. He's probably going to go back to New York and find some high-society girl and end up marrying her because it's convenient."

This time Jenna's agreement was a little less enthusiastic as the tightness in her chest increased. She felt Kathy's hand curl around hers, and she saw the trace of sadness in her friend's eyes.

She shouldn't be upset about this, Jenna told herself. Even if there had been an opportunity, it wouldn't be fair to Lee to build something with him and then have it taken away. Maybe if she wasn't dying and if she had a softer tongue and was more like Kathy or Laurel, she would have been able to reciprocate. But she knew in her hearts of her hearts that whatever charm had attracted Lee to her would fade away when he got tired of her sharp tongue.

He wasn't the same Lee anymore, and she definitely wasn't the same Jenna.

And that hurt.

That really hurt.

"You okay?" Laurel's voice broke into her thoughts, and Jenna blinked.

"What?"

Kathy wrapped her arm around her shoulders, her voice soft. "You looked like you were thinking about something serious."

Jenna shook her head. "Sorry. I have to meet Lee today for the interviews. I'm thinking of taking a spray bottle."

When Laurel laughed, she felt a little better.

But as she left for the ranch, her heart was a little heavy. This was why she'd never wanted to get involved with Lee to begin with. The minute she had laid eyes on him, all those feelings that she had deep inside, under the hurt of his betrayal, had stirred, and she had known that he would be dangerous to her.

"I can't do this," she murmured as she drove out of town toward the ranches. Her heart was beating so painfully that she stopped by the side of the road to calm herself down.

"Don't make me go through this," she pleaded in a broken voice. "Haven't I been through enough?"

Her prayer went unanswered, and she ultimately wiped her eyes and continued on her way.

Tomorrow she would have to go back to the hospital to start a new treatment. Her doctor had told her that she would be getting injections and that they would be painful and would hinder her daily routine. If she didn't have the shots, her organs would begin to fail and shut down.

So she just had to bear with it.

A part of her knew that she would never get matched with a donor. Her name was far from the top of the list, and her doctor had told her that she had a very rare blood type, which made it difficult to find a suitable match.

Her hands shook as she tightened them on the steering wheel and whispered another prayer, this time for peace and acceptance.

As she pulled up toward the main house, Jenna saw another car parked there. When she got out, she saw a woman standing on the steps of the porch, talking to Lee.

Wondering what was going on, Jenna approached them and frowned when she saw the gaunt look on Lee's face.

"What's going on?" she asked, and the woman turned around to face her.

"Sharon?" Jenna felt even more puzzled. "Why are you here?"

Sharon looked a little uneasy as she glanced toward Lee.

But it was Lee who spoke, his voice hoarse. "They performed an autopsy on Gramps. He didn't die of a stroke or a heart attack."

Jenna frowned. "What do you mean? He had a heart attack, didn't he?"

Sharon pursed her lips. "We still don't know the

culprit, but we think Ben's vital organs show signs of poisoning."

Jenna looked between the two, trying to come to grips with what she was hearing. "Wait, what does this mean then?"

Sharon's voice was grim. "It means that the police are now considering Ben's death a homicide."

7
LEE

When Sharon had called to ask for a meeting, Lee hadn't thought much of it. He had assumed that the doctor just wanted to hand over his grandfather's remaining medical reports.

"What do you mean 'homicide'?" Jenna stared at Sharon, her voice tense. "Who would want to kill Ben?"

Sharon looked just as upset. "I don't know what to tell you. The coroner didn't release the reports to anyone but the hospital chief and the police until now."

"So, what? He's been sitting on those reports for all this time?" Jenna sounded furious. "It's been weeks! Lee deserved to know. And why did they want to suddenly conduct an autopsy?"

Sharon shoved her hands in her pockets. "When the ambulance transports someone who is deceased, there is always an initial examination. The doctor who was on duty at the time felt that something was off. While Ben was showing all the symptoms of having suffered another heart attack, there were a few abnormalities that the doctor noticed. That's why he ordered an autopsy."

Lee sat down heavily on the porch steps, staring at nothing. "So, Gramps was killed." His voice was dazed. "Who would want to kill him? He didn't have any enemies. Everybody loved him."

Sharon's voice was cautious. "My personal belief is that it might've been a slow-acting poison. But I can't say anything for sure. The police are handling the case right now. I just wanted to come tell you in person so that it didn't come as a surprise. The sheriff's going to come and see you today."

It had been hard enough to come to terms with his grandfather's death, but to find out that it might've been murder was shaking Lee up all over again.

Then he felt Jenna's hand on his shoulder, and her touch was grounding. "We'll figure it out from here," she said. "Thanks, Sharon."

Once again, despite her snarky attitude toward him, Jenna was acting as his shield. Lee didn't need protection, but he did appreciate having her by his side.

He looked at Sharon and nodded. "Thanks for letting me know."

Sharon hesitated. "Sorry I couldn't do more."

She left almost immediately after that, and Jenna's hand tightened on his shoulder. "Come on. Let's go inside."

Lee followed her into the living room and let her turn on the air conditioning before asking tiredly, "Why are you even here?"

She sat down on one of the couches. "The interviews. They're today. If you want, I can postpone them."

"No," Lee shook his head. "They drove up all the way from different towns. It wouldn't be fair on them." He could see Jenna watching him, and he muttered, "Why would anybody try to kill Gramps?"

Jenna tapped her finger on the arm of the couch. "We don't know if they did. Unknown causes don't automatically mean murder. They're going to investigate it as such, but let's hope that's not the case. Benjamin didn't have any enemies though. I'm sure of that."

"Maybe it was business dealings?" Lee said quietly, trying to think past his shock and rack his brain for a reason.

"Have you gone through all his books?"

"Not yet," Lee glanced toward the study. "I've gone through a few of them, but Gramps had a system that I'm still trying to figure out."

"Let me take a look at them," Jenna said, frowning. "I've seen his books before, so I might be able to help out."

"We can do tha—"

His words were interrupted when there was a knock on the door. Jenna immediately got up. "They're here." She looked toward him, hesitating. "If you don't feel up to the interviews, I can take care of them myself."

"No," Lee stood up. "I'm fine. I'll be fine. Let's do this."

THE REST OF THE AFTERNOON PASSED BY IN interviews and tours of the ranch. By the end of it, Jenna was beginning to look exhausted. However, she didn't utter a word.

The sun was setting when they finally trudged back.

"What do you think?" Jenna asked as she sank into the kitchen chair to pour herself some of the cold tea that the housekeeper had left in the fridge for them. "I think Andrew has a better understanding of the ranch and the side businesses. He's also smart enough to drum up more business. As long as you maintain your own records and have an audit conducted once every few years, you should be good. You might just have to come to town every few years to keep an eye on things, but aside from that, you won't have to bother with the ranch."

Lee leaned against the countertop, watching her. "I'm leaning toward Andrew myself." He paused, digesting her words. "It's not like I'm just abandoning the ranch."

"I never said you were." Jenna shrugged. "Your life in New York is waiting for you. You have nothing here."

Lee's jaw tightened. "I thought you said I had you."

He watched her blink, and then an uneasy expression crossed her face. "I mean, you have nothing here to tie you to Sunset Ridge. Your life and your business are there."

"But you're here."

"This is not about me, Lee!" Jenna snapped. "I'm not tying you anywhere."

Lee had the urge to shake her, tired as she looked. The woman had a knack for pressing his buttons. At this point, any other woman would have lowered her shields, but not Jenna. She refused to budge an inch. It was as if she was determined not to let him into her life in any way.

He wanted to say more, but there was yet another knock on the door.

This time it was the sheriff.

Sheriff Stiles was a middle-aged man who used to work on the ranch as a teenager. Lee had seen him at the funeral and the wake. This time, however, the sheriff was here on official business.

He took off his hat as he stepped inside. "I'm real sorry about this, Lee."

Lee nodded his thanks. "Sharon already told me. Come in. You want something to drink?"

"Want some iced tea, Sheriff?" Jenna asked from the kitchen doorway.

Sheriff Stiles looked surprised to see her there and then said, "Yes, please."

Lee waited for Jenna, who sat down next to him after handing over the beverage to the flushed-looking sheriff. It was hot outside, so the redness of the man's face wasn't surprising.

"The coroner thinks it might have been a slow-acting poison," Sheriff Stiles said. "That means that you're not completely off the suspect list."

Lee had had an inkling that his name might be on that list since he was the only one who could financially gain from his grandfather's death.

"I appreciate your honesty, but anyone who knows me would tell you I never wanted the ranch," Lee told him. "My company is worth a lot of money, and even while Hillside Ranch is worth plenty, I'm worth far more."

The sheriff nodded gravely. "I did consider that, which is why you're not on top of the list. I still have to interview you though."

"I understand," Lee said calmly. "If you need any documents from me, I can have my assistant mail you copies of everything."

"I'd appreciate that. How long do you plan to stay in town?"

That question had Lee pausing. "Well, I took a few weeks off from the office. I'm still working from here, and I'll make sure I'm here until the end of the investigation. I also have to hand over the ranch to a manager before I leave."

"That'll take a month, tops," Jenna interjected, and Lee had to refrain from scowling. Why was she so eager to get rid of him?

He glowered in her direction, but she just ignored him.

"Anyway," he growled. "I'm here for as long as I'm needed—"

"Which isn't long—"

"That's up to me to decide, Jenna," Lee said through gritted teeth.

The sheriff looked between the two of them and lifted a brow. "So you two really are together?"

"No!"

"I'm working on it."

The two responses were almost instantaneous, and the sheriff blinked, and then comprehension dawned on him. "Oh, I see."

He cleared his throat and then asked, "Moving back to the topic at hand, I'd like to get a list of all the clients Benjamin had."

There were other questions as well, but it seemed to Lee that Sheriff Stiles had already crossed him off his list, and this interview was just a formality. When the sheriff was done, Lee walked him out. When he returned, he didn't see Jenna in the living room. When he entered the kitchen, he saw her putting a pill in her mouth before swallowing it with water.

"What is that?"

He saw her freeze, and panic washed over her face. "What?"

Lee's instincts told him to press the topic, and he stepped closer. "What was that medicine?"

He saw her hands tighten on the back of the chair, and her face relaxed with deliberate effort. "An aspirin."

"I didn't know they made aspirin that size." He watched her carefully.

"Well, now you do."

As she went to put the glass in the sink, Lee felt a strange sinking sensation in the pit of his stomach. Something was wrong with Jenna. He suddenly felt sure of it.

THE WHOLE TOWN BEGAN TO BUZZ WITH THE news of the investigation.

Midge had been devastated, and Lee had chosen to break the news to her first.

"It'll be fine," he told her. "We'll get through this."

Her sobs had broken his heart. "Who would do this to Ben?"

But Lee had no answers for her.

"So, it's true then?" Kathy murmured, putting Lee's cappuccino down on the small round table in the corner of the café.

Lee had brought his laptop to the café to work since the internet at the ranch wasn't very good. He had to get that fixed, among a laundry list of other things on the to-do list.

"Yeah," he said heavily. "One of the deputies interviewed Midge yesterday at the station, and she just burst into tears."

Kathy clasped the small round tray to her chest, her lips pressed into a thin line. "Midge is a sensitive soul. Why didn't they just interview her at the ranch?"

Lee had been pretty annoyed by that himself.

He had driven the old housekeeper to the station because she had been devastated.

"I don't know. I offered that they could interview her there. But since she handled all the food in the house, they are still looking at her."

Kathy let out a disbelieving noise. "That poor dear. I'll drop by after work and check up on her."

"She's been with us for years," Lee sighed. "She and Gramps used to be friends when they were kids. His death hit her harder than anybody. She was inconsolable at the funeral."

Since the café only had a few customers for now, Kathy sat down. "I heard you finally hired a manager for the ranch."

Lee nodded. "Jenna told you?"

Kathy blinked. "Jenna? No. I heard it from Billy, your foreman. I haven't seen Jenna in a few days."

Lee, who had been about to take a sip of his drink, paused, his hand hovering in midair. "I thought she came here every day."

"She does, but she went to Rock Springs for some meetings."

Lee set down his cup. "For a few days?"

Kathy wouldn't meet his eyes. "She's taking a few days to rest. Things have been hectic."

Lee didn't know why, but for some reason, he felt that Kathy was hiding something from him. However, he kept his tone casual. "Does Jenna usually get tired easily?"

Kathy gave him a wary look. "What do you mean?"

Lee kept his eyes pinned on her. "Just a question. The other day she didn't look so good, and then I saw her half passed out in the middle of the road in her car. I find it odd because Cole never mentioned anything."

He saw Kathy hesitate before she said, "Well, she works eighteen hours a day. Anybody would get tired."

"Then she should talk to somebody about reducing her workload."

Lee wasn't buying her explanation. Kathy was not that good of a liar. He could see the guilt on her face, but he also knew that she was loyal to Jenna, so whatever the problem was, she would never tell him, even if he confronted her. But now, at least he knew for certain something was wrong.

However, he had come to this café with another specific goal in mind.

"Does Jenna date a lot?"

The sudden change in topic clearly threw Kathy, and she was about to answer when the door opened and Pastor Dean walked in.

"What's going on?"

"I thought you had Bible study until three?" Kathy gave him a confused look.

Her brother shrugged. "I did. But the kids kept complaining about how hot it was, so I told them we'd have a make-up class on the weekend."

"You know they're fleecing you, right?" Kathy studied him. "They're not going to show up."

Her twin smiled, a sinister smile that didn't quite suit a man of God. "I always keep my weekends free. Their parents will appreciate a little free time if I have to corral the kids to teach them."

Lee didn't know whether to be amused or concerned. "That sounds a little threatening."

"It's all about perspective," Pastor Dean said, sinking into the armchair across from Lee. "So, what were you talking about?"

"Lee wanted to know if Jenna goes on many dates," Kathy explained.

Pastor Dean snorted. "No one has ever managed to get a second date with her."

Kathy frowned. "Well, that's just not true. She used to go out with Bobby Barnes until—"

Her sentence stopped abruptly as an almost sad expression crossed her face. Lee would almost call it grief. But her voice was steady as she continued, "She went out with him a couple of times."

"That was years ago," her twin argued. "She stopped dating after that. Now, she just goes out with a different guy every few weeks."

Kathy frowned. her voice tinged with disapproval. "I don't like the way you phrased that."

Pastor Dean's eyes widened at the reprimand. "I'm not implying anything. She's just not looking for any long-term relationship. Even you know that. How many of her dates have tried to ask her out again? There's nothing wrong with enjoying life. Jenna is a good Christian. She just goes out with them for dinner and dancing."

Kathy gave him a long look. "Fine, you're forgiven."

"Who's Bobby Barnes?" Lee asked.

"One of the deputies," Pastor Dean responded. "Was madly in love with Jenna at some point. He's married now. Got a baby girl on the way any day now."

Lee tried to rack his brains, but he couldn't really remember if Jenna had been dating anybody when he had left. But then again, after middle school, Jenna hadn't really dated at all. The two of them had always been stuck together at the hip.

"What about when I left?"

He saw Kathy go still at his question, and she asked cautiously, "What do you mean?"

"Did she date somebody?"

He saw Pastor Dean stare at him with an incredulous look, and he said, even as Kathy tried to stop him, "Are you really that stupid? She was madly in love with you when you left. You broke her heart, man. Why do you think she hates you so much now?"

Everything inside of Lee went still.

"*What?*" he croaked.

"Dean!" Kathy hit her brother on the back side of his head. "Do you ever shut up?!"

Her brother gave her an offended look. "Why does it matter if he knows? Secrets are the devil's work. Plus, that was ten years ago!"

His sister picked up the small cushion from behind her and hit him with it. "You don't go around spilling other people's secrets!"

Pastor Dean grimaced as he fended for himself. "I didn't think it was that big of a—"

He looked toward Lee as he was about to finish his sentence, and his voice faded as he saw the expression on Lee's face. "…deal. Oh boy."

"Jenna was in love with me?" Lee echoed, feeling numb.

Kathy sighed, hitting her brother one more time before tucking the cushion behind her back. "Yeah. But it was a long time ago."

"Why didn't she ever say anything?" Lee couldn't understand this hollow feeling inside of him.

"You never told her that you planned to leave," Kathy murmured. "And the day that you left, she was waiting for you at your old spot. She wanted to tell you, but you left. She waited for hours until the sun went down, and then she went looking for you only to find out that you had left without even saying goodbye."

Each word was like a stab to his heart.

Jenna's reaction to his return was making so much more sense now.

"She waited for weeks to hear from you," Kathy finally said, a hint of anger in her voice now. "And then, on her birthday, you sent an email to Cole, but you sent nothing for her. That really broke her heart."

Lee's hands felt cold at this revelation, and he recalled what his grandfather had said. Jenna had visited him every day. Even after she had figured out that he wanted nothing to do with her, she had still looked after his grandfather.

"I'm not—That birthday message—I wanted to call Jenna," Lee murmured, remembering how long he had gazed at the phone. "But I knew that if I heard her voice, I would want to come back and abandon everything I was working for. I missed her more than anything. She was the only one who could make me come back, and I was determined not to."

"Well," Kathy stood up, her voice uncharacteristically cold now. "You got everything you worked for, but you lost Jenna. Hope you're happy, Lee."

Lee stared down at his laptop, his heart feeling utterly empty.

LEE TRIED TO FIND JENNA, BUT SHE EXTENDED her stay in Rock Springs for a few more days. Not even her family knew where she was staying.

"She said it was at some motel," Cole said, his voice uncharacteristically quiet, as he twirled the fork around his pasta.

They were sitting at the diner, grabbing dinner together.

"Everything okay with you?" Lee asked, studying his unnaturally subdued friend.

"I don't know, man," Cole met his gaze. "Jenna's been acting a bit off for a while now."

"What do you mean?"

Cole shrugged. "We used to be really tight. But she started pulling away a few years ago. At first I thought, you know, she just wanted her space, but now it feels different. I barely see her once or twice a week, although we live on the same ranch. She suddenly decided to move out of the main house. Our parents were upset, but, once again, we thought she wanted some space. I called her yesterday, asking her which motel she was staying at, but she just avoided the question. She said she'd be back the day after tomorrow."

That didn't sound like the Jenna Lee knew.

"Have you tried talking to her?"

"I did," Cole muttered. "But you know how she is. She just told me I'm imagining it and that everything's fine. But it's not just me. Ma and Dad also think she's pushing us away."

There was a strange feeling forming in Lee's gut and he said, his voice terse. "I found her on the side of the road a few weeks back. She was half unconscious in her car. She said she was tired. It's not the first time I've come across her in that kind of state. The other day, Kathy insisted I drive her home, and she could barely walk."

Lee saw the alarm seep into Cole's eyes. "You think something is wrong with her and she's hiding it from us?"

"That would be my guess. Have you noticed anything strange about her lately?"

Cole's brows knit together as he racked his brains. Then he said slowly, "She's become less energetic over the past few years. And she's begun to go into the city a lot. She makes different excuses every time, but we never know where she's staying or what she's doing."

The pit forming in Lee's stomach was growing larger by the second. Jenna was clearly hiding something from her family.

"I'll talk to he—"

"I doubt it will help," Lee said slowly. "I have a feeling Kathy knows, but she won't give Jenna away."

"You want me to go behind Jenna's back and find out what she's hiding?" Cole asked quietly. "She'll consider it a betrayal."

Lee knew that Cole had a point, but he also knew that Jenna would not tell them anything if she could avoid it.

"Maybe an outright confrontation might help," he muttered. "But—"

His words faded when he saw the door to the diner open, and Vicky walked in.

He scowled.

His friend looked over his shoulder to see who it was, and Cole grimaced. "Why did you ever go out with her?"

"To get on your sister's nerves, mostly," Lee admitted without thinking, and it was only when he heard the fork fall with a clang onto Cole's plate that he realized what he had just said.

His friend was watching him with wide eyes. "You did it to make Jenna jealous?"

Lee winced. "Well, kind of."

"Did it work?" Cole grinned, some of his worry seeming to lift at least a little bit.

Lee gave him a dry look. "Have you not heard the rumors?"

Cole's expression darkened. "Oh yeah. I can't believe you kissed my sister. I should shoot you."

"At times like these, I can really see the resemblance between the two of you," Lee muttered. "She threatens to shoot me every time she sees me."

"But still. *Vicky*?" Cole made a face.

The woman in question saw them and sauntered over, her voice bright. "Lee!"

Lee gave her a cold look. "Vicky."

She batted her eyes and said, her voice soft, "I've been looking for you."

"Have you?" Lee asked, recalling all the vicious rumors that this woman had been spreading about Jenna.

However, either Vicky was just determined to overlook his lack of interest, or she was really that dense because she leaned forward and said in a coy tone, "I know you must be embarrassed by what happened the other night, but I just wanted to tell you that I understand it wasn't your fault. I saw the way Jenna was eyeing you."

Lee saw Cole stir in his seat, and he kicked his friend in the leg to keep him from interrupting.

"Really?"

"I thought about it and decided that I'll let you take me out for another date to make up for running out on me," Vicky smiled at him.

Lee wasn't one to be nasty to women, but he had an intense dislike for this particular "lady."

"Well," he said coolly. "Isn't that just gracious of you? But I'm afraid I'm not interested."

He saw Vicky's face fall. "Excuse me?"

Lee raised his voice slightly so that the people around them could listen in as he stood up. "It was never a date when we went out the other day. You just wanted to catch up. I was very clear on that. It's not my fault you kept insisting it was a date. Then you went on to spread false rumors about Jenna after what happened. You attempted to trash her reputation, and that is not okay with me. Jenna is more than just a friend to me, which I explained to you after she left."

Lily stood behind the counter, a satisfied smile on her face that was mirrored on Cole's own lips.

Vicky's face was growing red. "How can you even look at that woman, if you want to call her a woman? She works with men all day long! How do you know that she's not —"

"Finish that sentence, Vicky. I dare you," came a cool voice from the doorway.

Lee's head jerked up, as did Cole's, when they recognized the voice.

Jenna stood in the doorway of the diner, her arms crossed over her chest as she watched Vicky with a ruthless gaze.

She had almost purplish bags under eyes, and her cheeks were a little sunken.

Lee's heart almost stopped at the sight. She looked incredibly sick.

One glance at Cole revealed that he was thinking the same thing.

He saw Vicky take a step back and then square her shoulders. "Am I wrong? Who knows what you get up to at that ranch. And it's not like you don't have a reputation in town for dating around."

Jenna lifted a brow. "Since when is my dating life your concern?"

"I'm just looking out for Lee!" Vicky said angrily. "He doesn't need a loose woman like you in his life."

Jenna's smile was vicious. "Seems to me that's exactly what he wants. He went out with you, didn't he?"

Under Jenna's haggard appearance and sharp smile, Lee could see the burning anger. He wanted to defuse the situation, but he wasn't stupid enough to get in between Jenna and her target. Jenna was no docile kitten. She had claws sharp enough to draw blood.

The whole diner had fallen silent, and Lee could see Vicky tremble in rage. "I love him!"

Jenna's eyes widened, and Vicky continued, "I have always loved him!"

Jenna stared at her, as did Lee, stunned.

"Oh, really?" Jenna blinked. "You've always loved him? What do you love about him?"

When Vicky struggled with an answer, Jenna urged her in a mocking tone, "Go ahead. You've always loved him. It can't be that hard."

"He—I love how hard he works!"

Jenna rolled her eyes. "Give me a better reason than something so generic."

Lee winced, and Cole made a pitying sound.

"I—I don't have to explain my love to you!" Vicky finally cried out, her hands curled into fists.

People around them were snickering.

"Why don't I clarify then?" Jenna said pleasantly. "You suddenly love him because he's rich. Because he can give you the lifestyle that you think you deserve. You're not in love with him. You're in love with his money. You need to grow up, Vicky. You're not in high school anymore. If you want money so much, get a better-paying job. Don't expect a man to be a walking, talking bank account."

"You can't talk to me like that!" Vicky hissed, and Jenna gave her an amused look.

"I can't tell you to get a job?"

"You can't dictate my feelings for me!"

Lee could see that Jenna had just about had enough. "Listen. I don't care about you or Lee or whatever feelings you're trying to convince anyone that you have. But I do care if you go around trying to drag my name through the mud. This isn't high school. You keep slandering me, and I'll either pummel you into the ground or throw a lawsuit at you. Depends on what mood I'm in."

Vicky's face was red with a mixture of fear and fury.

If she was smart, she'd back down, but Jenna had thoroughly humiliated her in a room full of people. Even Lee knew that she wasn't going to do the smart thing.

He just sighed quietly, stepping back to watch the drama unfold.

He glanced toward Cole, who was shoving pasta into his mouth, watching the entire show with anticipation.

"You think that just because you and he were friends ten years ago, he'll just fall at your feet!" Vicky spat out. "I know you've been going to his ranch every day. Only God knows what your intentions are. You're always going to be that ill-mannered tomboy who he can never hold on his arm in the kinds of circles he's accustomed to moving in."

Lee frowned at her words. Vicky was going too far.

But she wasn't done yet.

"You'll never be anything more to him than an embarrassment. You talk and dress like a man. You don't have an ounce of grace in you! We all know the real reason you've never been in a long-term relationship. You're good enough to have a good time with but never good enough to take home to a family."

Jenna's face was turning pale, and Lee's blood began to boil.

"Everyone knows it, Jenna," Vicky sneered. "A man wants a soft woman who can nurture his house and welcome him. He doesn't want a woman who curses and spends the whole day sitting with men. Lee isn't any different. No matter your history with him, at the end of the day, you're just a woman he can have a good time with, not marry."

"That's enough!" Lee roared.

He didn't mind being passive around Jenna when she dug into him, but having anyone insult Jenna and put that look on her face was unacceptable.

He saw Vicky's frightened face at his loud voice, and he was about to step forward when he heard someone laughing.

It was Jenna.

8
JENNA

It had been Cole's constant badgering that had made Jenna decide to push for an earlier discharge from the hospital.

Knowing her persistent twin, he would track her down.

The decision to grab a bite from the diner had been a stupid one, Jenna sighed internally as the crazy-eyed woman in front of her shrieked like a banshee.

But there was no way that Jenna could just stand aside and let this woman destroy her reputation.

She had walked in on the last leg of the conversation when Lee had been telling Vicky off and standing up for her. It had taken a heroic effort to stomp down on those traitorous feelings that had tried to worm their way into her heart on hearing that exchange.

It was difficult to keep a straight face as Vicky's words stabbed her.

Jenna knew that nobody considered her to be a loose woman. Most people respected her. It had taken Jenna years, but she had carved a place for herself in this town.

Vicky was right. Jenna was never going to be the kind of woman who a man could show off.

But she couldn't help but laugh at how ridiculous this whole thing was.

She wasn't even going to live long enough to worry about any of this.

The laughter that bubbled out of her mouth was filled with self-mockery, but she wasn't going to let anybody know that.

So, she straightened up and shook her head at Vicky, who was looking at her as if she had finally gone crazy.

"Those things don't matter to me, Vicky. I have earned my place in this town. I don't need a man's approval to make me feel better about myself. And I certainly don't need his parents' approval. Those are things *you* worry about. Your insecurities are not mine to be concerned about. But—" She took a step closer to Vicky and saw her flinch. "If I ever hear you talking trash about me again, you'd best believe that you will be hearing from my lawyer. I'm not going to stoop to your level and engage in a catfight. I've got better things to do with my time."

She saw the blood drain out of Vicky's face.

However, Jenna was not planning to stick around to see the aftermath of the whole confrontation. She was beginning to feel sick to the stomach after all the exertion.

Turning around, she walked out of the diner, leaving Lee to handle Vicky.

But Lee was a step behind her, grabbing her arm as she was about to turn the corner into the parking lot.

"Jenna!" he growled. "Wait!"

Let him leave me be, Jenna prayed silently, but she had no strength to engage in another confrontation at the moment, and so she stopped.

"What? Why do you keep grabbing me? Benjamin raised you better, Lee!"

Lee wasn't listening as he turned her around. "Where have you been?"

"Excuse me?"

"You heard me," he growled. "Where have you been for this past week?!"

Jenna's brows knit together. "I was in the city, not that it's any of your business."

"Why?"

"You may refer to the second part of my statem—"

"Now is not the time to be a smart mouth," Lee glared at her. "You look terrible. What happened to you?"

Jenna looked toward the diner and saw her brother sitting there, watching the two.

"Help me," she mouthed, glowering at him.

Cole very conveniently turned his head and decided to finish his meal.

"Will you let me go?" She yanked her arm away. "I was busy. Working."

When Lee didn't say anything, she glanced toward him and saw a cold look in his eyes. "When did you become such a good liar?"

Jenna went still.

Uneasiness filled her, and she took a step back. "Look, I don't know what your problem is—"

"My problem is that the woman I'm interested in looks like death warmed over. My problem is that she's lying to me, and she has no hesitation in doing so."

"Didn't you just hear Vicky?" Jenna made a face. "I'm not the right woman to be interested in. Apparently, I have no class and no manners. Don't waste your time here, Lee. I'm not interest—"

"Why didn't you tell me you were in love with me?"

Jenna stared at him, shock filtering through her. "What?"

He took a step toward her and without thinking, she took one back, her heart racing at the gleam in his eyes.

Lee was rarely angry.

His patience was never-ending, especially with her, and seeing him like this, advancing on her, his eyes intent, made her stomach tighten.

"Before I left," he said, his voice heavy. "Why didn't you tell me that you were in love with me?"

"I—" Jenna tried to think up of a quick-witted reply to save her from this situation, but her brain was coming up empty. "I—Who told you that?"

"An extremely reliable source."

The confidence in his voice told her that there was no getting out of this. He knew what he knew; no matter what Jenna said, he wouldn't believe it.

"It was a long time ago."

"But you've still held a grudge all these years."

"Well," Jenna was moving backward into the

parking lot as Lee just kept walking toward her. "I'm a petty person."

"You're not *that* petty," Lee said in an almost reasonable voice.

"You don't —"

"So, what is it?" he said abruptly. "Have you been trying to push me away because you still have feelings for me, or do you truly despise me?"

"Despise is a strong word," Jenna muttered, trying to calm her wildly beating heart.

"So then I should assume you have feelings for me."

"No?" She cursed herself for the indecisive-sounding word.

Before she could say anything else, Lee responded, "Are you trying to convince yourself or me?"

Jenna didn't like being cornered like this. She narrowed her eyes at him. "Why do you care? You're going to be gone in a few weeks. I'm not going to be your summer fling—"

"You have some gall to assume that I would treat you with that much disrespect," He smiled at her, but for some reason, that smile, accompanied by the predatory look in his eyes, made a shiver run down Jenna's spine.

"Back off, Evans," she warned, suddenly feeling that she was losing ground.

But Lee, who would usually sigh and let her be, or at least retaliate, just smiled. "Why? What are you going to do?"

They were in full view of the diner's large windows, and when Jenna glanced toward them, she saw people watching.

"People are looking at us!" she growled.

"Good," was all Lee said before he took advantage of her momentary distraction and covered the distance between them, one hand wrapping around her waist and the other holding her in place by her nape.

This time, the kiss was gentle and soft. Almost drugging.

Jenna wasn't even given an opportunity to fight back. She fell victim to the tender assault and went limp in his arms almost instantly. Even when she felt his lips curve against her mouth in triumphant satisfaction, she was unable to summon any amount of anger to push him away.

It was then that she began to realize that ever since Lee had shown up, he had been patiently whittling away at her walls.

When she had seen him staring at her that first day, it felt like something inside of her had come back to life. She had shoved that feeling inside a box in her heart and sealed it away. But Lee had been determined from the start to get back into her life.

She should never have been kind to him.

She should never have offered him her help.

Hating herself for the way her heart pounded at the way he so gently kissed her, Jenna tried to bury those feelings again. But she could no longer stuff them in the box that was overflowing. It wouldn't close.

When Lee pulled away, Jenna felt dazed, and she felt her hand curled in some fabric, only to realize that it was his shirt.

She immediately released the fistful of fabric, her cheeks turning bright red when it dawned on her what had just taken place.

"You!" she swore.

Lee grinned at her, dancing out of reach. "You kissed me back again!"

"I'm going to stab you, Evans!" she growled, both flustered and angry.

"No, you won't," Lee looked smug. "You like me."

"I never said that!"

"You just let me kiss you," he pointed out to her utter mortification. "In front of quite a few witnesses, might I add."

"You—It wasn't—You're insufferable!" Jenna wanted to wring his neck even as her lips tingled at the memory of the kiss. "You are the worst—"

"And yet you let me kiss you both times," Lee waggled his brows. "The more you try to push me away, Jenna, the more I want you."

"You don't always get what you want," Jenna muttered, a painful throbbing in her chest.

"You're an idiot, Lee. You're just setting yourself up for heartbreak."

She saw his expression change, but Jenna was already striding toward her truck and getting in.

Her heart was pounding painfully as the truck roared out of the parking lot. She ground her teeth until she hit the dirt road that led toward the ranches, and then she stopped the truck, putting it in park.

She blindly stared out at the empty road, her ears roaring and her heart pounding.

What was she doing?

Why was she letting this man get under her skin?

She had built these walls for a reason.

But patient, stubborn Lee, with his warm smiles, had managed to dig a small hole and found a way inside.

The tears leaked out, hot and scalding.

Jenna leaned her head against the steering wheel, swamped by bitter sobs.

"Lord, help me!" she cried brokenly. She hit the dashboard with the heel of her hand, weeping in frustration and pain.

"Please help me, Lord. I don't want to be sick. And I don't want to still love him. Why won't you help me?"

She didn't want these kisses that stole her breath, and she didn't want to think about a future that would never come to pass.

Three years.

Her doctor had given her a prognosis of three years.

"You're a fool, Lee Evans," she said hoarsely, staring out the windshield, her eyes bruised. "You're going down a path with no future."

THE NEXT FEW DAYS, JENNA FOUND HERSELF coping with the side effects of the injection.

Her balance was a little off, so she decided not to ride any of the horses. Instead, she delegated work to her subordinates. However, she still had to check on Hillside Ranch.

She really didn't want to go there, knowing that Lee would be there.

So, she chose a time when she was sure he wouldn't be around.

She knew from Kathy that Lee would often go to the coffee shop to work. He would be there in the afternoons, which was why Jenna chose to drive all the way to the ranch in the middle of the afternoon. She just had to have a quick conversation with the foreman.

But, when she arrived, there was a car parked in the driveway and two men stood on the porch, knocking on the door. They were wearing suits and didn't seem to be from town.

Cautiously, Jenna walked over to them. "Can I help you gentlemen?"

They looked over at her, and she could see them studying her, trying to figure out who she was.

"We're looking for Lee Evans," one of them said. "You know where we can find him?"

Jenna crossed her arms over her chest. "Might I know what this is for?"

The two men exchanged a look, and then the taller one said, "It's a private matter. We need to talk to—"

Their eyes instantly went to the side of the house to the right, and when Jenna followed their gaze, she saw Lee coming around the side, talking to the foreman, Billy. She went still, as did Lee when he saw her.

But then he looked in the direction of the two men, and a heavy frown settled on his face. "Can I help you?"

"Are you Lee Evans?" the man who had spoken first asked.

"I am." Lee studied him.

Jenna watched him take a card from his suit's front pocket. "I'm a representative of Forrest Development. We sent you an email, but there was no response—"

"Because I'm not interested," Lee said shortly.

Interested in what? Jenna looked between the two.

"My buyer is willing to make a higher offer," the man said quickly.

"I'm not willing to sell the ranch," Lee said, his voice hard as he began walking.

Toward her, Jenna realized.

She immediately took a step back, and annoyance flared within her when she saw a smile form on his lips at her actions. But then, when he got closer, his smile faded when he got a good look at her face.

Jenna already knew what he was looking at.

Her cheeks were sunken in, and her clothes were hanging off her frame slightly.

She hadn't had much of an appetite recently, and whatever she was eating, she was throwing up. It was only yesterday that she had begun to adapt to the pills she had been given along with the injection. Her appetite was slightly back, and she was no longer throwing up. She was more energetic as well.

"What happened to you?"

Lee's eyes were wide, and she saw fear in them.

"Nothing," Jenna shook her head. "You go deal with your guests. I have to talk to Billy."

She didn't want to talk to Lee. It was difficult to keep herself in check with him around.

She started to walk away, but Lee was quick to grab her wrist and pull her into his side, securing her with his arm around her waist.

Jenna saw the foreman's eyes widen, and she scowled. "Let me go, Evans."

"We need to talk," Lee said quietly.

This time Jenna didn't hesitate. She was letting him get away with far too much lately. She lifted her boot and stomped on his foot. "Hands off, Evans. I've told you to quit manhandling me. I'm not your property."

He winced and let her go, glaring. "You're not anybody else's either."

"Don't tempt me," Jenna said, narrowing her eyes. "Billy! With me."

Billy looked between the two, and he trudged after her, shooting an apologetic look toward his cursing boss.

A silent prayer left Jenna's heart. *Just give me the willpower I need right now.*

"What is being done about the replacement of the two trucks?" Jenna got straight down to business as they approached the large barn where most of the farm equipment was kept.

Billy reached into his pocket and took out a folded paper. "I was just talking to Mr. Lee about this."

Jenna blinked. "I thought he wasn't interested in the ranch operations."

The foreman beamed with a hint of pride. "He's gotten involved lately. He's been spending hours on the business records, and he's been getting to know everyone working here."

Jenna stopped in her tracks. "Why? But he's going back!"

Billy gave her an odd look and then a knowing smile. "It seems he's set his heart on something here. Who knows? He might just decide to stay."

Jenna's hands began to tremble, and she shoved them in her pockets, not wanting to reveal her agitation.

She watched a barn cat rub itself against her legs before darting out after a grasshopper.

Jenna vaguely listened to Billy as he talked about costs and repairs. Lee had begun to take an interest in the ranch, and he had begun looking at the things that she was overseeing until the ranch manager stepped in.

Jenna could see the ranch hands were more relaxed, and she knew this was because Lee was playing the role he was meant to.

"I guess I won't need to come by all that much anymore," she commented as she walked back to her truck with Billy. "Lee seems to have a pretty good understanding of how to run things here now."

"I wasn't expecting that," Billy confessed. "He's changed since he got back."

"Really?" Jenna asked idly.

She wasn't surprised. After all, he had changed from a mild-mannered man into a more forceful one who had no problem pushing back when she herself got aggressive.

"He used to be so sweet back when he was young," Jenna muttered, annoyed.

When the man walking with her laughed, she gave him an annoyed look.

He just chuckled. "He grew up, Ms. Miles. In my opinion, his decision to go to New York was a good one."

Jenna didn't say anything.

Billy touched his hat. "The way I see it, it was important for him to go and discover himself. He was always such an awkward kid. Never really fit in anywhere. He's grown more confident now. If he had stayed here, I doubt he would have changed."

Jenna knew he was right. The Lee that had returned had a different look in his eyes altogether. He hadn't completely shed his past self, but he had built upon it. He was happier now, more confident and sure of himself.

And he had had to abandon her to do it.

Suddenly the pang in her heart made her stop in her tracks.

Great, Jenna scowled internally. *Now I've gone and hurt my own feelings.*

"Ms. Miles?" Billy looked over his shoulder at her.

"Sorry," she muttered. "I was thinking about something."

She caught up to him, but he stopped. "Mr. Lee's waiting for you, it seems."

Jenna glanced in the direction he was pointing, and she saw Lee leaning against her truck, eyebrows raised.

Her chest tightened, and she had to force herself to keep walking. "I'll see you next week then."

Walking over to the truck, she did her best to ignore Lee, but he stepped in front of Jenna as her hand went to the door handle.

"We need to talk."

"About what?"

"About what you're not telling me," Lee said tightly, standing in front of her now.

Jenna gave him a steady look. "Bold of you to assume that I should tell you things."

"Jenna," Lee's voice had a warning note to it.

Jenna shrugged, returning her hands to her pockets. "What?"

"What's wrong with you?"

"You're going to have to be more specific," Jenna gave him a scoffing look.

She saw Lee's jaw pulse in anger now. "You look sick!"

Jenna made a deliberate show of looking at her reflection in the car window. "I was trying to lose weight. Seems like I did a good job of—"

"You're lying."

"Listen—"

"I know you're hiding something from all of us," he said slowly, and Jenna fell silent.

When she didn't say anything, Lee added, "Even Cole has begun to notice your odd behavior."

"Maybe all of you need to start minding your own business," Jenna said, alarm seeping into her.

"We care about you!" Lee snarled.

She stepped back, suddenly feeling unsure. This was getting out of control.

So, Jenna decided to be cruel. As long as it got him out of her hair and out of her sight.

"You need to stay away from me, Lee. I've been telling you all along that I don't want anything to do with you outside of work. A few kisses mean nothing. And what happened in the past is over and done with. You decided to leave. And I moved on. I'm not the same girl you left behind. So, stop looking for her in me."

She saw Lee's eyes widen, and she forced herself on ruthlessly. "The only reason that you're so adamant about pursuing me is because I'm not simpering after you. But your bruised ego is not a reason to make me uncomfortable. You don't know a darned thing about me. You say you're interested in me, but you know next to nothing about me. I am not interested in a city slicker. And that is what you've become. So, leave me alone. Leave me and my problems alone."

She saw the hurt in his eyes, and something within her desperately wanted to wipe that look away. But this had to be done. Because if she let this go on any longer, both of them would suffer. There was nothing she could give Lee aside from a painful future.

So even as her heart throbbed, she brushed past him and entered her truck.

The only thing she saw as she drove away was his pale face.

Her face was wet as her fingers clenched and unclenched on the steering wheel. But Jenna kept driving. She didn't stop at home to grab some lunch. She drove straight up to her cottage and parked next to it.

Her breathing was shallow as she lowered her head to rest it against the steering wheel.

"You had to do it," she whispered. "You had to. It's for his own good."

But the reassurances did nothing to calm her aching heart. When she had seen Lee for the first time after he had returned, she'd vowed to never get entangled with him. And look at her now.

Here she was, crying in her truck over the man who had once again stolen her heart.

She slammed her hand down on the dashboard, cursing. "Stupid. Stupid, stupid, stupid! How could you let him do that to you again?!"

Her vision was half blurred with the tears as she finally leaned her head back against the seat, acknowledging her own feelings.

You were the only person who could make me stay.

She recalled the words he had spoken to her a while ago, and she closed her eyes miserably. The best way to deal with this was to break Lee's heart the way he had broken hers all those years ago.

"It's not like he loves you now," Jenna told herself. "He's just interested in you, most probably because you've given him the cold shoulder so much. Men always want what they can't have. His heart isn't going to break that much."

But mine is, she added silently.

Even so, it was going to be fine.

She had to keep telling herself that.

God will get me through this, she told herself fiercely. *He's gotten me through everything else, hasn't He?*

Wiping her eyes, she got out of the truck.

It was about time to take her medicine. She decided to make herself a cup of tea and a sandwich to go along with it.

But when she reached the gate of the cottage, she went still.

Somebody had trampled all over her precious flowers.

Jenna's heart crawled into her mouth as she looked around at the devastation that had been wrought on her carefully maintained garden. Then, her eyes went to the front door, and she saw that it stood open.

Jenna didn't hesitate, striding over and walking into the living room.

Chaos.

She saw how everything had been broken. Her table lay on its side, her dinnerware broken into pieces. Not a single chair had been spared.

The kitchen appliances that she had maintained with such care were all broken, their parts crushed under somebody's foot. Her bedroom, her living room, and her kitchen had all suffered the wrath of somebody.

Jenna moved through her home numbly, her eyes taking in the damage.

It was when she saw the door of the bathroom, half open, that a terrible thought occurred to her. She ignored the broken sink and opened the cabinet.

Her lips parted in horror when she saw that her medicines were no longer there.

"No. No. No!" she whispered, looking around.

She saw the edge of the orange bottle next to the toilet, and it was when she stepped toward the toilet bowl that she saw small white tablets floating in the water.

Jenna nearly sank to the floor in shock.

She scrambled to pick up the prescription bottle, but it was empty.

Her hands were shaking as she stared blankly at the eroding tablets in the toilet bowl. Even if she overlooked the damage to her house, throwing away her medicine was a malicious act.

She was supposed to take her medicine at a certain time to control the side effects.

There was no way she could get the prescription filled again without speaking to the doctor. And she knew exactly what would happen if she missed even one dose of the medicine.

Jenna didn't hesitate.

There was no time to cry about what had just happened. She had to get to Rock Springs Hospital immediately.

9
LEE

Jenna was many things.

But she wasn't cruel.

Lee stood in his kitchen, staring at his laptop at the number of emails he had begun to receive. However, his eyes were glazed over as he thought about Jenna's reaction this afternoon.

Three hours had passed, and Lee could still not get over the words she had spit out at him.

He could also not get the image of her eyes out of his head. Even when her words had been harsh, there had been something akin to devastation in her eyes.

He was angry and hurt.

But he couldn't help but think there was a deeper meaning to this. Jenna never did anything without purpose. For her to push him away like this, in the cruelest manner she possibly could, was off.

She could be curt, but cruel wasn't in her vocabulary.

Lee closed the laptop with a frustrated growl.

He couldn't focus on anything with the way she had barged out on him.

"Everything okay, Lee?" Midge asked from where she was slicing some potatoes for dinner.

"Yes, no—I don't know," Lee muttered.

He saw Midge smile at him. "It's Jenna, isn't it?"

Lee sank into the chair across from her. "I don't know what to do about her. I tried to tell her how I feel, but she made it sound like I was just interested in her because of my ego. But that's not true. The way I feel about her is—I've never felt that way about any other woman. But she refuses to see it."

Midge deftly moved her knife over the potato. "Jenna is a sweet girl. Under all that bravado, she has a sensitive soul. Sometimes when someone hurts you, it's not easy to forgive. You need to earn that forgiveness. Trust isn't something that just comes to you. Especially when you've broken it once."

Lee stared at her. "What do you want me to do?"

"You need to be sure of your feelings." Midge set down her knife. "Do you see a future with Jenna down the road? What do you see in your future in the next five or ten years? Is she in there?"

"She's always been there. Never once did her image waver when I thought about my future." Admittedly, that hadn't been romantic. Lee had simply imagined someday retiring back home... and Jenna would be there, of course. He'd taken it for granted. Problematically, now he found himself thinking of having her in his life in a whole new light...

But Jenna wouldn't care.

She didn't care about how he felt, and she

refused to even give him a chance. Today had been the last straw.

It was time they had a long conversation.

On one hand, he was hearing accounts of how Jenna looked out for everyone. She was very respected in town. People turned to her for the smallest of things, and while she could be a little bad-tempered, she was always kind.

But that was never the woman who stood before him. It was as if Jenna was determined to portray the worst side of herself to make him run away.

Lee grabbed his keys and phone.

He didn't know what was true. Which side of her was really real? But he was done letting her push him around.

He wanted answers.

Getting into his car, he decided to drive all the way to Jenna's cottage. But to his surprise, her truck wasn't there. And when he got out, he noticed the destroyed flowers.

He froze.

He knew Jenna loved her garden.

Lee called Cole.

When his friend picked up after one ring, Lee said in a grim tone, "You need to get down here to Jenna's place. I think somebody broke in… and I don't see her truck anywhere, so she's not home."

He didn't wait for a response, tucking the phone back into his pocket and walking inside, only to be greeted by even worse damage.

His blood was icy as he looked around, wading through the broken furniture. Every single thing had been destroyed with great deliberation.

It was as he was walking toward the bedroom and bathroom that he heard a soft sound of horror from behind him.

Kathy stood in the entrance, her face shocked, her voice a whisper. "What happened here?!"

"I don't know," Lee said, his voice tight. "I found it like this. Why are you here?" He saw two bags in her hands and frowned. "Are those groceries?"

He saw an uneasy look cross Kathy's face. "Yeah."

"Why are you bringing Jenna groceries?"

"She was feeling a bit off," Kathy replied. "I'll call the sher—" Just then her phone began to ring.

She set down the two bags and dug into her purse for her phone. "Hello, Kathy speaking— What? Yes. Yes, that's right." Her expression was growing paler and paler by the second. "What do you mean she's—"

Her eyes widened, and she suddenly rushed past Lee into the bathroom. Lee didn't know what was going on, but he followed her and saw her crouch down next to the toilet bowl and pick up an orange-colored bottle, which looked like a prescription bottle.

"Yes. Yes, she was telling the truth." Kathy looked into the toilet bowl, and Lee followed her gaze to see white tablets floating in it. "I'll be right there. Her doctor is Dr. Ralph. No. Yes. I'm on my way. I have her insurance information with me."

When she ended the call, Lee stepped in her path. "What's going on?"

Kathy turned pale. "Look, I need to go—"

"What's happening with Jenna?" Lee's voice was cold. "Where is she, and what is wrong with her?"

Kathy bit her lower lip. "It's really not my place to say, Lee."

"I don't care," Lee said shortly. "You either tell me here, or I will follow you to whichever hospital you're going and I'll bring along her entire family. I have a feeling they're in the dark as well."

He saw Kathy hesitate, and then grief filled her eyes as she whispered, "Jenna was diagnosed with liver cancer a while ago. They can't find a transplant match for her, and the doctor has given her three more years."

All the blood drained from Lee's face as he whispered hoarsely, "What?"

He heard someone behind him and looked over his shoulder to see Cole standing there, his face pale.

It was as if somebody had ripped Lee's heart out of his chest.

Jenna was dying.

THE DOCTOR ON DUTY ALLOWED THEM TO SEE Jenna, who was unconscious.

Cole was talking to Jenna's doctor while Kathy talked to the nurse.

Jenna looked haggard. Her weight loss made so much more sense now, as did her surly attitude. According to the doctor, she was in constant pain.

She had been trying to push Lee away all this time, and now he knew why.

The doctor on duty had told them that Jenna had barely managed to reach the nurses' station and give them some information before she passed out. Her doctor had had her admitted, and she was now on pain medication along with some antibiotics.

The hospital gown she had been put in had short sleeves, and Lee saw the bruises on her arms, including fresh ones on her upper arms. He felt sick. *Did I…*

Lee lowered his head and tried to keep it together. *Forgive me, Lord. And save her. Please. I already lost Gramps…not her too. Please.*

He heard a soft groan and lifted his head to see Jenna open her eyes, her expression dazed.

"Hey," he said softly, lifting her hand in both of his and bringing it to his lips. "How are you feeling?"

She looked at him, her expression confused. "What happened?"

Lee had imagined plenty of times how he would confront her for lying to him, but right now, watching her look so confused and vulnerable, such a far cry from her usually strong, stoic self, he couldn't muster any strength to argue with her.

"You passed out at the nurses' station," he said gently.

Jenna let out another groan and curled into a ball. "Oh!"

Lee's hand was going toward the buzzer when she shook her head. "It'll pass. Don't."

Each second that Lee waited for her pain to subside was a different sort of agony to him. Jenna wasn't crying. Her eyes were closed, squeezed shut, her jaw clenched as she breathed past the pain. As if she had a lot of experience doing that over and over again.

When her body finally relaxed, she slowly straightened herself before letting out a long sigh. "Well, this is just great."

"How long did you plan to hide this from everyone?" Lee asked, watching her, trying to keep his voice steady.

"Well," Jenna just looked tired now, as if the fight had left her. "I had a plan."

"Yes," Lee narrowed his eyes at her. "We know all about your plan. Kathy was very forthcoming."

"Kathy and her big mouth," Jenna sighed again.

Lee stood up, unable to keep sitting. "Dr. Ralph said that you're on the list for a transplant."

"I am far down the list."

"What about your family?" Lee persisted. "Surely one of them can be a match."

"They aren't," Jenna replied, her voice tired in a way that was making his heart ache. Gone were the scowls and the bad-tempered responses. She looked like a woman who had been on the battlefield. "I checked."

"There have to be other ways—"

He saw Jenna hesitate, and then she just looked away, "You shouldn't interfere in this. I'll figure this out."

"You mean by dying?" Lee snarled at her. "*That's* your strategy?"

"Well," Jenna muttered. "It's one of them."

"This is not the time for jokes, Jenna!"

"I'm not joking!" Jenna finally burst out. "I'm trying to deal with the situation the best way I can. I have considered my options. This is my problem, Lee. Kathy should never have told you!"

Lee wanted to shake her. "You are the most stubborn person I've ever met in my life!"

He saw Jenna purse her lips tight at his words, and for a moment he thought he saw a glimmer of tears in her eyes before she turned her head away from him.

"So, then, leave," she said, her voice harsh. "Walk out the door. You're so good at it, after all."

Lee winced.

The silence that followed their exchange was almost deafening.

"I'm sorry," Lee finally said. "I understand why you didn't tell anybody. And I am sorry for leaving, Jenna. I'm sorry for not saying goodbye. I'm sorry for not wishing you a happy birthday after I left. I'm sorry for making you feel like I abandoned you. And I'm sorry for breaking your heart."

He heard a soft sniffle, and his own heart splintered at the sad sound.

"Will you please look at me?"

"I don't want to," Jenna replied, her voice thick. Her hands were clenched in the white sheet as they shook.

So Lee very gently pulled her to him, letting go of his anger at her attempt to hide something like this. "I'm sorry that you had to brave all this alone." His voice shook.

Jenna was stiff in his arms, and then her form relaxed and she curled into him.

His shirt was growing wet, and Lee closed his eyes in prayer.

He heard a soft scuffle and looked up to see Cole standing in the doorway. His usual bright smile was missing, and there was devastation in his eyes as he looked at his sister.

"Jenna," he whispered, and when Jenna looked up, he rushed forward to take his twin into his arms.

Lee decided to step out and let the siblings have a moment to themselves. His heart heavy, he went in search of Dr. Ralph.

He found the man in his office.

"There has to be a way to bump her up on the waiting list," Lee demanded.

The doctor studied him. "The fastest way is to

find somebody to donate to her solely. But we checked her relatives, and nobody's a match."

"What about me?" Lee said. "You can check me, right? What if I'm a match?"

Dr. Ralph paused. "If you want to check that, I can arrange for some labs. But Jenna's insurance doesn't cover this expense. It was one of the primary concerns she had. I just talked to her brother. He said he'd arrange for —"

"Whatever the cost, I'll pay for it," Lee said coolly. "I just want her alive and well."

Although he knew money wasn't the issue here. Not for the Miles family.

The doctor looked like he wanted to argue, but common sense won over, and he simply led Lee to a nurse, who took some of his blood to test.

"It'll take a few weeks for us to get back to you," Dr. Ralph said as they rounded the corner together. "But I'll let you know."

Lee nodded and returned to Jenna's hospital room. Jenna now looked calmer, as did Cole.

"So, what's the plan?" Lee asked.

"Plan?" Jenna asked. Her color was better, and the doctor had handed Lee the refilled prescription for her medicine. The small paper was tucked into his pocket.

"Somebody trashed your place," Lee said abruptly. "They threw away your medicines. This doesn't seem like a normal home invasion. This seems personal."

"Did either of you call the sheriff?" Jenna looked between the two men.

"I did," Cole replied. "He said he'd go there personally with a few deputies and check out the place. He also wanted to talk to you, Lee."

Lee knew what it was about. The sheriff hadn't found much with regard to his grandfather's death. The police were investigating, but there were currently no leads. Most days, Lee tried very hard just to pretend the investigation wasn't happening. The thought that his grandfather could have been murdered was several steps past bearable. Add Jenna's illness, and Lee really couldn't cope with anything else.

"I handed over some of Gramps's books to the sheriff," Lee murmured. "It must be about that."

When he saw Jenna climb out of bed, he immediately blocked her path, growling. "And just where do you think you're going?"

Jenna stared at him. "To get changed? To go home? They've already discharged me."

"So quickly?" Lee scowled. "You can't be feeling better already."

Jenna pushed past him, and he caught her arm, incredibly gently this time. "Get back into bed. You're still too pale for my liking."

"Don't make me fight you, Evans," Jenna snapped. "The doctor said I'm fine now, and Kathy is bringing around the car. I need to go look after my house." She then groaned. "I have to buy everything all over again."

Her twin grimaced. "I think you do. It was a mess. They used your dinner plates as frisbees."

Unexpectedly, Jenna leaned against Lee. His arms closed around her on pure instinct, holding her close. "How am I supposed to buy everything from scratch? It'll take forever."

"You can always move back into the main house," Cole suggested, and Lee saw the way Jenna glared at him.

"No, thank you. I know you'll tell Ma and Dad. They'll be beside themselves. I'd rather sleep—"

"You can stay with me for a few days," Lee suggested. "You can help me out with the books for a while. And I'll help you replace everything."

"I'm not staying with you. I don't trust you. You don't have good intentions when it comes to me."

"Well, that goes without saying," Lee teased, hoping to make her laugh. "But it's your parents or me. And I promise not to smother you. Plus, it'll just be for a week. And I really do need the help."

He wasn't lying, but his biggest motivation was to have Jenna near him. He intended to replace everything in that cottage, down to planting the flowers all over again. Whenever he looked at that small house with a beautiful garden, it reminded him of when they had made plans to live together. It wasn't just the garden. It was everything in that house that reminded him of that one evening. In his eyes, it felt like the house those two children had dreamed of, and Jenna had ended up building it for herself alone. This time, he wanted to help build it.

"A week," he said again, and he could see the struggle on Jenna's face.

"Ma won't let me breathe," she finally said. "I'll take you up on your offer. But just for a week."

Lee knew that Jenna was using her absence to allow her parents to come to terms with the news.

"They need to see me as I am and not as somebody who needs round-the-clock care," she murmured, pulling away from him.

When she looked at Cole, he nodded. "I'll handle them. Don't worry."

Lee didn't know what they had talked about in the half hour that he had been gone, but Cole looked less tense, and even Jenna looked like a huge burden had been lifted from her shoulders.

She left for the bathroom to change her clothes, and Lee turned toward his friend. "What's going to happen now?"

Cole pursed his lips, his shoulders slumping. "I don't know, man. I think I'll quit my daytime job and start to take over the ranch. We don't know how long Jenna ha—"

"I asked them to check if I was a match," Lee said quietly. "And if I'm not, I have enough resources to look for one. She's not going to die. I won't let that happen, Cole. Let me contact some people."

He saw Cole let out a heavy breath. "I have some resources too. I'll ask around. Jenna has never once asked for anything. As long as my parents are still running the ranch, the money is in the family account. Which is probably why Jenna never asked for it for treatment."

"Your sister is a very complicated woman," Lee said slowly.

"Some would even call her difficult," Cole said with a wobbly smile.

"But I like her because of the way she is," Lee met his friend's gaze.

Cole's eyes widened, and Lee continued quietly. "I think I love her, Cole. When Kathy told me that the doctor had given Jenna few years, it hit me like a ton of bricks. I can't live without that woman. I loved her back then, and I love her now."

Cole was silent, just watching him. "You broke her heart. You don't know what she went through back then. I'm not going to be your friend right now. I have to be Jenna's brother first."

"I made a mistake back then," Lee said, his voice hard. "I messed up, but I don't intend to make the same mistake again." He glanced toward the closed door. "My feelings never changed for her. And this time, I don't want to mess up."

Cole gave him a steady look. "What about when you have to go back? You know she's never going to go with you. She loves the small-town life. She loves working at the ranch. Asking her to leave her life here is never going to work. Jenna is not a city girl."

"Then I'll change," Lee stuck his hands in his pockets. "I can't leave her, Cole. From the moment I arrived in town, she's been pushing me away, but it's never worked. I never had eyes for any other woman aside from her, even when we were teenagers. I was just too dumb to realize it."

"She'll fight you tooth and nail," Cole warned him. "I know she seems harsh, but—"

Lee let out a small laugh. "Harsh? She told me I was setting myself up for heartbreak. And when she did, there were tears in her eyes. That woman inside that room doesn't hate me. She was trying to protect me from what's to come."

His chest felt tight. "I'm not going to let go of her. No matter what happens. Even if God has other plans, I will stay with her until the very end."

He saw Cole look away in obvious distress, and Lee steadied his breathing.

Both of them had to stay strong for Jenna.

"I can't believe she went through all of this by herself," Cole said heavily.

"She wanted to spare all of you the pain."

"It was a stupid idea!" Cole growled.

Lee had to agree with him, but he knew that Jenna wouldn't have been able to see her parents and brother suffer. She had always been that way. She had always hidden her pain to protect the people around her. Fierce, strong, independent Jenna with a heart of gold, which she protected with a sharp tongue.

People liked her because she wore her honesty and character on her sleeve. People trusted her because she was dependable. People loved her because she also loved unreservedly in her own loyal way.

"She's not going to say yes to you," Cole looked away. "She hates being a burden on anybody."

"I'll win her over no matter what I have to do."

Lee was done playing nice. He wasn't going to win over Jenna with patience alone. He needed to play dirty to get her to agree to him. He refused to believe that she didn't have feelings for him. She hid them, buried them, tried her best to hide them, but Lee had grown up with Jenna. Even if they had spent ten years apart, he knew her better than herself. That was why he had been able to pick apart her lies when few others had.

Just as he heard the bathroom door open, his cell phone began to ring.

It was Gramps's lawyer.

"Mr. Collin," Lee frowned. "How can I help you?"

The lawyer's voice was tense. "Can you come to my office today? I have to discuss something regarding your grandfather's will. It's urgent. I can keep my office open late for you."

"Well, I'm already in Rock Springs," Lee said, wondering what could have the lawyer so worked up. "I can be at your office in twenty minutes. Can you tell me what happened though?"

The lawyer let out a heavy breath, and his voice was grim as he said, "Your grandfather's will is being challenged."

EDGAR COLLIN WAS A REPUTABLE FAMILY lawyer. Lee had seen him plenty of times while growing up.

"I don't understand," Lee studied the man. "Who is Paul Evans? I've lived with my grandfather since I was ten. I've never even seen a picture of this man."

Edgar handed over a thin file, speaking as he did. "He's your step-uncle in a way."

Lee opened the file and studied it. It was all the information that Edgar had gathered about this man. Paul Evans was the son of Benjamin and Cecilia Evans. He lived in Chicago and had no employment status. But what was interesting was that there were no siblings listed.

"Wait, why isn't my father listed in his siblings?" Lee asked, the wheels in his head turning.

Edgar pressed his lips together. "That is actually the grounds of the case that Paul is presenting. Your father was not Benjamin's biological son. He was his first wife's son from another marriage. Cecelia Evans was your grandfather's second wife. His first wife, Jane, died a few years after their marriage, and Benjamin raised Jordan."

Lee found himself reeling with all this information. "Why did Gramps never mention this?"

Edgar steepled his fingers together. "Benjamin had the misfortune of being forced to break ties with both his sons. When his second wife passed, Paul was fifteen, and your father, Mark, was in his early twenties. Your uncle and your father were always at odds, even more so when Paul discovered that your father was not truly his brother."

"Gramps never adopted him?" Lee asked slowly.

"He did," the lawyer replied hesitantly. "But your father and Benjamin had a huge argument just before he left to get married. I can't say that I know what it was about, but it was enough that your grandfather disowned Mark on the spot. He even went as far as removing him from the family register."

Lee stared down blankly at the paper in his hands.

He didn't have good memories of his father. Both his parents had been madly in love with each other and had no space for a child in their relationship, so he had been neglected often.

"I don't mean to talk ill about your father, Lee, but from what I know, Mark was a very self-absorbed man. I don't know much about Paul, however. He just disappeared one day. People became concerned, and the sheriff approached your grandfather. I don't know what conversation they had, but the sheriff was satisfied with it and left. Paul never reached out to your grandfather again. I assume they had a falling out."

Lee stared down at the picture, his mouth dry. "Is that why Gramps took me in when my parents died? Because he had no one left?"

"No," Edgar's voice was firm. "Your grandfather started looking for Mark a few years before your parents' death. He wanted to make amends. However, your father was not willing to do so. Benjamin asked Mark to let him meet you at least. Your father took great satisfaction in denying him access to you. Since Benjamin had disowned him, he had no legal right to try and meet you. But your grandfather had been trying to get to know you for years before your parents' death. He loved you dearly."

The small pang in Lee's chest settled on hearing that. "So, what's going on now?"

"Well," Edgar sighed, leaning back in his leather chair. "Paul claims that the ranch belongs to him since he is Benjamin's only blood relative. The fact that your grandfather disowned your father is his biggest card."

"How strong is his case?"

"Well, your grandfather did name you in the will, so while he does have a case and he might win at least half the ranch, there's another issue."

"Which is?" Lee asked warily.

"I don't know how much of this is true, but when you turned eighteen and left, your grandfather made another will. He was upset, and he was always a hasty man. In it, he claimed that you would not inherit the ranch. Of course, a few years later, he took it back and changed the will again, but the original copy of that second will went missing from his safe. He never found it. Now, if Paul has managed to get a copy of that will, he can use it to try and overthrow the current will."

"What are the chances of that happening?" Lee asked, his tone hard.

"Fifty-fifty," Edgar replied. "It depends on a lot of factors. But it is imperative that the investigation into Benjamin's death is completed as soon as possible."

Lee narrowed his eyes. "Why?"

Edgar's face was worried. "I have a bad feeling about Paul returning so soon after Benjamin's death was declared a homicide."

10
JENNA

"This is the last of it," Jenna said, closing the record book. "I think we have a list of all of Ben's business dealings."

Lee, who was sprawled in a chair, stirred. "Are we done?"

Jenna gave him a dirty look. "*I'm* done. Your nap is over."

He grinned. "I helped."

"By sleeping," Jenna gave him an annoyed look. "How are you running your company when you're so lazy?"

Lee sat up. "I'm not lazy, and I have people who run my company as needed."

Jenna gave him a disbelieving look, and he just smiled. "Come on. I'll make you lunch. My treat."

As he walked out of the room, Jenna shouted after him, "You made me do your share of the work. Don't make it sound as if lunch is a treat! I earned it!"

She heard him snicker and realized she had been duped. He had intended to take a nap all along.

"One of these days, Evans, I'm going to smother you with a pillow," she growled as she set down the last of the books and picked up the laptop.

She looked around the room. It had been a few days since she arrived. She'd gone to see her parents after leaving the hospital. It was only right that she break the news to them herself.

Jenna let out a heavy breath, recalling her mother's tears.

She had stayed with them for a few hours, and they had fought with her when they realized that she wasn't going to move in with them. But Jenna knew that they needed time to come to terms with this whole thing. It was Cole and Lee who had stepped in and talked to them.

Jenna had to confess to herself that now that her parents knew, she wanted to go hide in their arms like a child. She wanted them to pat her head and tell her that everything was going to be okay.

And that was the second reason she had to leave.

She would have allowed herself to become dependent on them, and she needed normalcy. She didn't need tears. She needed to be tough right now.

When she entered the kitchen, she saw Lee throwing things into a pan. "What are you making?"

"My famous egg fried rice," he told her. "What are you doing on the laptop now? Aren't you done?"

Jenna sat down at the kitchen table. "Ben refused to automate anything. He did all his business on paper, the old-fashioned way. I'm trying to create a system for you."

As the oil heated up in the pan, Lee wandered over, his voice thoughtful. "You know, if you tell me what exactly you need the system to do, I can create software for it."

Jenna lifted her brows. That wasn't the worst idea. She had been the one to automate everything for her family ranch, and even then, there were glitches, and she had to handle everything herself. But if Lee could create software that would be easy to use for everyone, that would be helpful.

Before she could say anything, however, Lee closed the lid on the laptop, his face so close to hers that Jenna froze. "You've worked long enough. Sit down and watch me cook."

When he carried the laptop away, Jenna had no choice but to do as he said.

It was her third day here.

She had expected things to be awkward, but Lee was going out of his way to make her comfortable. He hadn't once brought up their conversation in the hospital room. And for that she was grateful.

But the white elephant in the room was growing larger and larger.

She watched Lee cook and rested her chin on her folded arms on the table. "I got a call from the sheriff today."

Lee looked over his shoulder at her. "Yeah?"

"They didn't find fingerprints, but one of the ranch hands saw somebody walking in the area around my cottage. He was pretty far off, so the ranch hand didn't get a good look. I was thinking of going over there after lunch—"

"I'll come with you," Lee said without hesitation as he tossed some vegetables into the wok.

"I can go by—"

This time his voice was quiet as he looked at her. "You're not pushing me away, Jenna. You have no reason to do so anymore."

Usually Jenna's reaction would have been volatile, but the truth was already out, and she stared at him. "I can think of plenty of reasons."

He set the wok aside and turned to face her. "Name one."

"I'm dying."

"Not if you find a donor."

"The likelihood of that is rare," Jenna snapped.

"Never say never," Lee responded lightly. "I have plenty of people who owe me favors in some very prominent hospitals. I've already gotten in touch with them."

Jenna froze. "What?"

Lee gave her a look. "What? Did you think I would just sit on my hands and do nothing?"

She opened her mouth and then snapped it shut. "Oh. Thanks, I guess."

"So, your chances are much better now." He smiled. "What other reason is there?"

Jenna stared at him, trying to think of another one and coming up with nothing.

"You have no other reason," he said softly.

"You're going to leave," Jenna said, panic beginning to form in her gut. "I know you are because—"

"I know Billy told you that I've begun to learn the ropes of running the ranch," Lee replied calmly, standing in front of her and leaving her no choice but to look up at him. "I never hired that guy for the position of ranch manager. You never asked me why."

Jenna gave him a cautious look.

Lee studied her, and then he said, "You know, when you look at me like that, it feels as if you're just waiting for me to hurt you."

Jenna froze. He was right. She was waiting for him to hurt her. Even if she had moved past when he had left her ten years ago, she still remembered the pain of being deliberately erased from his life.

Lee let out a heavy sigh before crouching down before her. "I made a mistake, Jenna. Not in leaving, but in the way I behaved toward you. I was so terrified that if I talked to you or contacted you, I would be beyond homesick."

His voice was tight, and his eyes remorseful. "I made a mistake. And then when I came back, I expected things to be fine, and I thought that you would be happy to see me because I had been looking forward to seeing you and showing you what I had made of myself. I convinced myself that my actions would not have any consequences."

Jenna was quiet.

"At first I got angry when you refused to look at me," Lee said, frowning. "And then I began to realize what I had done, and I didn't know how to fix it. No matter what I said or did, I couldn't take back my mistake and how I had made you feel. So, today I made the calls to sell my company—"

"What?!" Jenna shot to her feet, horrified. "What do you mean 'sell your company'?!"

Lee got to his feet, his jaw tight. "I'm going to stay here and make things right. I'll learn to run the ranch like Gramps wanted, and I want to build a life with you here."

"Have you gone insane?" Jenna stammered, panicking. "You can't—You can't do something like that! You spent ten years building that company!"

"It doesn't compare to you," Lee said quietly. "At the end of the day, I have to go back alone, without you by my side. Everything I did, Jenna, was to prove to you that I was a man worthy of standing by you. I never understood it before, but you were always the one protecting me. I wanted to be your shield. I had to leave to become somebody who could stand in front of you and keep you safe. I became that man, and now I want to stand next to you."

Jenna's chest tightened at his confession. "You can't say these things to me." Her voice was thick as she took a step back, her heart pounding. "You can't just—"

"I can. I've already done it!"

"Then change it!" Jenna shouted at him. "You built that company from scratch! I'm not letting you sell it just because you want to make a point!"

"It's not about making a point!" Lee roared. "I'm willing to do whatever it takes to stay here with you!"

"So, what?!" Jenna shouted. "You're going to make yourself miserable running a ranch that you hate?"

"I don't hate it! And if that means I can keep you by my side, then yes!"

"I don't want that! I don't want you to be miserable!" Jenna shoved at him.

"Why?" Lee demanded, grabbing her hands and pinning them to his chest as his eyes bored into hers. "Why do you care if I'm miserable or not? Wouldn't it make you happy? I hurt you so badly when I left. This is the least I can—"

"I do care." Jenna pushed back the tears that were burning her eyes, refusing to cry. "I care if you're miserable because I care about you! You can't be that dense!"

Lee went still, staring down at her. "You care about me?"

"Of course I do!" Jenna's heart was pounding against her rib cage as she began to lose control of the situation.

"Care about me how?" Lee demanded, his hands tightening on hers. "I'm not interested in being your friend anymore, Jenna. I want all of it. I want all of you. I want a future with you, children with you, a lifetime together."

Jenna's mouth was dry at his words. She no longer had the strength to bury the flicker of hope inside of her.

"I don't think I can give you all of that," she whispered. "I don't know what the future holds anymore."

"But if you could, would you?" Lee asked, his voice not quite steady. "If you knew what the future held and if you were confident that you would recover, would you promise your future to me?"

"Lee." A tear slipped down Jenna's cheek. "What if I die?"

"Then let me marry you tomorrow. Give me whatever time you have left. Stop pushing me away."

Lee rested his forehead against hers, and Jenna closed her eyes, the ache in her chest growing with every word of his.

"You're not being fair," she mumbled.

"I know," he responded. "But I've lost too much already with you. And I need some starting point to fix everything and earn your forgiveness."

"It's not about forgiveness, Lee," Jenna sighed, pulling her head back to look at him.

"It's not," he agreed. "But it's a starting point."

"You're not going to sell your company. You're not going to run this ranch. We'll figure things out, but this is not the way I want things between us to start."

She felt Lee go still. "Wait, you're saying—"

"I'm saying I'll give us a try," Jenna finally lowered her last shield. "I'll give us a shot, but not like this. You put years of effort into that company, and I'm not going to be the one who takes it away from you. We'll figure everything out along the way, but I don't want you to do something you hate. I know I can be nasty, but I'm not a monster—"

"You're not nasty," Lee said, frowning.

"I've been pretty mean to you," Jenna lifted a brow. "It's not like I'm not aware of what I do."

She saw a smile form on Lee's face. "Well, you have been mean to me." He lowered his head and kissed the tip of her nose, whispering, "But I kind of like it." Jenna tried to wiggle out of his arms, but he held onto her. "Where are you going?"

"You're crazy."

Lee laughed, and this time he kissed her firmly on the mouth. "And you agreed to be mine. You can't undo promises, Jenna. It's not nice."

"I said I'd try—I never said I'd be yours." Jenna squirmed in his hold, her cheeks flushing. "Stop it!"

But Lee finally had her where he wanted her, and she knew all her efforts would be fruitless because he didn't seem to have any intention of letting her go. And secretly, she was so very, very grateful for that blessing.

The cottage was still in shambles.

Jenna waded through it and sighed when she looked at the broken appliances still on the floor. Her tone was bitter. "I saved money for each and every thing in this house. And this person broke everything with so much ease."

She looked over her shoulder to see Lee crouching down and picking up the shattered picture frames. His voice was low. "This was definitely an attack on you.'

"I know. Nothing was stolen. I already talked to Laurel about replacing the furniture. She has pending orders, but she put me on the list. It's going to take a few months though. I could just get some cheap—"

"Why don't you let me handle this?"

"What?" Jenna glanced at Lee, who was gazing out the window at her garden.

He looked back at her. "Let me fix up this place and the garden."

Jenna's brow furrowed. "That doesn't make any sense."

Lee shoved his hands in his pockets. "I want to. This entire house, from the garden to the interior, looks just like how we dreamed our home would be."

"We didn't even know what it meant when we said we would live together," Jenna muttered. "We were so young. Just babies, really."

Lee's look was filled with meaning as he said slowly, "I think we did. I think we both did, but we just didn't want to admit to it."

Jenna fell silent.

"I want to rebuild the garden with you and the house. I want to pick out the furniture with you. I want to be involved."

Jenna's lips quirked. "You're acting as if we're preparing our shared home."

Lee narrowed his eyes at her. "You can laugh at me, but this was a dream home, and you stole our idea."

"I didn't steal anything!" Jenna scowled.

"Did too," Lee argued, walking over and bending down until he was eye level with her. His voice was smooth as he said, "There are going to be penalties, just so you know."

"Penalt—"

Jenna's words were cut off when he stole a kiss from her, grinning wickedly.

Pulling away with a smug look on his face, he said, "You'd better be prepared to pay up."

Jenna flushed, glowering at him. She felt flustered when he did things like this with such ease and confidence. She wasn't a romantic person by nature, and Lee had a habit of throwing her off balance.

She pushed him back.

But as she was walking away, she heard Lee ask her in a strange voice, "You sure the sheriff combed over the entire place?"

Jenna blinked. "Yeah. He and another deputy searched for any hints of—What are you looking at?"

But Lee was already on the phone.

AN HOUR LATER, SHERIFF STILES LOOKED DOWN at the black glove, which had been at the bottom of an upended pile of dirty laundry.

"Well," he said. "This shouldn't have happened. How did I miss this?"

"It doesn't belong to Jenna," Lee said, and Jenna wondered how he knew that. He hadn't uttered a word while they had waited for the sheriff.

"She's allergic to this material." He shoved his hands in his pockets and looked at the sheriff, his face cold. "Doesn't this look familiar to you?"

Jenna saw a strange expression cross the sheriff's face. "Oh."

The glove was a thick one. It looked kind of familiar, but Jenna couldn't place it.

"Are either of you going to tell me what's going on?" She frowned.

The sheriff reached down and bagged the item. "The person who trampled the flower beds was wearing heavy boots, large ones, but most of the pressure of the boots was centered around the heel. We think that the person wore a larger size to confuse us. But this is definitely going to help."

"About the glove—"

The sheriff hesitated. "If you don't mind, Jenna, I need to make sure that my suspicions are correct before I talk to you about it. If I'm right, this matter is a little delicate, and I cannot afford to have you get involved."

Jenna gave him a long look before she said, "I am going to pretend that you didn't just imply that I'm going to go off my rocker if I discover who this was and hinder your investigation."

Sheriff Stiles flushed. "Sorry. I didn't mean to imply that. What I meant was that I do have a few people in mind, but until I'm sure, I don't want to mention any names. Of course, I'll keep you updated." He turned around and then hesitated. "Lee, about Benjamin's —"

"I know you're looking into it," Lee said, his voice tight.

The sheriff shook his head. "It's about your uncle. After what you told me, I talked to a few people. His old classmates and people he interacted with when he still lived in town. He wasn't a very likable person, but a few of the people who still refer to him as their friend…their behavior was a little unsettling. I've been trying to look into Paul's life, but I can't find anything. It's almost as if when he left town, he wiped his entire existence. There's no trace of him anywhere, not even in Chicago. He never lived at the apartment that was registered in his name. He's never held down any job. He has no credit cards to his name. The man has no online activity whatsoever. I have a very bad feeling about this, so be careful."

Jenna knew that this whole matter bothered Lee, especially given how they still didn't know what had happened to Ben. She touched his hand, and he immediately wrapped his hand around hers.

"I'll keep an eye out," Lee murmured. "I have a meeting with Sharon today. I sent Gramps's reports to a cardiologist in London, and he faxed her his findings."

"Yeah," the sheriff nodded. "She called me about it. I'll be seeing her tomorrow morning as well. She's sent me the reports."

Jenna tightened her hold on Lee's hand.

While the matter of her home being trashed was a grave one, right now it was Lee who needed the most support. If she was going to take this massive step of agreeing to stand by his side, then she wasn't going to let him suffer alone. Benjamin's passing was horrible enough, but to have someone attempt to take Lee's family home away from him only compounded the horror.

Sick as I am, Lord, let me still be strong for him. Please.

When the sheriff left, Jenna turned to face Lee. "You okay?"

Lee sighed. "I'm fine. I talked to Mr. Collin today. Apparently Paul has gone ahead with contesting the will. He's communicating through his lawyer so far."

"Benjamin had a safety deposit box—"

"I looked in it," Lee said heavily. "The will isn't there."

Lee had told her about what his lawyer had said.

"I asked my parents about Paul," Jenna said as they walked toward the car. "Dad knew him. He said that Paul was a very standoffish kid. He and your father never got along. Apparently, Paul used to bring up how the ranch was always going to be his because he was Benjamin's actual child."

"Sounds like a delight," Lee muttered, opening the door for her.

Jenna didn't sit, her hands on the top of the car door as she looked at him. "We'll figure it out. Whatever happens, we'll figure it out. He won't get the ranch."

It was when Lee sat down in the driver's seat that he said, "I hired a private detective agency in Chicago to look into Paul's past." He started the car and turned it toward the town, "This whole business about the second will is a little too shady for my liking."

Jenna silently agreed.

They drove together into town and made a stop at the hospital first to meet up with Sharon.

"It's definitely poisoning," Sharon said grimly. "But it's not a store-bought variety. We tested everything that you can buy at a pharmacy, but the results are inconclusive."

"Then what are you thinking?" Lee asked, exchanging a look with Jenna.

Sharon steepled her fingers together and looked at the two before saying slowly, "Have you ever heard of Mad Hatter disease?"

When Lee was silent, she continued, "I believe that he was consuming some natural form of poison in extremely small doses that led to his eventual death. Mercury, possibly, but not definitively."

Jenna grew still. "Nobody went in and out of that house except for a handful of people. Ben wasn't very social."

Sharon pressed her lips into a thin line. "Which is why I gave the sheriff a list of names this morning."

Jenna stared at her and then asked slowly, "You didn't put Midge's name on it, did you?"

Sharon winced. "I had no choice. She was the only one who handled food in the house."

Jenna wanted to defend the sweet old housekeeper, but she didn't have any words. Sharon had done nothing wrong. Her actions had been logical in every way.

Jenna saw the weariness leak into Lee's eyes, and when they walked out, he let out a heavy breath. While she had an explosive personality, Lee was the polar opposite. He held everything in.

Jenna hesitated at what she was about to do since she wasn't a very emotionally available person. But it was different where Lee was concerned. So, as they walked toward the car, she grabbed his hand, stopping him.

When he looked at her, she said, "Tell me what's going on in your head."

"I'm fi—"

"You're not fine," she said shortly. "You are the farthest thing from fine, Lee. If you want us to stand a chance as a couple, you have to put in some effort. And that means talking to me when you're upset."

He stared at her, and then his shoulders slumped. "I was too late. I waited too long to come home, and somebody poisoned him. There's so much guilt inside of me that I don't even know where to begin."

Jenna closed her eyes, her chest tightening at his pain. "You blame yourself. But I was here. I should've known."

"How can I not blame myself, Jenna?" he growled, his eyes filling with pain. "That man protected me. He gave me a roof over my head. He raised me. And in return, I walked away and let him die."

"You know that's not true," Jenna said quietly. "The minute you heard that Ben was sick, you dropped everything and returned. You didn't abandon him. Nobody knew what was going on. But I'll tell you something—the last few weeks of Ben's life, he was the happiest I've ever seen him. And when you were gone, he was so proud of everything you achieved. You never let him down. You didn't leave him to die."

She saw Lee close his eyes, and she tightened her hands around his, her voice firm. "I was very close to Ben, Lee. So, you need to trust me when I say that he never held your leaving against you. He recorded every single one of your achievements. He read and reread every article about you. And you weren't the ungrateful grandson that you're trying to portray yourself as being. You came back. You didn't have to. But you did. And he knew you would. Despite his harsh words to you every now and then, Ben knew you loved him."

Lee swallowed, and when he opened his eyes, there was a sheen of tears in them. "I know." His voice was thick. "I know you're right. I keep thinking I could have done more."

"If Sharon couldn't figure out that he was being poisoned, you wouldn't have been able to either," Jenna told him.

Jenna knew that while her words might have some impact, it was Lee who had to make peace with himself over the events that were occurring. She pulled him toward the car, a silent prayer leaving her heart.

Let him heal.

They stopped for dinner at the diner, and Jenna deliberately ignored the people who watched them with curious eyes. The day Lee had kissed her outside of the diner in full view of everyone in it, she had known people would talk. She had expected shock and disbelief but not approval and support.

An older woman smiled at her from the next sink when she went to wash her hands in the bathroom. "I always knew you two would end up together. Despite the odds, you and Ben's boy were always meant for each other."

Jenna blushed at that, and when she returned, no amount of Lee's teasing would make her tell him what had her face so red.

Lily kept beaming in their direction, especially when Lee put one of his chicken wings on Jenna's plate and insisted she eat.

"You're doing this deliberately," Jenna hissed at him.

When Lee just gave her an innocent smile, she wanted to wring his neck. "Doing what?"

"Putting on a show for everyone to see." Jenna stabbed the piece of chicken he had just given her.

He just shrugged. "Of course. How else am I going to let everybody else know that you're off the market?"

Jenna's eyes widened. "Excuse me?"

He gave her a pleasant smile that made her shiver for some reason, perhaps because his voice was deceptively soft as he spoke. "You don't seem to have noticed, but more than five men have been watching you ever since we walked in. They keep glancing in your direction every now and then. Feel happy that I'm feeding you rather than going and having a word with them."

Seeing this transformation from mild-mannered man into territorial predator had Jenna blinking. She looked over his shoulder at one of the men and shrugged. "You could take him. I mean, you won't come out of it unscathed, but you could take him."

Lee shot her an amused look. "I'm sure you'd have my back."

Jenna grinned. "I'll throw in a kick or two if it looks like he's getting the upper hand."

Lee nudged her lightly under the table. "Thanks for your support."

His smile had Jenna feeling a little flustered, and she looked down at her plate. Even when they had been young, Lee had always had a habit of looking her directly in the eyes as he smiled, and not once had she been able to resist that charm of his.

"Why are you making that face?" she heard him ask, his voice curious.

"Shut up." Jenna could feel her ears heat up.

It wasn't as if she wasn't accustomed to dating. She was always confident when she went out with men. She was never one to be shy. It was Lee who flipped the cards on her every time.

"So this is where you two have been," Pastor Dean slid in next to Lee. "What are we having?"

Jenna gave him a steady look. "I'm not buying

you dinner. You still owe me twenty bucks from last month. And where's my truck, Dean?"

"*Pastor* Dean," her friend corrected nonchalantly. "And the truck is nearly done. It's still at the shop. I left it with Dylan."

He droned on and on, but Jenna had stopped listening to him. She suddenly remembered something.

The glove.

It had looked familiar for a reason.

She had seen it before.

It was a mechanic's glove.

11
LEE

"I CAN'T BELIEVE THIS!" JENNA SNARLED.

Lee watched her pace the study as he leaned against the desk, his arms folded over his chest.

"I'm sorry, but I can't let you go and bash his head in. If you touch him, this whole thing is going to get worse."

His voice sounded calm, but Lee was anything but.

From the moment he had seen the glove in Jenna's house, he had known. He was a cautious man by nature, which was why he had asked around after the whole showdown with Vicky had taken place. He knew that Vicky had started dating Dylan again. Also, from the conversation he had had with the sheriff, Lee knew the damage at the cottage had not been a one-man job.

Dylan was definitely going to pay, and so was Vicky. But not in the way that the sheriff thought.

Jenna had suffered because of one woman's insane jealousy and pettiness.

Lee planned to answer in kind.

"I won't hurt him," Jenna snapped. "Just… damage him a little."

"You don't have to fight every battle alone, Jenna," Lee finally got up and crossed the room to her. "You should let me fight some of them for you. Trust me, the result will be much more satisfying."

Jenna stopped and looked up at him warily. "Why? What are you planning?"

Lee just smiled at her coldly, his fingers gently brushing against her cheek. "You didn't think that Dylan and Vicky could do something to you, and I'd just let them get away with it."

He saw Jenna shudder, and she murmured, "Sometimes you seem like a villain when you talk like that."

Lee's lips curved, and he wrapped his arms around her waist. "What if I was a villain for everyone but you?"

She grinned, as if amused by the thought. "You're too soft to be a villain. You were always the nice guy."

Lee watched her leave the room, and his own smile faded.

He had stopped being nice a long time ago. You couldn't survive in the business world by being a pushover. The people around him, including Cole, had begun to notice that he was no longer the same person he was when he had left. But Jenna didn't mind.

She clearly noticed that he was different, but Lee had never changed his behavior around her. He was still patient and calm around her, egging her on, stepping on her toes. He was the same childhood friend she had fallen in love with. He wanted to be that person.

But sometimes he found himself slipping, especially when someone came at Jenna. His protective streak when it came to this woman had just grown. While Jenna was still hotheaded, she was smart and resourceful. She had grown a lot in these past ten years, and she had also suffered a lot.

Despite her sharp tongue and short fuse, Lee never felt the least bit intimidated by her, which plenty of men did. He adored Jenna. He loved her temper, her reluctant sweetness, her protective nature, and her ability to make him smile.

Ever since that day at the hospital, her tone had softened toward him, and Lee had noticed. She had forgiven him.

Lee stared at the door through which Jenna had just left.

He had meant it when he had told her that he was planning to sell his company. It was still something he was willing to do if it meant winning over her heart.

"Lee." Jenna's voice came from the front door, and she sounded tense. "You'd better come out here!"

Lee didn't hesitate, making his way over to the foyer where Jenna stood with the door open, looking outside.

"What is—"

He paused when he saw a few men standing near three cars. One of them looked vaguely familiar, and it took Lee a second to place him as the representative of Forrest Development.

"What're you doing back here?" Lee gave him a cool look. "I told you I wasn't interested in selling the ranch."

The man gave him a dismissive look. "I'm here at the owner's request."

Lee's brow lifted. "I am the owner."

"The real owner," the man said, a smug smile on his face.

That was when Lee noticed a tall man approaching the porch. He froze at the sight of him, knowing immediately who he was.

Looking at Paul Evans was like looking at a younger version of his grandfather. Lee had never realized how much his uncle would resemble Ben, and he felt a pain in his chest.

"You must be Lee," the man introduced himself, taking off his sunglasses and holding out his hand.

The eyes.

The eyes were wrong.

It was there that the resemblance stopped.

Paul Evans had a certain meanness in his eyes, a craftiness that Lee's grandfather had never possessed.

"And you must be Paul." Lee didn't accept his hand.

Lee had seen enough people like Paul to know that this man was dangerous.

A cold look entered his uncle's eyes when Lee refused to shake his hand. "I see you take after your father then."

"No," Lee responded. "I take after my grandfather."

Paul cleared his throat. "I don't think you can call Benjamin your grandfather. He disowned your father."

"And yet he raised me," Lee smiled casually. "Go figure. Now, what are you doing here? And what are those men doing here?"

Paul's lips curled into a light smile. "I'm selling the ranch, so I'm showing around prospective buyers."

Lee felt his blood boil at the statement, but he heard Jenna shuffle forward and immediately lifted his hand discreetly to stop her.

"This ranch isn't yours to sell," he said. "It was left to me. By name. As Ben's grandson."

"I think we both know that this ranch isn't yours. My father may have left it to you in his later years, but he was mentally not all that there when he wrote that will. He would have never left me out of it. The ranch belongs to me because I am an Evans by blood."

"Be that as it may," Lee replied. "The ranch has been transferred into my name. And your lawsuit is still in the works. You are legally not allowed to be in my home. You're trespassing."

Lee saw Paul stiffen, and he smiled internally.

"The ranch is still my home," Paul said tightly.

Lee shrugged. "That's a matter of opinion. I lived here for more than a decade and never saw a single picture of you inside this house. As far as I know, my grandfather didn't have a second son. I mean, after all, you would have shown up at his funeral if that had been the case. I don't remember seeing you there. In fact, I don't remember ever seeing you. Awfully convenient how you just showed up now, wanting to sell the only thing my grandfather held dear."

Paul's face turned white in anger, and he snarled, "You'd better watch your mouth, boy—"

Lee picked up the rifle on the stand just inside the door and stepped down until he was a few steps away from Paul. Lifting the rifle, he pointed it straight at Paul's face. "I repeat. You're trespassing. Unless you want me to shoot you, you'll leave. The same goes for all of you. My grandfather's ranch is not for sale."

The men that accompanied Paul glanced at him before hurrying to their cars. As they drove away, it was only Paul left, and he glared at Lee. "You think you're very smart, but I'm the one holding all the cards. By the time I'm done, this ranch and your little company are both going to be mine." With that, he walked toward his car, got in, and drove away.

"What did he mean by 'your company'?" Jenna finally asked. "He can't take your company, can he? It's yours. It's got nothing to do with Ben."

Lee stared after the car that was growing smaller in the distance. "I didn't think he would be this bold." When Jenna did not respond, Lee looked over his shoulder at her. She was staring at him. "What?"

She blinked. "You pointed the gun straight at his face."

"He was on my property," Lee said calmly.

She shrugged, climbing down the steps of the porch until she was next to him, "Yeah, I know. It's just that I never took you to be so comfortable with a gun."

Lee had to resist the urge to smile. "Does it bother you?"

She shoved her hands in her pockets. "Not really. I was just surprised." She looked in the direction of the dirt road leading away from the ranch. "It bothers me that he was so confident."

Lee followed her gaze, murmuring, "I don't think that Mr. Collin is equipped to handle something like this. I'm going to make a few calls."

IT WAS TWO DAYS LATER THAT LEE FOUND himself meeting up with his grandfather's lawyer once again. Only this time, it was at the diner.

It was late in the afternoon, and the diner just had a few stragglers.

"Why did you want to meet here?" Lee asked. "I could have driven up to your office."

Mr. Collin looked a little uneasy. "I was already in town, and I got a call. This is an emergency meeting."

"What happened?"

The lawyer took out a handkerchief and wiped his brow. "Paul has put in a claim that you stole a quarter of a million dollars from his father. I have yet to see the evidence, but he's handed it to his lawyer. He is trying to get ahold of your company as well."

Lee blinked. "What?"

"This is what I've been told today. Apparently, according to him, you stole the money and started up your own company. He says, by default, since the money never belonged to you, the company belongs to his grandfather since it was his money that was used to start it."

"That's a pile of horse manure," Lee growled. "I didn't take a dime from Gramps, even when he offered it! And the only way I managed to start the company was because I patented my software. I borrowed money from people, and then I returned it."

"We're going to need proof of that," Edgar said, his voice tense. "When I first heard about this, I thought he was reaching. But, I put in a request for Benjamin's financial records. A quarter of a million dollars did go missing from his bank account two years after you left, and according to your company's public books, that was the exact amount of your investment. Which is why I need you to give me evidence and receipts."

Lee's hand curled into a fist under the table. Going after his grandfather's ranch was one thing. He could understand that Paul wanted what he considered rightfully his. But going after his company was just greed and manipulation.

"Lee?"

Lee pressed his lips together, and the hand that was on the table began to tap in agitation. "I'm going to have to get ahold of all my investors. I'll also have my company lawyers reach out to you, and I would like you to coordinate with them. I hope you understand when I say that I would like you to take a backseat and act as a consultant rather than as the primary lawyer. I don't know what my uncle is trying to do, but this whole situation is getting messy. I'm not going to risk my company as well."

Mr. Collin actually looked relieved. "I'm just a family lawyer. I have studied corporate law, but not to deal with such things. I'll happily act as a consultant."

When he left, Lee remained sitting there, his fingers tapping on the table, a thousand scenarios running through his mind.

He was so lost in his thoughts that he didn't

even notice when another person took the seat across from him.

It was only when Cole called out his name that Lee blinked. "Oh, it's you."

"It's always a warm welcome with you." His friend waggled his brows. "What's going on?"

Lee caught him up to date as Lily brought over three pieces of pie and grabbed a seat to join them.

"I heard he's staying at the motel down the street," Lily chewed a forkful of the pie. "Your uncle, that is."

Lee glanced out the window. He could see the edge of the motel rooftop from where he was sitting.

"The man is shameless enough to demand to stay at the ranch," he muttered. "Honestly, if he hadn't approached this whole thing the way he has, I wouldn't have minded giving him half the ranch since Gramps was his father. But not only does he want to sell the place, but he wants my company as well."

Cole whistled in anger. "Going for your company is taking it too far."

Lily was more curious about something else. "Doesn't it seem strange to you that nobody ever mentioned Paul to you while growing up? It just seems odd that you spent all these years here, and not a single person brought his name up."

Now that Lily mentioned it, Lee did find it a little odd. "Maybe Gramps had a hand in that. Apparently, the relationship between my father and Paul wasn't a good one. He probably just didn't want—"

His words trailed off because even his excuse sounded flimsy. What exactly had Paul done that had made his grandfather refuse to even utter his name in the house?

"There are no family pictures either," Lee murmured. "There's one of my father, but it was in Gramps's study. While I was going through Gramps's stuff, I didn't find any trace of Paul. It's almost as if Gramps tried to erase his very existence."

"I asked my parents about the fight between Benjamin and Paul, but they didn't know. But they did say that Ben refused to even listen to Paul's name."

As Lee listened, he mused that it wouldn't be a bad idea to talk to Cole's parents. Since the ranch was right next to his, there was a good chance that the Mileses would know more about the kind of person his uncle was.

As a customer arrived and Lily left, Lee looked toward Cole. "How are your parents taking everything?"

He saw the instant shift in his friend's eyes. "Not well. They want Jenna to move back in, but I understand why she doesn't want to. My dad tried to take back control of the ranch, and she refused to let him. Has she mentioned anything to you?"

Lee shook his head. "I tried talking to her, but she just didn't want to. I told her she's welcome to stay at my place for as long as she needs to. The sheriff has given the go-ahead for us to fix everything up at the cottage. The furniture arrives today, so she's going to be getting it set up."

"Did you hear back from the hospital?" Cole asked, leaning forward.

"Not yet," Lee said, his voice tight. "But I had my assistant contact some top hospitals in New

York to put Jenna's name on the list. I have contacts in different hospitals because they use my software. What about you?"

"I don't understand why I'm not a match. She's my twin. Dad wanted to get tested, but the doctor refused since he's diabetic."

"We'll get through this," Lee said firmly, a silent prayer leaving his heart. *I need her. We all do. Don't take her from us, Lord.*

"Jenna doesn't want anybody in town to know about this, but Laurel found out, and she also went to get herself tested," Cole said. "Word was bound to leak out, and it has. Nobody said anything to Jenna, but Dr. Ralph told me that quite a few people have approached him to get tested to see if they're a match."

Lee wasn't surprised. Now that people knew, the town would invariably rally to help one of its own, especially someone as beloved as Jenna.

"I heard that the Saltwatz's mechanic shop is going under. Something about the bank foreclosing on it because of debt," Cole said slowly, watching Lee.

Lee just picked up his fork and took a bite of the pie, saying calmly, "That's unfortunate."

"You had something to do with this, didn't you?" Cole said after a heavy silence of him just watching his friend. "You suspect Dylan."

"I don't suspect him. I know it was him," Lee murmured. "Vicky's mother has one of the most popular salons in town. It's a pity that they failed their six-month hygiene check yesterday."

Cole's expression was lax with shock. "You did this?"

"I don't know what you're talking about," Lee shrugged. "It's not like I would stoop to reaching out to the bank manager who's a friend of the Saltwatz family and pointing out that using his position to let his friend not pay back a debt can get him fired."

Cole just stared at him, stunned. "No, you didn't."

"I just said I didn't," Lee replied, unfazed. "Are you going to finish that pie?"

Cole just pushed his plate toward Lee, muttering, "You really are vicious, aren't you?"

Lee stabbed the pie, his voice icy. "They hurt Jenna deliberately. Even if we overlook the trashing of her house, the act of throwing the medicines away, knowing that they were prescribed, was malicious."

"But it doesn't make sense," Cole scowled. "It was Vicky who started the confrontation in the diner the other day. Why go after Jenna like this?"

"Jenna told me that Dylan used to beat up on her when they were in high school," Lee said coldly. "At Vicky's behest. None of us noticed what Jenna was going through."

He looked up to meet Cole's horrified gaze. "We never saw a single bruise on her face because Dylan was very careful about not putting marks anywhere that were visible. It wasn't like she took everything like a sitting duck, but I asked around recently. Since she told me, I've been reaching out to people we went to school with. It was Vicky who told him where to hit her. Apparently she was jealous of Jenna's grades. She hated that Jenna was the only one who stood up to her. I thought jealousy like that died down after people graduated from school, but that's not true for Vicky. While she grudgingly went to work in her mother's salon and did a terrible job on people's hair, mostly because she's lazy and doesn't care, Jenna earned the respect of the townspeople. She's well-liked and respected. It seems that Vicky doesn't like that."

When Cole gaped at him, Lee just gave him a small smile. "Sounds unbelievable, doesn't it? I'm not basing this off just hearsay. I went around following up on every rumor that Jenna has been dragged into over the past few years, and there have been plenty."

"That's some kind of time you have on your hands," Cole muttered.

"I don't like anyone tarnishing her name," Lee replied shortly. "The sheriff is going to arrest Dylan. He left behind his glove at the cottage. And I'm pretty sure that Vicky was conveniently absent from work that day. She bought oversized boots at a mall a day before."

Cole raised an eyebrow. "I'm surprised that my sister let you handle this."

That had Lee's eyes widening. "Are you kidding me? She wanted to rip their heads off. It took a lot of convincing and bribing to get her to not go after them. Who did she get her temper from?"

"Dad says she inherited it from his great-great-grandmother. According to him, she used to be a bullfighter. I don't buy it, but he believes it."

Despite his light words, Lee could see a trace of anger in Cole's eyes. His friend was not a violent man. In fact, he was the complete opposite of his twin, and the only time he ever got fired up was when it came to Jenna. Similar to Lee in that respect, really. One more reason the men had always been close friends.

Lee glanced outside the window, and his brow furrowed when he saw the sheriff's car parking outside. He saw the sheriff look in his direction. There was no nod of greeting.

Instead, the man walked toward the diner, and when he entered, he made a beeline toward him.

His voice was grim. "You need to come with me, Evans."

Lee lifted a brow. "What's going on?"

The sheriff didn't look very happy. "I have a search warrant for your house."

Lee went still. "If you want to search the main house, you didn't have to get a warrant for it. I offered to let you do it before, remember?"

His words made the sheriff look a little relieved. "There are some special circumstances now. I don't want you coming home and finding out, so I'm giving you the courtesy of telling you right now. If you want to be present while the search is being conducted, you have to come with me."

Cole stood up. "I'll go as well."

Lee had more questions, but he decided to wait until they got to the ranch. The drive up there was tense.

"That's a strange request," Cole said tightly. "Why would the sheriff want to search the main house?"

Lee stared out the window. "I don't know, but I have a bad feeling about this. I think I'll call my lawyer."

By the time he got through to his lawyer, who agreed to jump on the first flight out to Sunset Ridge, they had already reached the ranch.

Jenna was waiting in the driveway, along with a trembling Midge.

Jenna looked a little pale, her arms crossed over her chest. "What's going on?"

Lee didn't want to have this conversation in front of the elderly woman, so he said gently, "Why don't you go home, Midge? You don't have to be here for this."

Midge shook her head. "I'm not leaving you, Lee. Why do they want to search the house?"

She looked close to tears, and Jenna put her arm around the older woman. "Why don't you go wait in the car? It's hot out here."

Lee watched her guide the old housekeeper to the car.

She had just returned when the sheriff and the deputies pulled up after them, and she demanded, "What's going on, Sheriff Stiles? What's this about you getting a warrant for the house?"

The deputies entered the house while the sheriff explained in a tight voice, "I'm sure you know by now about the money that Lee's uncle claims he stole."

He held up a piece of paper, "This is a warrant for all your bank statements, Lee, going back ten years. I also got a tip that you purchased aconite recently. That's not illegal, mind you. It could just be suspicious."

Lee frowned. "What's that?"

It was Jenna who replied. "You can't be serious? He'd be suffering from the side effects of it for weeks. We would all have noticed!"

"Wait," Lee touched her arm, confused. "What's aconite?"

"It's a plant," Jenna growled. "A very poisonous plant. And we both know where that tip came from, Sheriff."

The sheriff stiffened. "I don't have a choice. I still have to search the house."

"It's fine," Lee said slowly. "But I will be upfront with you. If Paul sent in a tip, I have a feeling you're going to find something in the house."

From the look on the sheriff's face, Lee could tell that the thought had already occurred to the man.

"You've called your lawyer, haven't you?" the sheriff asked quietly.

Lee nodded.

He watched the sheriff, and then Jenna turned to him, worry in her eyes. "They're going to find something, aren't they?"

Cole shoved his hands in his pockets, his voice grim. "Seems that way."

Jenna looked frustrated. "I don't understand. The ranch, I get. But why is he coming for your company? And why you? It's like he's out to get revenge or something."

Lee had no answer to her question because it was bothering him as well.

If Paul had managed to plant something in his home, then he would have been able to obtain access to the building, and having Paul snooping around inside didn't sit well with Lee.

"It's going to be fine," he told Jenna, who looked tense.

She didn't look very convinced, but she relaxed when he curled his hand around hers. It was astounding how comfortable she had become with the slightest touch from him. Despite everything that had happened, she now trusted him.

It was humbling and also a blessing Lee didn't ever forget to thank God for.

Half an hour later, the sheriff walked out of the house, his face grim.

"I'm sorry, Lee." Lee already knew what he was going to say. "I'm placing you under arrest."

Lee didn't argue since he knew that the odds were not in his favor, but he also saw the unwilling look on the sheriff's face. He found it considerate that Sheriff Stiles didn't handcuff him.

He saw the way Jenna watched him, her face white. Her brother put his arm around her shoulders, possibly to comfort her, or more likely to restrain her.

"It'll be fine," Lee told her. "I'll be out in no time. My lawyer will be here soon."

As he sat in the patrol car, he saw Midge's terrified face watching him from close by.

12
JENNA

THE WHOLE TOWN WAS BUZZING WITH THE NEWS of the arrest.

Lee was quite well-liked, so most of the townspeople were in disbelief.

"Is his lawyer here?" Kathy asked as she flipped the "Closed" sign. Lily and Laurel were sitting on the couch while Jenna glanced at her phone as she sat perched on the edge of the coffee table.

"He's here." Jenna kept looking at her screen.

Her jaw was tight with anger from the events of this morning. She had gone to talk to Billy, and she had seen Paul Evans walk around the property, showing it off to prospective buyers like he owned the place.

She hadn't hesitated in calling the police and getting all the men escorted off the property. But it still boiled her blood to see the man trying to ruin Lee's life. There was no logical reason for it. The man had never even laid eyes on Lee before.

"What's the word in town right now?" She looked at Lily.

The diner was the hub of gossip for the entire town, and Lily would know better than anyone the general opinion about the ongoing matter.

"A lot of people think that he was framed," Lily said with grim satisfaction. "That those financial documents and aconite seeds were planted. Especially now that Paul has started showing up everywhere, making claims against Lee, people are siding with Lee even more. Nobody really likes Paul."

Laurel leaned forward. "I heard something interesting today. I don't know how authentic this is, but before Lee's father left town, he and Paul had a massive falling out. It was over a girl, apparently."

Jenna frowned. "Which girl? Lee's mother?"

"I mean, that would be the obvious option," Laurel murmured. "But I don't think so. I was just prying because I'm nosy that way, but the woman who told me just laughed and said that Lee's mother was madly in love with Mark. She never had eyes for anybody else. The fight was bad enough that Ben got involved."

"If Paul held a grudge all these years—and he definitely seems to be the type," Jenna said thoughtfully, "Then he might be punishing Lee for his father's actions. It sounds insane, but then the man isn't exactly the poster boy for sanity."

"He came to the diner today," Lily told them. "He's creepy. That's the only way I can describe it. Very soft-spoken, but just being in his presence made me uncomfortable. It's his eyes. They're just *wrong*."

Jenna wasn't surprised. She didn't get good vibes from the man either. But before she could say anything, her phone pinged, and she immediately jumped to her feet and made her way toward the front door of the coffee shop.

"Are you expecting someone?" Kathy asked.

But Jenna just opened the door.

A minute later, a tall, fair-headed man entered the coffee shop. With startling blue eyes and a head full of golden curls, he was quite handsome with his strong features.

He looked around and nodded. "Ladies."

"Vince?" Laurel looked surprised. "When did you get back in town?"

Vince Kells was among the wealthier men in Sunset Ridge, and all of the women present had known him since they were young.

"I flew in yesterday," Vince closed the door behind him. "Jenna contacted me about Lee. I wanted to help."

He dug into his pocket and retrieved a silver flash drive. "I did what you asked. Here is all the information that you need. You can give it to his lawyer, and Lee will be out in a heartbeat."

"What did you ask him to get?" Kathy looked between the two.

Jenna just smiled, a triumphant expression on her face. "Paul is underestimating all of us.."

"I have a few friends who are botanists," Vince explained. "I called in a few favors to see whether they could track down any recent sales of aconite seeds in bulk. The sale of the plant itself isn't illegal, but given its toxicity, it could be a red flag if someone buys large quantities. They located the place they think the seeds found in Lee's house may have originated. There's surveillance camera footage that proves he never visited any of the suspected stores."

"So, why don't you just take this to the sheriff now?" Laurel asked anxiously. "He'll release Lee, right?"

Jenna, who was usually the more impulsive one in the group, shook her head. "I can't do that. It has to be done through the proper channels; otherwise evidence can be discarded in court. I'm not going to play around with Lee's freedom. I will meet his lawyer tomorrow morning and hand the evidence to him."

She looked toward Vince. "Thanks for coming through."

Vince grinned. "The least I could do. I haven't seen Lee in years. Makes sense that the first time we cross paths in ten years, he's in jail."

Jenna put the flash drive in her bag and saw Vince stealing glances at Laurel, who was also catching on.

"She's not in town, Vince," Laurel finally sighed.

"Oh, you're asking about Naomi?" Lily's eyes widened. "She's at some conference thing."

Naomi Higbee was Laurel's childhood friend. She was also Vince's ex-fiancée.

"I wasn't asking about her," Vince shoved his hands in his pockets, his ears bright red. "I was just wondering about Nick."

"Really?" Laurel drawled. "Is that so? Since when do you care about my son?"

"I care!" Vince spluttered. "He's a good kid."

"Oh yeah?" Laurel narrowed her eyes at him. "How old is he?"

"Ten?"

"He's six, you moron!" Laurel threw a cushion at him.

Vince caught the cushion, saying in a sulky voice, "You know how kids grow. One minute they're tiny bundles that barely fit in your arms, and the next, they're suddenly taller than you."

"A smarter man would stop talking," Kathy advised, her eyes laughing. "Come on. Sit down. I'll get you a muffin. That'll make you feel better about making that blunder."

"I'm not sitting next to you," Vince muttered at Laurel, who scowled.

"You're supposed to be his godfather."

"You fired me from that position!" Vince complained, choosing a seat far away from Laurel.

"And this is why!" Laurel retorted.

Jenna ignored the two friends' bickering. She had more important things on her mind

Like getting Lee released from jail.

Lee's lawyer, Alexander Millerton, was a gray-haired man with sharp eyes who looked like he came into this world wearing a suit.

Jenna met him at the diner, right after the morning rush, and Lily ushered them into a corner booth to avoid spying eyes and ears.

"How reliable is this?" Mr. Millerton asked, studying the flash drive before him.

Jenna didn't get annoyed that he was questioning her, and she quickly explained her sources.

"We can definitely use this," the lawyer said as he plugged the flash drive into his laptop and went over the contents. "Of course, I'll have to verify the sources."

Jenna waited for him to get done looking over the documents, and then she asked, "How soon do you think Lee can be released?"

"This afternoon," Mr. Millerton said calmly. "Thank you for collecting this data. I had people looking into it, but it was going to take us a few more days. This is very helpful."

Jenna watched him leave a few moments later. She had just stood up when a wave of dizziness overtook her, and she grabbed the edge of the table. Her vision blurred, and she heard Lily shouting her name as she shook her head to clear the sudden cloud of fogginess.

She felt Lily's arms around her, and another customer rushed toward Jenna to help her sit down.

"You okay?" the man asked, his voice horrified. "Should I get a doctor?"

"Give me a second," Jenna gestured with her hand.

The spell of dizziness slowly faded, and she wiped the corner of her mouth, suddenly feeling a wet sensation.

"You're bleeding," Lily said tightly before Jenna could check what it was.

"Don't make a scene, please," Jenna said in a quiet voice, and Lily reached out to grab a few paper napkins from the table and wiped her lips with it.

"You need something?" the man, Riley, asked.

It was one of her ranch hands, Jenna realized.

"Don't tel—" her words drifted off, and she had to force them back. Her family didn't want her hiding anything from them any longer. She let out a long breath. "I'm fine. Just a side effect."

She already knew from the look in Riley's eyes that he would be running straight to Cole to tell him what had happened. She waved him away. "Thanks. Stop worrying. I'm fine."

No matter how hard she had tried, word had leaked out.

It was once Riley left that Lily said, her voice heavy, "I also got myself tested, Jenna. I'm waiting on the results."

Jenna felt her heart clench. It was always overwhelming to see how her friends loved her.

"Thanks."

"Now, now," Lily patted her shoulder, her voice dry. "No need to get so emotional."

Jenna grinned. "Sorry. I'm still not used to people knowing."

"I should kick you in the behind for hiding something like this from me. You're lucky Laurel didn't just murder you."

"My parents already attempted that, thank you very much," Jenna grumbled.

But it wasn't like she didn't understand where they were coming from. She knew she shouldn't have hidden it, but she just hadn't wanted them to see her when her body started deteriorating.

"Has the doctor said anything?" Lily asked.

"Not yet," Jenna shook her head. "It takes some time for the lab results to come back, especially for something like this. And I haven't really called back since Lee was arrested. I've been occupied with that."

When Lily frowned, worry in her eyes, Jenna patted her hand, trying to comfort her. "I know it looks bad, but it's really not right now. This is just a side effect from the treatment I'm undergoing."

Lily looked around before sitting across from her. "Did you hear about what happened to Vicky's family salon?"

Jenna frowned. "No. What happened?"

As Lily began to tell her an odd story, Jenna's eyes widened. "What? Why are they suing out of the blue?"

Lily leaned forward, her eyes gleaming. "So, according to one of the women, Lee approached them and promised to cover their lawyer fees for all the times Vicky botched their hair horribly. But before he did so, apparently the sheriff confronted Vicky about her role in what happened to your home. She was very smug about it, but the sheriff couldn't find the boots in her home despite the fact that he knew she had bought them. And her parents—you know how spoiled she is—defended her and called you nasty names in front of the sheriff. Lee was seething."

Jenna found herself reeling with all this information as her friend continued. "You know how Tom Green, the deputy, comes in here every morning for his coffee and breakfast? So, he told me today that he heard this from his aunt, who heard it from her neighbor that not only are those clients suing the salon, but it's assumed that they'll win. The salon is going to go bankrupt—rightly so, mind you, given how often they provided terrible service. And Lee made that happen because he got angry about what they did to you."

Jenna's heart was pounding. "He did that for me?"

Lily scoffed. "Honey, the man only sees shades of black and white when it comes to you. He made the bank foreclose on the mechanic shop. They couldn't find Dylan's other glove, but the sheriff had proof of a new purchase. And when Lee found out, I don't know what he said to the bank manager, but he scared him enough to demand the family pay its debt. It's insane."

"Dylan's father is a decent man," Jenna muttered. "He shouldn't have to —"

Lily's eyes grew cold. "Dylan's dad is definitely not that nice. Apparently he's been embezzling from his clients. He also told the sheriff that you had it coming and that since you are a woman, you belong in the kitchen, not doing a man's job. He wouldn't dare say any of that to your face."

Jenna fell silent.

"So both of them got rid of the evidence," Jenna murmured.

Lily smiled fiercely. "I'd say this was better than going to jail."

Jenna recalled the calm expression on Lee's face

as he had assured her that he would make things right and that she shouldn't step in.

This level of viciousness was something she had never expected from him.

I wanted to become someone who could stand in front of you and protect you.

Recalling his words, Jenna's cheeks felt hot.

She had greatly underestimated Lee. While she knew he had changed, she hadn't realized how much. This was not the boy she remembered.

"You look happy," Lily murmured.

"I've never had somebody do something like this for me," Jenna said without thinking, and her friend smiled.

"You should see the way he looks at you," Lily told her. "It's like his whole world begins and ends with you. You are a very lucky woman."

I am, Jenna thought to herself.

She had always put on such a tough exterior for the world to see. But Lee, with his calm smiles and vague answers, had chosen the role of her defender, and he had made sure she didn't know.

That touched her more.

He had wanted to protect her pride at the same time.

She took a deep breath. "He never said a word to me." Lily just shot her a look. "Does everyone know?"

Lily shrugged. "It's like an open secret. Nobody's talking about it, but we all know. But what has happened is that the few people who used to badmouth you have stopped. They're fearful of Lee's retaliation. He used to be so quiet and restrained that nobody ever expected him to turn out like this. Mind you, he'd never hurt an innocent business. He's not like that. These people were hurting both their customers and you. They deserved what they got."

Jenna left the diner after a while. As she was walking to her truck, she saw a familiar figure standing in the shade under the oak tree, just out of sight of the main road.

Jenna's eyes widened with surprise at seeing Midge out and about when the elderly woman very rarely left the ranch. She was about to call out to her when she saw someone approaching.

Jenna froze.

It was Paul.

To Jenna's utter shock, Midge reached out and hugged the man. He smiled down at her, and they began talking. She saw Midge getting upset as the conversation continued, and at one point she burst into tears. Paul kept shaking his head and gesturing. He finally wrapped his arms around Midge's slumped shoulders and guided her away.

Jenna stood there, frozen.

Midge had been with the Evans family since she was young. She and Benjamin had grown up together. Why hadn't it occurred to anyone to ask Midge about Paul? She would have known about him.

But seeing how lovingly she treated Paul, doubts began to form in Jenna's head.

She had to tell Lee or the sheriff.

She turned around and lifted her phone. Seeing the lawyer's number pop up on her screen, she was about to answer when she heard the screeching of tires. Jenna was slow to turn around, and she saw a car barreling toward her.

Someone screamed her name from the sidewalk, and Jenna knew that if the car made impact with her, it would crush her against the side of her truck.

Jenna knew that she had seconds to act if she wanted to survive. She jumped out of the way, and she heard a loud crash just as another vehicle whizzed past her, slamming into the car, making it spin and crash against the wall of the diner.

She heard screams, and people began running over. Someone was helping her up, and Jenna's heart was pounding fiercely as she looked toward the damage. The door of the second truck flew open, and Pastor Dean stumbled out, his forehead bleeding. "Is she okay? *Is she okay?!*"

Two people rushed over and helped him stand up, but he was looking around for her. "Is Jenna okay?"

"I'm fine!" Jenna gasped, stumbling over to him and grabbing his arm. "You're bleeding!"

"So are you," Pastor Dean gestured toward her grazed hands and knees. "Who was that?"

Thank you for saving me, Lord, Jenna prayed gratefully.

They looked over at the car, both of them shaken. Three men had gathered around the car that had been aiming toward Jenna, and they were wearing shocked expressions on their faces.

"Well, who is it?" Jenna demanded, but they just shared uneasy glances with each other.

Having been left with no choice, Jenna pushed them aside to see who it was who had tried to kill her. Her lips pressed together into a thin line when she saw an unconscious woman behind the wheel. She had no problem recognizing Vicky.

She was also bleeding from a cut on her head, and Jenna growled, "What are you all waiting for? Get her to the hospital and call the sheriff!"

The people around her stirred into action, and Jenna just stared at the woman who had been about to crush her spine.

VICKY SURVIVED.

She was patched up in the hospital, along with Pastor Dean, who was beaming at everyone who called him a hero, basking in the credit even as he also reminded them God was the one really responsible for saving Jenna's life.

Vicky's family arrived before the sheriff did. Jenna had never truly liked the Torres family. They considered themselves superior to most folks in town, and Jenna blamed them for what Vicky had become.

"You!" Vicky's mother, Susannah, advanced on her. "You did this! Why is my daughter getting arrested? You go and make this right!"

Sharon, who had been standing next to Jenna, stepped forward. "You should talk to the sher—"

Jenna wasn't someone who hid behind people, so she spoke coldly. "Your daughter just tried to murder me in front of a whole lot of witnesses."

"That's not true!" Henry Torres growled, wrapping his arm around his hysterical wife. "My Vicky would never do that. She just lost control of the wheel!"

Jenna shrugged. "That's up to the sheriff to prove."

Vicky's father puffed up his chest, trying to seem intimidating. "I'm telling you, girl. You go in there, and you take back your charges. You've made my daughter's life miserable enough. Vicky's a good child!"

"Are you threatening my daughter, Henry?" came a roar from the end of the hallway, and Jenna's eyes widened as she saw her father charging forward.

Henry froze momentarily, and then he regained his senses. "She's accusing my daughter of trying to kill her!"

"There were witnesses, Dad," Jenna told her father. "People were standing on the sidewalk and saw Vicky parked across the road from the diner. When I left, she drove straight at me."

"They're all lying!" Mrs. Torres half sobbed and half shrieked. "You probably paid all those people to say such things! That man of yours used my Vicky and broke her heart, and now you're trying to send her to jail and ruin her reputation!"

"Hey!" Jenna snapped. "Don't you dare talk about Lee. If you have something to say, you say it to me! Don't act like your daughter is some angel!"

"I've got this, Jenna." Her father pushed her aside gently before growling at the couple. "Your daughter insulted mine in the middle of the diner a few weeks ago! Then she and that ex-boyfriend of hers destroyed her home and flushed her life-saving medicines! Do you think I don't know that? Two men from the farm across the road saw the car. They came forward today. Both your daughter and that Dylan boy were in there. They saw them getting into the car and leaving!"

Jenna went still.

She saw the Torres couple pale before Susannah blurted out, "So what if she did?! It was just a matter between girls! How do I know you haven't paid—"

"Because I interviewed them myself," Sheriff Stiles's voice came from a few feet away. "If all of you don't stop shouting, I'm going to arrest everyone, regardless of who you are."

Everyone fell silent, and Jenna squeezed her father's wrist as he glowered at Henry.

"Vicky confessed," Sheriff Stiles said. "She confessed to everything. For now, I'm taking her in. The rest depends on the Miles family. If they don't want to press charges, we can proceed from there. But this case will go to court because this is the second time that your daughter has attempted to harm Jenna."

Jenna didn't feel sorry for the Torres couple when they went pale at the sheriff's words.

"You take back the charges!" Mrs. Torres suddenly shrieked, trying to dart toward Jenna. "You take them back! She didn't do anything wrong! You made her do this! I'll kill you!"

The sheriff grabbed Vicky's mother. "Control yourself, Mrs. Torres! I don't want to have to arrest you!"

But Susannah was hysterical. "How are you sure she's not being coerced into seeing all this?! Lee killed his grandfather! What if he's threatening my—"

Jenna cut in, "I warn you not to say another word about Lee. If you want to go down this path, I'll throw a defamation suit at you. After everything that has happened, do you really think you can afford to offend Lee Evans? Or me? Your daughter just tried to kill me." She began to roll up her sleeves with her bandaged hands. "I don't even care if I go to jail for this."

It was Pastor Dean who grabbed her from the middle. "All right now. We've had enough violence for today."

"Let me go!" Jenna snarled. "I'm going to teach this woman a thing or two about respect!"

Sheriff Stiles sighed. "Cool it, Jenna. Otherwise I'll throw you in a cell to cool your heels."

Jenna shut up, scowling at the frightened-looking woman, who took a few steps back.

"Mr. and Mrs. Torres, I need you to speak with you privately."

Jenna watched the reluctant couple leave with the sheriff into Vicky's room, and she only relaxed when the door closed behind them.

Her father sighed heavily before turning to face her. "You're not hurt, right?"

Jenna shook her head. "Dean saved me in time."

"*Pastor* Dean."

Jenna ignored her friend's comment. "Thanks for that."

The pastor looked worried. "I'm just glad you're okay."

Jenna heard approaching footsteps, and when she looked over, she saw a familiar figure approaching her.

"Lee?" she managed to stammer before Lee had her in his arms, his hold tight.

"Are you okay?" he demanded fiercely.

Jenna was too stunned to do anything but stare at him.

It was Pastor Dean who asked in a scandalized voice, "Did you break out of jail?"

"I got released," Lee said. "My own lawyer turned up evidence the planted financial documents were fakes. And thanks to the evidence that Jenna's friend gave my lawyer about the aconite seeds, he got me out. I heard about the accident! How badly are you hurt?"

"I'm fine." Jenna had never been happier to see his handsome face. Without thinking, she flung her arms around his neck. "I'm just glad you're out!"

When Lee froze, Jenna realized what she had just done. She tried to untangle herself from him, but he wasn't having it. He wrapped his arms around her waist, holding her to him.

They stayed like that for a few seconds until her father cleared his throat in a disapproving sound. "I'm still here."

Jenna had to step on Lee's toes to convince him to let her go. She looked at her father. "So, the sheriff really did find witnesses?"

Her father nodded, pulling her to his side and glaring at Lee. "You want my girl; you'd better buy her a ring. None of these public displays of affection. This is my baby girl."

"Dad!" Jenna groaned in mortification.

Her father glared at her. "I don't care what you say. Nobody's good enough for you. It's bad enough he's making you stay at his house."

"As a guest, Dad!" Jenna hissed. "And I just needed a place to stay for a while."

"You have a home!"

"You guys are smothering me!"

"Because you're sick!" Jenna saw her father's expression morph into one of grief. "You need to let us do something to make us feel like we're helping. Come back home, please, honey."

Jenna's heart ached as she saw the anguish in his eyes.

But before she could say anything, it was Lee who said, "She'll move back in today. Jenna was helping me sort out Gramps's things. I didn't want to do it alone."

Her father gave him a weary look. "I understand. But I want my baby home now. We need her around us."

Jenna's heart broke, and she saw the glimpse of understanding and sadness in Lee's eyes. Then he said, "I get it. But I do have a ring. You only have her until I marry her."

"Hey!" Jenna glared at him. "What are you—"

"It had better be a decent ring, and I want you two to date a proper amount of time before you pop the question. And no late-night drives. I was young, too, once. I know all about what happens!" her father warned.

"*Dad!*" Jenna wanted the ground to open up and swallow her whole. When she saw Pastor Dean and Sharon snickering in a corner, she growled at them, "This isn't funny."

"It's funny when it's happening to you," Pastor Dean teased.

Jenna gave him a cold look. "You just wait until somebody comes sniffing around your sister."

The look of horror on her friend's face was satisfying.

"I'm a grown woman," Jenna interjected in the heated discussion going on between her father and Lee. "I'll move back home for a bit, but stop this. I'm not a child, Dad. You can't make the rules for me. And don't go announcing things like you've gotten a ring, Lee. We have not even gone out on a date yet. Marriage is way down the line."

Both men shut up and gave her guilty looks.

Jenna had more to say, but her phone began to ring just then. When she dug it out of her pocket, she saw that it was Dr. Ralph. Hesitant, she answered.

"Hello?"

The doctor's voice sounded strange. "I have some news, Ms. Miles."

Jenna glanced at her father and Lee before asking slowly, "What is it?"

"I think we've found a match."

13
LEE

"I'm a match?"

Lee stared at the doctor, stunned, unable to process the multiple emotions running through him.

"I can save Jenna?"

Dr. Ralph smiled at him. "It's not going to be a fast or easy process, obviously. But, yes. God heard your prayers. You're going to be a living donor for her, and we'll just take a small portion of your liver. You have to know that these procedures don't mean that the problem is fixed. But her life span is going to be expanded, and as long as she keeps receiving treatment, she can live relatively normally."

Lee's heart was pounding in a mixture of excitement and hope. Jenna's hand was cold in his as he held onto it. "So, she'll be fine?"

"Yes," the doctor said cautiously. "But there are certain risks when it comes to you. You need to keep in mind that it's going to have an impact on you, at least temporarily. I want to give you a few pamphlets to go through, and if you have any questions, you can always ask me. If you still want to go ahead with this—"

"I don't need to read anything," Lee shook his head. "When can we do the procedure?"

Dr. Ralph looked hesitant. "I would really suggest that you read—"

"I already told you—"

"He'll read them," Jenna said firmly. "I'll make sure of it."

Dr. Ralph visibly relaxed, and then he said, "Once you sign the agreement, we will begin. The surgery can take place a week after the signing. We need to go through some preparatory procedures."

Once he left the office, Lee turned around to

face Jenna. "I don't care what the pamphlets say. This is happening."

Jenna pressed her lips together. "Lee—You need to understand. There are a lot of health complications that come with being a donor. You should at least be aware of them. Don't just go into something blind—"

Lee felt his anger stir. "I can fix this. I can fix whatever is killing you. What is there to think about?"

Jenna hesitated, and then she said quietly, "Just read them. I know you won't understand, but I just want you to read them, and I still want you to have the option of backing out."

Lee wanted to shake her, but he refrained from doing so for the sake of Jenna's health.

"Fine," he said tersely. "I'll read them. But it'll change nothing."

When Jenna didn't say anything, he tilted her chin up, making her look at him, "It won't change anything. We are still going through with this."

"Just read them," she repeated.

They got into his car, and then she said, "There's something I have to tell you. I saw something just before Vicky tried to kill me."

When Lee studied her, she said, "I saw Midge meet Paul. You should've seen the way they interacted. She was very affectionate toward him."

Lee's face went blank. "Did you hear what they were talking about?"

Jenna shook her head. "They were too far away. But, Lee—Do you want to tell the sheriff?"

Lee shook his head. "I want to talk to my lawyer first."

As they began the drive back to town, Lee said, "I was looking into Paul's life in Chicago. I hired a PI there. Paul is involved with some shady people, and he's in a lot of debt. But when he first arrived in Chicago, he was looking for somebody. He was looking for some girl. He moved around cities for a few years before coming back to Chicago and settling down. He has an alias there, which is why we never found any digital footprint. It was too late when he heard about Gramps's death because Gramps had already begun the transfer of his property to me without me knowing. That's why it was so easy to get everything in my name just weeks after his passing. I think Paul anticipated that the entire ranch would be stuck in a dispute, and it would be easier for him to gain control of it. He didn't think the ranch would be in my name by the time he arrived."

"It still doesn't explain why he's coming after your company and why he's trying to frame you for murder."

"If he can prove that I had something to do with my grandfather's death, he'll get all the property, excluding my company. I don't know why he's looking at my company. It could be simple greed, or he might have more sinister motives. Either way, I should have thought about his connection to Midge."

"What if we just ask her?" Jenna said slowly, but Lee could hear the doubt in her voice.

"We don't know how loyal to him she is," he murmured. "I think it was Midge who put the plant seeds in my house. And if she did it deliberately, under his instructions, and she never said a word after I was arrested, I think we both know where she stands."

It hurt, knowing that she had just watched him get arrested.

Midge had been a huge part of his life growing up. She had been warm and affectionate to him. She had been a mother figure in his life. She had been the one to hug Lee when he was upset and put him to bed when he was sick.

He used to spend hours with her in the kitchen, peeling potatoes and talking to her about how his day went. He would spend his weekends watching her cook and asking her to read him stories.

Lee felt heartsick at knowing she had betrayed him like this.

He didn't want to think about whether Midge had played a role in Gramps's death.

A hand curled around his, and Jenna's voice was firm. "We'll get through this. Whatever comes, we'll face it together. I'll be right with you."

It felt different having somebody right by you, supporting you. In all his years, Lee had never had someone who had stood by him so staunchly. Jenna had begun to soften up around him, just for him, and it made his heart tighten in his chest.

"I love you," he murmured, glancing at her.

When he saw the shock in her eyes, he continued, "You can hit me because I might've said it too soon, but I'm not going to lie to you about my feelings. I loved you back then, and I love you now. I don't care if you don't say it back, and I don't care if you think I'm not being sincere—"

"I can't say it back," Jenna said, a heavy emotion moving through her eyes. "I won't say it back until I know that I will survive. I won't do that to you."

He saw the sheen of tears in her eyes as she turned her head to look out the window, and he squeezed her hand, his voice hoarse. "That means you do, doesn't it?"

When she just shuddered, he let out a breath he didn't know he had been holding. "Fine. Fine, you don't have to say it right now. But I want you to know where I stand. But once the surgery is over and the first words out of your mouth are 'give me water' and not an undying confession of love for me, we're over."

He saw Jenna's shoulders shake from sudden laughter, and he grinned.

She didn't have to say it for him to know how she felt.

He was grateful for her.

Thank you for this second chance, Lord, he whispered. *Now please help me find justice for Gramps.*

He entwined his fingers with Jenna's and lifted their hands, pressing a kiss on the back of hers. "As long as you're next to me, I'll be fine."

He saw her flush from the corner of his eye, but she didn't pull her hand away, and that said a lot.

It was the lawyer who told Lee that surveillance footage had captured Paul buying the aconite seeds in bulk quite a while back, meaning Ben could have been poisoned very slowly and steadily over the course of at least a year.

"Is this enough to get him arrested?" Lee asked.

"For now, yes," Mr. Millerton said. "Even though we're still not sure it was actually aconite that killed Ben, the very act of trying to frame you and/or misdirect the investigation is illegal. Otherwise he technically did nothing wrong in purchasing the aconite. But…I do have some concerns about your housekeeper. I think it's best if you fire her or at least remove her from the ranch until you figure out what her role in this is."

"She lives on the ranch," Lee said heavily. "She's got no children and no family left. I can't just throw her out."

His lawyer studied him, "I understand that you might have emotional ties to this woman, and you might not want to prosecute her. But if her only crime is helping your uncle, that's still a crime. You should remove her from your surroundings, even if it means helping her settle elsewhere."

Lee watched the lawyer leave the diner and then sighed.

He knew that Mr. Millerton had a point, but he couldn't bear to hurt Midge. Even so, he had to do something.

"Everything okay?" Lily came up to him and refilled his empty coffee mug.

Lee pondered the situation before asking, "What do you know about Midge, Lily?"

"Midge?" His friend's brow furrowed. "Same as you, I guess. I would say less than you. Her husband died a decade after the marriage, and then her daughter passed away at age seventeen. She's worked as a housekeeper at your place for as long as I can remember."

"She had a daughter," Lee repeated slowly. "What was her name again?"

"Henrietta, I think," Lily said after some thought. "My dad used to be crazy about her. But then a lot of guys were. Apparently she was beautiful. She had a lot of suitors."

"She must have grown up around my father and uncle." Lee was trying to piece together a narrative that was still too thready.

Lily shrugged. "I would think so."

"Yeah," Lee murmured.

A beautiful girl, two brothers who despised each other's existence…what was to say that this girl was not the object of both their affections?

It could explain a lot about the fallout between the entire family.

But Lee didn't want to make assumptions. He needed to find out the truth. He could either directly confront Midge or ask somebody who knew the entire family.

Which was why Lee made his way to Fairweather Ranch in the middle of the afternoon. He found Glenda Miles at home, and Jenna's mother beamed at him. "Lee, sweetheart, come in. What brings you here?"

Glenda looked weary under her smile, and Lee knew the reason. Her daughter's illness had rocked her world. But she was cheerful as ever.

"Did you come to visit me?" She was clearly joking, but when Lee said yes, she looked surprised.

"Really?"

Lee sat down at the kitchen table at her urging. "I had some questions, which I think you can answer."

He watched her pour him a glass of juice before taking the seat across from him. "Of course. What can I help you with?"

Lee hesitated. "Do you remember Henrietta?"

He saw a strange expression cross Glenda's face. "Why are you asking about Henrietta?"

The shift in her tone strengthened Lee's conviction that he was on the right track. "How close was she to my father and my uncle?"

Glenda's face went blank. "Lee, I don't think you should be asking these questions."

"I wouldn't ask if it wasn't important. Some things have happened that have brought me to this point."

Glenda sighed. "I doubt Henrietta has anything to do with what's going on right now. But I'll answer all your questions. She was my younger sister's best friend. When I married Roland, Henrietta was fifteen. She was close to both your father and Paul. They worshipped the ground she walked on. They hated each other, but they cared about her."

"Was either one of them in love with her?"

Glenda glanced out the window for a long moment before she said, "You have to understand, Lee. Henrietta had a very certain kind of beauty. Men were taken with her at a single glance. She had many suitors. Paul wasn't particularly close to anyone, not even us, so I can't say for sure. But you can't spend that much time around a woman like her and not fall in love with her."

"What about my father?"

Glenda rubbed her temple. "I don't like to talk ill about the dead, but Mark had a kind of reputation in town that had fathers locking away their daughters when he was around. He wasn't just flirtatious; he was utterly charming. He went through girls with a recklessness that was frowned upon. It was only when he met your mother that he settled down. But I will say this: while I don't know how your father felt about Henrietta, I do remember the way she looked at him. I think Henrietta had feelings for him."

"What about Midge?" Lee said thoughtfully. "She would have known."

This time, Jenna's mother stood up and walked over to the window, her expression agitated. "One can never understand what goes on in a mother's heart."

Her answer was too vague, but Lee needed facts. "Did she encourage Henrietta?"

Glenda was silent before she said slowly, "I think she thought that if Henrietta married into the Evans family, she would be loved and happy. But she didn't like your father."

"She preferred Paul," Lee completed her sentence, his voice heavy.

"It's just my opinion," Glenda said carefully. "But I always believed, or at least I felt, that Midge was partial toward Paul because he was Benjamin's son. I think she would have liked Henrietta to marry him."

But Henrietta might not have been interested in Paul, Lee mused silently. She might have been more attracted to the older, adopted Evans.

This was turning out to be a mess.

"How did she die?"

Glenda let out a heavy sigh filled with regret. "It was around the time that your father left. I would say a week after. Details were never shared with anyone. But it was a closed casket. The rumor at the time was that she died of a broken heart because she was in love with Mark, but then at the end of the day, rumors stay rumors. Paul was devastated, but more than that, he was angry. And Midge—"

"She must have been brokenhearted," Lee said quietly.

"It was more than that," Glenda said. "It was a small funeral. Only a handful of people were invited, and there was no wake. It was almost as if Midge wanted no one to talk about it. She didn't cry at the funeral, but Paul stood next to her."

"Did my father return for the funeral?"

"No," Glenda said shortly. "He never came back. Nobody ever saw him again after that until Benjamin brought you home."

When Lee was silent, Glenda said, "Paul left for a few months after the funeral. I think he went to travel to get over his loss. And then he returned, and he stayed until he and your grandfather parted ways."

Lee was beginning to understand why nobody ever talked about both his father and uncle. The tragic story that surrounded them painted his father in an ugly light. But that did not mean that his uncle had any right to try and ruin his life.

Lee let out a heavy sigh. "I know this must have been a difficult walk down memory lane."

Glenda did not say anything for a brief moment, and then she looked at him and said, "You might be Mark's son, but you're nothing like him. Which is why I'm so happy that you and Jenna are together. You got Benjamin's values. He did a fantastic job on you."

She bent down to kiss him on the forehead. "I can see the love you have for my daughter. Just don't ever hurt her."

Her eyes were shining, and Lee nodded, wrapping his arms around her in a brief hug, whispering, "Jenna is the one and only love of my life, Mrs. Miles. Hurting her is out of the question."

When he left, his mind was racing at this new turn of events.

Confronting Midge wasn't something Lee wanted to do, but Paul was arrested the next morning, and while his belongings were searched, a bunch of letters were found.

"They're between Midge and him," Sheriff Stiles told Lee, holding out the sheaf of letters. "He's a smart man. He blacked out parts of the letters in case anyone ever found them. I asked him what the redacted portions contained, but he refused to tell me. The only thing we can do is ask Midge."

The letters dated back years, to around the time that Paul left the house.

Aside from the redacted parts, it sounded like letters between a mother and her son, where Midge asked Paul if he was eating well and if he had found a job and whether he needed her to send him money. His responses were also loving and devoted, and for a moment, as Lee went through the letter, he couldn't find a trace of the greedy-eyed man anywhere in them.

He found himself confused and thrown off. The light he had painted Paul in was changing shades, and he didn't know how to react to it.

"Maybe let me ask her," Lee said quietly. "You know how old she is. She might be overwhelmed with you questioning her."

The sheriff eyed him, his voice careful. "You do know that there's a strong likelihood that it was she who planted the seeds in your room. And evidence is building that it wasn't aconite that killed him, Lee. You should know. That apparently would have killed Ben much faster. So the seeds may very well just have been a distraction from the true cause of his death. And a means of framing you easily."

Lee lowered his eyes to the desk. "I know." He then looked him square in the eye. "But that woman helped raise me. She was kind to me, and she loved me. I owe her this much courtesy."

When he got up, Sheriff Hale asked, his voice grim, "And what if she turns out to have something to do with Benjamin's death?"

Lee flinched, and his back was still to the man when he said, "If her crime involves hurting my grandfather, then I won't step in. But if it's just me, I'll drop the charges." He looked over his shoulder at the sheriff. "That woman was the only mother I knew. I don't think I can turn my back on her so easily."

Saying that, he left.

It was early evening when he called Jenna.

"I'm wrapping up some work at the ranch, and then I'll come by," she said.

"I'm going to talk to Midge," he replied, driving toward the ranch. "The sheriff gave me copies of the letters."

"Wait for me," Jenna said urgently. "Even if you want to do it alone, let me be around the area."

"I'm nearly there," Lee said quietly. "I'll meet you at the main house and tell you how it went."

It took him another half hour to reach the ranch, and when he did, Lee took off on foot in the direction of Midge's cottage.

She didn't live very far off from the main house, and when he arrived, he knocked on the door.

She looked taken aback to see him. "Lee? What are you doing here?"

Lee hesitated. "Can I come in?"

"Of course."

She let him in, and he closed the door behind him softly.

"Do you want something to drink?"

"I don't think that would be a good idea," Lee murmured. He didn't even know where to start the conversation.

"What brings you out here?" Midge asked slowly.

Lee reached into his pocket and brought out the letters, placing them carefully on the kitchen table. "This."

He saw Midge reach for her reading glasses, and his heart ached when he saw her expression change. "W-Where did you get these?"

Her hands were shaking as she dropped the letters onto the table.

"They were found in Paul's belongings after his arrest."

Midge paled. "What? What? Paul was arrested? Why?"

Lee studied her. "Because he tried to frame me for Gramps's death. But you knew he tried to do that, didn't you?"

When Midge didn't say anything, his heart sank. "You planted that large bag of seeds in my belongings, didn't you?"

Midge was silent, and Lee could hear the sound of his breaking heart echoing in his ears.

He moved away from the table toward the elongated couch and sat down on it heavily. "I just don't understand why. What did I do to make you hate me this much?" He looked toward Midge, who was watching him. "Does this have something to do with Henrietta—"

"Don't you dare speak my daughter's name!" Midge's voice shook with anger and grief. "Not you!"

Lee pressed his lips together to hold in the pain. "Why?"

"You—" Midge was shaking. "You're *his* blood! You don't get to speak my daughter's name! Ever!"

"You mean Mark's blood, don't you?" Lee asked quietly. "What did my father do that both you and my uncle are now trying to make me pay for his crimes?"

The woman staring at him with so much rage was not the gentle-natured person who had raised him all those years ago.

She was a stranger.

"Get out," Midge said, her voice unsteady. "Get out of my home! You can't be here!"

Lee stood up, forcing his voice to be stern. "I can't leave until I know what's going on. Did you and Paul conspire to kill Gramps? Is that why you called me to come home? So you could try and frame me for it?"

"I never harmed Benjamin!" Midge cried out. "He was a good man! He was always good to me!"

"Then what about me?!" Lee raised his voice. "What did I do to you that you tried to frame me for his death?"

Midge's hands tightened on the edge of the kitchen table. "You're *his* son. You're that monster's son! He got away—He destroyed my child's life! Why should his child live happily?"

Her face was twisted as she gazed at Lee, hatred in her eyes that he had never seen before.

It was difficult for Lee to keep his composure. "What did my father do?"

"He ruined her!" Midge howled, tears running down her face. "He destroyed her reputation, her honor, just to have a good time. He used her naivety against her, promising her marriage and a future! My Henrietta was just a child who looked up to him and admired him. She didn't know any better! Then he threw her aside once he was done with her, and he left with your mother!"

Lee had suspected something of this nature, but the shock still hit him at the cruelty of the man who had sired him.

"I begged Benjamin," Midge was struggling to stand, crying. "I begged him to convince Mark to save my daughter's honor and marry her, but Mark left. Paul is a good man. He was willing to marry my Henrietta. But she went mad out of grief. I tried to lock her in my house, to try and talk some sense into her, but she ran away. She ran away, and she died in a terrible accident. Her body was—If Paul hadn't brought her back, I wouldn't even have known it was my child. Her face…nothing was left of her. My baby died because your father was a cruel, heartless man who looked at women as playthings!"

Lee felt suffocated in the face of her agony. "He never loved me. You know that. I was half starved when I came here. Why are his sins mine to bear? I loved you as if you were my own."

"I could never love you," Midge shook her head, her hair falling out of its pins. "I can't love you because you are the monster's blood. A snake's child will always be a snake."

His heart was shattering so quickly that he didn't even know how to pick up the pieces. "So, you were okay with sending me to prison for a crime I never committed?" Lee murmured.

When Midge just stared at him in stony silence, he got the answers he needed.

"So, you and Paul were in cahoots the whole time," he said quietly. "Send me to prison and take over my ranch and my company. You were in the house all the time. It wouldn't have been very hard for you to get ahold of Gramps's bank information and give it to Paul to transfer that money. Then he had someone doctor the documents to make it look like I stole that money. You two must have been planning this for a very long time. Do you feel happy now? Did it bring Henrietta back?"

"You shut your mouth!" Midge shrieked. "My daughter—"

"*What about me?!*" Lee roared, suddenly unable to hold in his feelings. "What about my feelings? The man who hurt your daughter is dead! He died! He was a miserable, selfish excuse for a man! But I'm not! You and Gramps raised me to be a good man! You raised me to be a loving person! You taught me to respect women and everyone around me! And all for what? So you could take revenge for your daughter's death? So you could destroy me and feel satisfied that you raised a child and then killed him?!"

He saw Midge's face turn white as a sheet, and he continued, "Because you did raise me! Blood relation or not, I looked at you as a mother! I spent hours every day with you. My childhood was miserable until I met you and Gramps! Now you're telling me that I was just a sacrificial lamb for you to feel better about your daughter's death!"

He saw Midge stagger, and he moved toward the door, his own gait unsteady, "You certainly got your revenge, Midge. Is it satisfying?"

Drawing himself up straight, he looked her square in the eye. "I won't press charges. Unlike you, I know how to forgive. I'm going to cherish the memories I had with you. I won't taint them. I'll give you a week. Find a place for yourself in whichever part of the world you want. I'll pay the money and give you a monthly settlement amount. You will be well taken care of. I'll make sure of it. But I want you gone in a week."

"Lee." He heard her mumble his name.

"I'll have to tell the sheriff, of course. He will definitely investigate you, but I will not be pressing any charges for what you did to me or for stealing from Gramps."

"Wait—"

But Lee had had enough.

He opened the door and left.

His whole body was numb as he kept on walking for what seemed like hours. In the back of his mind, he heard a cry of his name, but it didn't register.

And then a pair of arms wrapped around him from behind. "Lee."

They were in the middle of a field, and Lee felt his cheeks turn wet with tears, but Jenna just held him, allowing him to grieve.

They stood like that for a long time until she finally released him. Coming around, she reached up and wiped his face tenderly. "It was bad, huh?"

Lee stared at her, feeling lost. "She hates me because of what my father did to her daughter. She wanted me to suffer."

The whole story came spilling out.

He saw Jenna's jaw tighten. "She's wrong for doing that."

"I told her to leave within a week. I'll pay her living expenses. I'll do that much for Gramps and for myself. But I never want to see her again."

Jenna sighed. "So you're not pressing charges?"

"She says she had nothing to do with Gramps's death, and I believe her. The sheriff can conduct his own investigation. But whatever she has done to me, I won't be the monster she thinks I am. I won't let her write my narrative for me. I'll forgive her because she suffered in her own way."

"What about Paul?"

Lee shrugged. "I guess he was in love with her, and he hated my father for what he did to Henrietta. Midge was her mother, so I can understand her hatred. But there was no reason for Paul to have the same motivation."

Jenna leaned her forehead against his. "I know it's hard."

"I should have listened to you," Lee mumbled. "I should have gone with you. I keep thinking I can do everything by myself, but I can't. There are some things I need to have you there for."

Jenna hugged his neck. "Well, I'm here now. And I'm not leaving."

Lee lowered his hands to her waist and leaned against her. "I love you. I know you're not ready to say it—"

"I love you, too, Lee," Jenna whispered. "I wouldn't have abandoned my work and raced all the way here if I didn't love you. I don't do that just for anybody."

Lee sighed, breathing in her scent. "I signed the document this morning for the surgery. You'd better be prepared, because as soon as you've recovered, I'm taking you out on our first date."

Jenna snickered. "If this is your way of asking—"

"I'm telling you," Lee said, his own lips curving as some of the pain in his heart lightened. "We had ten years apart. You have had plenty of time to find another man. Now you're stuck with me."

Jenna laughed lightly. "Not the worst scenario."

When Lee kissed her, it was a tender moment, both of them in need of healing, which only the other could provide.

He was now beginning to understand why he was brought back into Jenna's life now. He needed her. Everyone he'd ever called his own had left him, but he still had her and always would.

Thank you, he closed his eyes. *Thank you for bringing me back in time.*

EPILOGUE

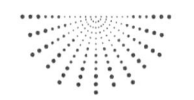

"I think she's awake."

The sounds of people talking were so annoying that Jenna had to resist the urge to throw something at them. But her body felt weak and heavy.

She slowly opened her eyes, and the first face she saw was Lee's.

He was lying on the bed next to her, watching her. His skin was a little pale, but he looked fine.

"You're finally awake," he grinned. "About time. I think Cole was planning to spray you with water."

Jenna looked around to see her family surrounding her, their eyes shining with relief.

"The doctor said the surgery was successful," Her mother beamed at her. "You're so brave, sweetheart. I'm so proud of you."

"You need some water?" Cole grabbed a glass, and Jenna shook her head.

"I can't. I have to confess my undying love for Lee before asking for water. He asked me to."

"Now that's just romantic," Lee said dryly. "Drink your water."

It was difficult to smile, but Jenna managed as she sipped the water through a straw.

She soon passed out again under the effects of morphine. The next two days were a blur as she dozed in and out.

Lee was discharged a few days earlier than her, but he remained with her as she became more lucid.

It was on one of those days, between the visits from various guests, that Jenna finally asked. "So what's going on with your case?"

"The judge threw out Paul's claims of Gramps being mentally unsound. I don't think that my uncle has the second will in hand, or he would have used it. But he's pressing for an appeal, so we don't know."

"I see," Jenna watched him play with her fingers.

"Midge posted bail for him, and he's out. The sheriff got a confession from both of them that he gave her the seeds to put in my bag, and Midge gave Paul the bank details to transfer the money to another account. It was an offshore account, so they couldn't track it. But Sharon said that while the seeds were poisonous, they weren't used on Gramps. It was just an attempt to go after me and frame me. So...still no idea what really killed him."

"Oh." Jenna saw sadness in his eyes. "What about Midge?"

Lee's fingers paused, and he shrugged. "According to your mother, she came to see me after my surgery. She sat with me throughout the time I was unconscious, but when I came to, she left. She's choosing to leave town. I am contacting her through my lawyer, and I told him to suggest Florida. It's a good place for people her age. It will be easier for her to spend the rest of the years she has in a place like that. I've already looked up some good condos. She always wanted to live next to a beach. She might be happy there."

"She came to see you," Jenna murmured. "I guess she didn't completely hate you like she thought."

Lee didn't say anything, and she touched his hand, squeezing it. "I know it hurts. It won't stop hurting, but I promise it'll get easier. Maybe after a few years, she might reach out to you."

Lee was silent, and Jenna could see the physical pain surrounding him.

"Can you give me a hug?" she asked.

That got Lee's attention. "What?"

She smiled at him. "I want to hug you because you're hurting, but I can't move."

"Did the surgery affect your personality at some point?" he asked, and Jenna flicked his finger, making him wince.

"How are you half drugged and still mean?" he complained.

She smiled at him. "It's an art."

He kissed her hand. "I can't bend that much. I can only sit or lie down, so you'll have to settle for this."

Jenna didn't mind. She believed that Midge would, at some point, realize the error of her actions and reach out to him. It would be up to Lee then whether he would forgive her or not.

"Vicky's trial is next month," Lee told her. "The sheriff conducted interviews of people who know her and her friends. As ridiculous as this sounds, she was just jealous of you. She hated how you were so easily accepted by everyone. It still doesn't make sense to me, but then you can never truly understand somebody's motives at times. Dylan is easier to understand. He already resented you for being his boss, and Vicky fed him some sob story about how you mistreated her, and he still had a thing for her, so he went along with her plan."

"So, brawn without brains," Jenna said, disgusted. "Well, hopefully they just get a few years, enough to knock some sense into them."

"Both sets of parents reached out to me to drop the cases, and I refused," Lee said with great satisfaction.

Jenna grinned. "I shouldn't feel attracted to you because you're being petty, but I love it."

Lee grinned. "It's not pettiness. They wronged their customers, too, and had for a long time. It's well-deserved justice." He looked at her, his smile fading. "I do hope they come out of this as better humans."

Jenna made a sound of agreement. "So, what's going to happen with Paul then?"

"I don't think he's going anywhere," Lee said thoughtfully. "I still don't understand his motives, but he's here to stay, apparently. The sheriff prefers it that way because he thinks that Paul had something to do with Gramps dying even if we don't know what yet."

Jenna sighed and looked up at the ceiling. "I know it's only been a few months, but it feels like a whole year. I never thought you'd come back. I never thought I'd survive."

Lee was quiet for a moment and then wrapped her braid around his hand. "Well, God works in mysterious ways. All those years away from you, I never once found myself looking at any woman. I kept comparing them all to you. And when I came back, I just wanted you to look at me."

"Well, I did," Jenna smiled. "Thank heaven for that. Stole your liver too."

When Lee laughed, she told herself that she'd make sure that smile always remained on his face. And as she grinned at him, a silent prayer left her heart to preserve their happiness so that she could heal both his heart and her own.

The fight for the ranch was far from over. Lee still had to figure out what his uncle's intentions were and who was really behind his grandfather's death. There were still a lot of unanswered questions. But as Jenna held his hand, she knew whatever came at them, they would figure it out together.

"Are you sure you want to go about this in this manner?"

"I know what I'm doing."

The motel room was dimly lit as the two men had a hushed conversation.

The older one, wearing a tense expression, strode over to the window, peering outside. "Did anybody see you when you came in?"

"No." The younger one gestured to his clothes. "Nobody ever looks at a repairman."

"Midge is leaving," Paul said. "I tried to convince her to stay, but she has regrets over her part in this. Lee got to her."

"I'm not surprised," his visitor sneered. "Old woman like her, I doubt she would have the stomach for this."

Paul's hands curled into fists by his side, but he didn't say anything. Finally, he asked, "Well, what's the next step now?"

The younger man stood up, putting on his cap, his voice vicious even as he smiled. "The game's just started."

TO CONTINUE ENJOYING BILLIONAIRE COWBOYS Second Chance Romance at Sunset Ridge **Go to**

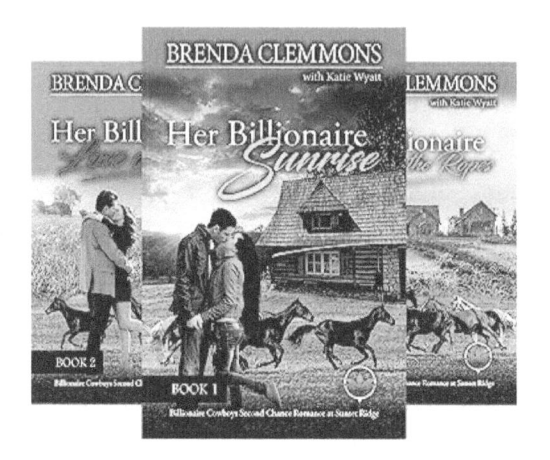

Thank you so much for reading our book. We sincerely hope you enjoyed every bit reading it. We had fun creating it and will surely create more.

SNEAK PEEK! BOOK 2

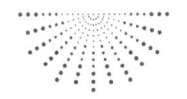

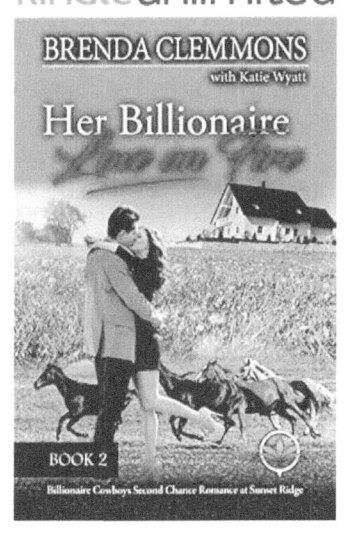

Her Billionaire Love on Fire: A Contemporary Billionaire Romance Novel (Billionaire Cowboys

Second Chance Romance at Sunset Ridge Book 2)

"Oh crap!" Irene gasped out, swerving the car to avoid the oncoming one.

Both her hands were clenching the wheel, her body tense as she diverted the rental to the side of the road.

"How do I park? How do I park?" she muttered to herself, her voice strained as she looked down at the gears to figure it out. Finally she saw the P for Park, and she brought the car to a stuttering halt.

Her heart was pounding, her hands shaking as she finally removed her foot from the brake.

She let out a shaky laugh. "Not bad for a first-time driver."

More cars whizzed by her, and she took a deep breath before looking in the mirror. With electric blue eyes, delicate features, pale skin, and a beauty mark at the corner of her lip, dying her hair hadn't done much to disguise her.

"My name is Irene Lopez." She stared at herself. "My name is Irene Lopez."

It was starting to sound almost natural at this point. She leaned over and picked up her driver's license, which looked a little faded around the edges. Despite how risky this whole situation was, she had to admire the thoroughness of the guy who had created the license for her. Her ID card also looked like it had been reissued a few months ago.

Irene found her eyes going to the rear-view mirror, the fear of being followed still thrumming in her veins. However, there was no one there.

Her heart in her throat, she swallowed, mumbling, "It's fine. You're safe."

Checking her watch, she realized that if she didn't start moving now, she'd be late for the meeting with her new employer. It was just an informal meeting at this stage, and then she had to sign the contract.

Lowering her head, she looked for the ignition keys and turned them. When the car made a spluttering noise, she nearly jumped out of her skin.

A nervous laugh left her lips. "If you keep jumping at every sound, you're going to lose your mind."

Talking to herself had become a habit now.

She turned the key again.

The strange sound came again, worrying her.

She didn't know much about cars, but she knew that this was a bad sign. Something flickered behind the wheel, and when she looked up, her heart sank.

The check engine light was on.

A prayer on her lips, Irene tried the keys again. However, no luck,

Without the heater, the cold was beginning to seep inside the car, and Irene began to shiver.

Reaching for her phone, she tried the number for the rental company in Rock Springs, but there was no response. Muttering under her breath, she tried to remain calm, but it was getting more and more difficult.

This job was her last chance.

Her last chance to shed her past and start anew.

She had spent every penny she had to create false ID documents, and then she had prayed. And her prayers had been answered.

Her heart was beating loudly, and she could feel the oncoming panic attack. Tightening her hands on the wheel, furious tears in her eyes, Irene tried the breathing exercises that her therapist had recommended.

But with her elevating panic and the fear of losing the only job she had managed to partially secure, the breathing exercises were pointless.

"Help me, please," she prayed aloud, her voice unsteady. "This is all I have. Please, I came here, trusting You."

Her trembling hand went to the key, and she twisted it.

It was the same spluttering sound and then nothing.

She let out a quiet tone of distress.

Maybe a tow truck would—

The thought wasn't even barely formed as she reached for her phone. However, in her panic, the battered old flip phone that she had bought second-hand to save herself some money knocked into the dashboard and snapped in two.

Horror filled her. "Oh no." She unbuckled her seat belt, leaning down to pick up the two pieces, muttering under her breath, "No, no, no. This is not happening!"

She tried turning it on, but the old phone was gone.

Her breaths were getting short, and suddenly the car felt too compact, too boxed in. *She was suffocating.*

Despite the icy winds blowing outside, Irene threw open the door, stumbling outside, drawing in loud, gasping breaths, overwhelmed by the severe claustrophobia. For a moment, it sent her back to a dark moment in her past, and she felt she was back in that box, scraping at the walls, hitting it, that stale air—

Black spots began appearing in front of her eyes as she tried to struggle past it.

"You need to breathe and empty your mind," her therapist had told her. *"Affirm everything positive that has happened within the past twenty-four hours."*

But right now, Irene couldn't even think of one positive thing.

Not since getting off the plane in Rock Springs and renting a car from the smarmy-looking person at the rental shop who had looked her up and down and just sneered at her drab clothes, plus the car breaking down.

These past twenty-four hours had been nothing short of hellish.

However, the slap of cold air helped, and Irene sank to the ground, her back against the car as she practiced the breathing exercises. It took her a good few minutes to calm down and begin to think about the situation rationally.

She couldn't stay here in the middle of nowhere like this. The nearest town was an hour away by car and a couple of hours if she decided to make the trek by foot. *Maybe if she hitched a ride?*

However, there were no more cars passing by.

Or at least she couldn't hear any.

Sighing, she pulled her knees to her chest and rested her forehead on them.

It was very cold, and the fact that she had left the car door open just meant that the car was just as frigid.

She hadn't slept for two days.

Her whole body ached.

Her phone was broken.

Her car didn't work.

She must have been lost in her miserable thoughts because she didn't hear someone approaching until two heavy brown leather boots planted themselves in front of her. Blinking, she looked up to be met by a pair of light green eyes.

The man was wearing a bulky black jacket, a beanie covering his hair, and there was a charming air about him. Perhaps it was the lopsided smile or the humorous twinkle in his eyes.

"Odd place to be taking a nap," the man commented, and Irene heard a hint of laughter in his voice, which she didn't quite appreciate.

"My car broke down," she replied slowly, as if

her brain was still processing the presence of another human being next to her.

"Tow truck?"

"My phone also broke." She held out the two pieces of the flip phone, which had him raising a brow.

"Whoa. I haven't seen one of these in ages!" He looked delighted as he took the pieces from her hand, examining them. "I used to have one of these when I was in high—"

His voice trailed off as he remembered the situation, and he gave her a sheepish look. "You okay? I can take a look at your car."

Relief filled her, and she whispered a silent prayer of thanks.

"T-Thank you."

He held out a hand to her and she stared at it, confused for a moment. He let out a chuckle and grabbed her hand, pulling her to her feet before he frowned. "Your hands are like ice. How long have you been out here?" He looked toward the car. "You would have been better off staying in the car."

He didn't really wait around for a response, making his way around the car and popping the hood. A few tense moments later, he let out a long whistle. "Well, I'll be."

The hood slammed back down with a large bang that made Irene jump. He gave her a strange look before saying, "The engine is fried. Look, I don't mean to be rude, but what were you thinking, driving this piece of scrap metal all the way—"

"I rented it," Irene said reluctantly. "The guy at the rental place swore I wouldn't have problems, and I don't know much about cars, so I thought…"

Her words trailed off, and by the look in the man's eyes, he knew something. "Let me guess. You went to Rover Rentals? The one right next to the airport?"

Irene nodded.

He shook his head in disgust. "They do this all the time. I can call you a tow truck, but the rental company is going to charge you for the 'damages.'"

Irene's heart sank. "How much money are we talking?"

The man shrugged, shoving his hands into his jacket pockets. "Anywhere between two to three thousand. They pull these kinds of stunts all the time with unsuspecting tourists."

Irene's mouth turned dry. "I don't—I don't have that kind of money. I have twenty dollars in total. I don't have that kind of money."

Her knees felt weak, and she nearly stumbled to the ground at the idea of that kind of money. She wasn't lying. All the money she had gotten in the settlement had gone into creating her new identity. She had nothing more than twenty dollars on her.

The man's eyes widened, and he hurried over to her, his voice kind. "Hey, no. Don't worry about it. Like I said, they do this all the time. I'll deal with them. Hey—"

Irene was beginning to feel nauseous at this point, and fear crept up on her at the idea of being so vulnerable around a stranger. But then, out of nowhere, the man was patting her on her back, lowering her to the car seat, ordering, "Breathe. In and out. Slow, deep breaths."

She found herself obeying, and to her surprise, his steady voice and calm demeanor actually helped.

When she lifted her gaze, he was crouching next to her. "Better?"

Irene nodded, flushing with shame, mumbling, "Sorry."

"It's okay." The man gave her a smile. "We all have our fair share of bad days."

When she didn't say anything, he grinned at her. "Come on. I'll give you a ride into town."

Irene felt uncomfortable. "But I'm heading to Sunset Ridge—"

"Clearly," the man replied, his voice filled with laughter. "This road leads straight to Sunset Ridge. You passed the turns for the other neighboring town way back, so I assume you were heading the same way I am. Come on."

Irene hesitated. Getting into a car with a stranger wasn't exactly safe.

Fortunately, the man misunderstood her reluctance for concern about the rental. "Don't worry about the car. I'll call a tow truck. I'll deal with the rental company myself. Bunch of no-good con artists."

Irene didn't have much of a choice at this point.

She looked over at the car parked behind hers and saw that it was a hefty-looking jeep.

"Do you think I can bring my suitcase?"

"Of course."

Irene wasn't used to kind and helpful men, and she felt unsure of how to react when he carried her suitcase to his car and then checked her car to make sure it was locked. The man even held the passenger side door of his car open for her.

Once in the car, the warmth of the heater began to thaw her out, and she felt the exhaustion of the past month creep up on her. It was getting difficult to keep her eyes open.

She could hear the man saying something, but her eyes were already fluttering shut.

As she drifted off, a vague thought moved in her head.

She hadn't even asked for his name.

She was in a car.

That was the first thought that hit Irene when she woke up, suddenly alert.

She was in a car, *and it was warm.*

Irene had taught herself to become a light sleeper over the past few years. And when she awoke, it was always with a sharp alertness.

Her eyes flew open, and before she could even turn her head, she heard a familiar voice say, "You must have been very tired."

Irene flushed at the man's amused tone. "S-Sorry."

"Not a problem." He grinned at her, his eyes dancing in merriment. "I just parked here a few minutes ago."

"Here…" Irene looked around and realized that they were in a large parking space. In front of them was a one-floor building with large windows. It looked like a diner, and she saw people conversing and eating.

It looked pleasant, and just like that, Irene's stomach grumbled. *Loudly.*

Her companion let out a bark of laughter. "Seems I picked the right spot to stop. Come on. Let's get something to eat. I have to call the tow truck. My phone battery ran out."

Irene checked her watch, belatedly remembering her meeting, and her heart sank. "I've got five minutes."

"To do what?" The man gave her a curious look.

"I have a meeting with Dorian Earl, the principal of Sunset Ridge High School," Irene said frantically. "It's for my—"

"Dorian?" The man laughed. "You mean *that* Dorian?"

He pointed toward a round, gray-haired woman who was standing in front of the restaurant with three men, engaged in conversation.

Irene felt dismayed. "My meeting was at the high school. Did she already lea—"

However, her sentence was barely finished when the man lowered his window and started waving his hand and calling out, "Hey, Dorian! Dorian! Over here! I've got your new interviewee here!"

Irene found her eyes widening as the principal of the school she was set to start working at turned her way.

And when the principal waved back, calling, "I'll be right there!" Irene found herself reeling with bewilderment.

Had she just been panicking for no reason this whole time?

"Cole, you're late!"

Irene saw a plump woman with platinum blonde hair and pink highlights call from behind the counter. She was a pretty thing with a sharp smile, light blue eyes, and a dimple in her right cheek as she grinned at something one of the customers sitting at the counter said. However, her attention was quickly diverted toward Irene's companion.

Cole beamed down at Irene. "Well, now you know my name."

He seemed to be a friendly person, and a popular one, Irene noted moments later as she saw people waving and greeting him. Irene had done her research on the town of Sunset Ridge. With a population of around ten thousand people, it would be easy to get lost in, which was the goal.

However, as she looked at Cole, catching up with nearly everybody in the diner, a hint of worry pierced her.

She had been banking on the fact that she could become a nobody here, a faceless individual in a random town. *Clearly, she hadn't done her research well enough.*

From the way she was being eyed with blatant curiosity, Irene knew that she was an outsider, and word would definitely spread. She wished she had a baseball cap to cover her face with, but she had a feeling that the woman approaching them might not appreciate it.

Dorian Earl had a grandmotherly look to her from a distance, but as she approached, Irene saw a predatory look in her eyes. The woman honed in on Cole as her target and beamed at the man. "When exactly are you taking my Rachel out again, Cole?"

Cole's laugh was a loud, pleasant sound, filling the room. "I barely get time to myself these days, what with Jenna recovering. I haven't gone on a date in ages."

Dorian grabbed his arm in what looked like a friendly manner, but Irene wasn't so sure. "Well, why don't you take some time out? My Rachel will ease your mind."

Irene saw Cole exchange an amused glance with the woman behind the counter as a few of the men leered at Dorian's words.

Irene felt her stomach turn.

The picture before her reminded her of someone, and she repressed the memory.

This was not the time or the place.

The woman behind the counter called out, wiping her hands on a cloth, "Who's your guest, Cole?"

Cole put his hand on her shoulder, and Irene flinched without thinking. However, when she looked at him, he hadn't caught it.

"I seem to have an eye for beautiful women in distress," he said jovially. "This is—"

He blinked, as if suddenly realizing he hadn't asked her name.

"Irene," she said quietly, and he gave her a grateful look before announcing,

"Irene. Where's Jimmy? I need him to tow a car back to the city. Lily, give him a call, will ya?"

The woman behind the bar, Lily, nodded and reached for the phone on the wall. As that was happening, Cole looked at Dorian. "It seems Irene was on her way to have a meeting with you. She had car troubles, so I gave her a ride."

Irene glanced at Dorian, about to introduce herself when she saw irritation in the woman's eyes. She had already met the woman on a video call for her interview, and she had expected the principal to greet her cordially at least.

Dorian frowned. "I'm very particular on timing—"

"Come on, Dorian." Cole put his hand on Irene's shoulder, his tone friendly. "She had a genuine emergency. Anybody's car can break down."

However, Irene could see the dislike harden within the eyes of the gray-haired woman looking at her, and she tried to speak up. "I'm really sorry, Mrs. Earl. I wasn't expecting car trouble—"

"How can I trust somebody with my students when they can't even plan in advance?"

Her words were curt, and Irene could see through the flimsy excuse.

Her heart sank when she realized that the woman had decided to form a strong dislike of her at their first in-person meeting for some reason. However, it seemed that Cole had come to the same conclusion, and this time there was an edge to his voice. "I never took you to be this unreasonable, Dorian."

His words apparently had an impact because Irene saw the woman get flustered. "You're misunderstanding, Cole. I just meant that I have high standards for my teachers. Ms. Lopez was supposed to be at my office for an informal meeting. The school board has already hired her. But I expected punctuality for the first time we met."

From the tone of her voice, Irene had a strong inkling that the principal wasn't very happy that the school board had hired her. On the video call, Mrs. Earl had sounded pleasant, and she had been particularly friendly toward Irene, even offering her the upper portion of her house to stay. She had made it seem like she would simply deduct the rent from Irene's salary.

But now, for some reason, Dorian had decided to dislike her at first sight.

Cole cleared a table for them, and Irene introduced herself to the older woman again. "We talked two weeks ago on the phone. You said you would like to meet me in person before signing the contrac—"

"I may look old, but my memory is still intact." Dorian's voice was sharp, and despite her best efforts, Irene couldn't stop herself from recoiling. She caught Cole's eyes and stiffened. Deciding to change tactics, she took a thin file from her purse.

"These are all the documents I couldn't send to you before. I worked for four years as a high school teacher, and I covered both English and mathematics and—"

"Why is there a five-year gap here?" Dorian asked, after glancing at the paperwork briefly. "It wasn't mentioned in your résumé."

It was.

Irene turned still, and her voice got quiet. "I was ill. I mentioned that before."

The lie came to her easily.

"What was wrong with you?"

The way Dorian was speaking to her, in this crass, rude manner, made Irene sink lower into her seat, familiar feelings of shame and self-doubt creeping up.

"It was—"

Irene paused, remembering the loud sirens, her limp body on the gurney, her fingers all but broken. Screaming.

So much screaming.

"It was a minor illness," she said, proud of how calm she sounded despite the storm raging inside.

"A minor illness that made you unable to work for five years?" Dorian gave her a disbelieving look. "You expect me to believe that?"

Irene's hands began to shake, and she put them in her lap. "I—I would prefer not to talk about it. It was personal. But I'm recovered now, and—"

It was clear that the high school principal could tell that Irene was uncomfortable with this topic, which was why Irene didn't understand why the woman insisted on pursuing this line of questioning.

"I have never heard of someone being bedridden for five years over a minor illness. It's best you come clean to me now."

That was the moment that Cole slid into the booth next to Irene. "It doesn't seem like you find my Irene good enough for the job, Dorian."

MY Irene?

Irene flushed, wanting to rebuke him but not knowing how.

"Since you don't want her, and she seems to be," he glanced at the certificates, "pretty qualified, how about she comes to work for me?"

Irene wondered if she was hearing things, and she saw the way Dorian's face tightened. However, she hesitantly asked, "D-Do you have a school?"

"Not exactly," Cole grinned at her. "But you seem smart, and I'm sure if somebody can teach math to teenagers, then they must have no problem handling some basic computer math. I'm in the market for an office assistant, and you have a trustworthy look about you, Ir—"

"She has the job!" Dorian said abruptly, her voice tight. "The school board and I have already hired her. We just wanted to get to know her better before we signed the contract."

Cole raised a brow. "Really? I got the impression that you were—"

"I need to be thorough." Dorian's smile was stiff. "You know how it is."

Relief filled Irene. "So can we sign the contract then?"

She had no hopes for a salary negotiation, what with Mrs. Earl's attitude.

Dorian nodded, but she didn't look very pleased.

However, that brought up the next question. "Mrs. Earl, you mentioned that you have an extra room—"

"Unfortunately, that's no longer available," Dorian said nastily.

Irene kept her composure even as she felt her mouth turn dry. She had only booked one night in the motel, and she had nowhere to stay after that. And she wouldn't get her salary until the next month.

Maybe she could try a homeless shelter in the town. They would allow her to stay for a month.

As she looked at Dorian, she had to wonder how people could be so hateful for no reason. Dorian knew her situation, or at least that she had no money and nowhere to stay. From the look in the woman's eyes, Irene knew that she expected her to beg.

This time, the bitterness was replaced by a hot flush of anger.

There was another reason, aside from the prominent one, that she had chosen to assume a new identity. She wanted to be stronger. She didn't want people to use her and hurt her anymore. She didn't want to grovel and beg in front of anyone anymore.

So, for the first time since she had started this whole journey, she smiled at Dorian and she meant it.

"It's all right. I'll make other arrangements."

She saw a flash of irritation in the woman's eyes, and it pleased her.

She had stood her ground, and while her new employer might not like it, it gave Irene a boost of confidence. *She'd sleep in a hundred homeless shelters before she bowed her head in front of anyone again!*

It was Cole's voice that jolted her out of her thoughts. "Well, now that that's done and dusted, why don't we have a meal to celebrate your new job, Irene?"

Irene looked at his beaming face, and she didn't quite know what to make of this man. She mentally counted the money in her wallet down to the last cent. Even if she wanted to thank Cole for everything he had done for her, there was no way she could buy him a thank-you meal.

For now, she was grateful to God that she at least had a place to sleep tonight.

"I would like to thank you for everything you've done." Her smile was unsteady. She didn't trust men, and even a kind gesture made her wary. But she couldn't deny that Cole had helped her, and she wasn't so ungrateful as to not acknowledge it. "But perhaps another time. I'm very tired today."

His smile was gentle. "Of course. Do you have a place to stay tonight? I can drive you there."

Once again, Irene felt burdened by his kindness. "I have a room at the motel. If you give me my suitcase, I can walk."

"I'll drive—"

But Irene shook her head, her voice a little firmer this time. "Thank you, but you've done enough. Have a good day, Mrs. Earl."

She didn't let Cole walk her or drive her, only accepting his instructions on where the motel was before she walked the fifteen minutes to the Sunset Ridge Motel.

Her feet were aching by the time she reached the place, her breath short, tears of exhaustion in her eyes. The man at the reception took one look at her and sped up the entire process of check-in, allowing her to be in her room within minutes.

Stomach grumbling, Irene staggered toward the bed. She didn't mind being hungry.

At least she was free.

Ignoring her desire to sleep, she stripped off her clothes and took a long hot shower that gave her some strength back. Clad in a surprisingly soft robe that the motel had in the bathroom, she eyed the bed, but she had more important things to do first.

She opened her laptop, and her fingers hesitated on the keypad before she logged into her old email. As soon as she did, she saw a bunch of new emails. All of them from the same person.

The person she was running from.

Against her better judgment, she opened and read each email, and with every minute that passed by, fear was thick on her tongue, her heart beating so loudly she was sure the people in the next room could hear.

At some point, she slammed the laptop shut, trembling at the promised violence in the messages.

Stumbling to her feet, she made her way to the bathroom, where she splashed water on her face to jolt herself out of her terror-stricken state.

Her eyes were wild when she met her gaze in the mirror.

However, underneath the fear was a new determination.

"My name is Irene Lopez, and I am not a victim."

Not anymore.

To continue enjoying Billionaire Cowboys Second Chance Romance at Sunset Ridge **Go to**

DID YOU KNOW?

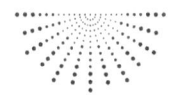

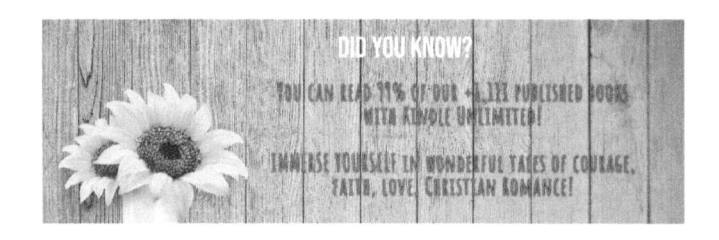

> **DID YOU KNOW?**
> YOU CAN READ 99% OF OUR +1,111 PUBLISHED BOOKS WITH KINDLE UNLIMITED!
>
> IMMERSE YOURSELF IN WONDERFUL TALES OF COURAGE, FAITH, LOVE, CHRISTIAN ROMANCE!

ROYCE CARDIFF PUBLISHING HOUSE, WE specialize in delivering heartwarming tales filled with love, hope, and positivity—stories that will leave you smiling long after you turn the last page.

With over **1,111 published books**, including **value-packed box sets**, there's always something new and exciting for you to discover. Whether you're looking for a cozy afternoon read or an uplifting series to binge, our stories are designed to entertain, inspire, and touch your heart.

And here's the best part: If you're a Kindle Unlimited subscriber, you can enjoy **99% of our books absolutely FREE**!

That means nearly all of our titles are ready for you to explore at no extra cost, making it easier than ever to find your next favorite love story.

Start your next reading adventure today—**where clean**, heartfelt romance meets endless inspiration. Dive into our library, and let us remind you why falling in love (with a great book) is one of life's sweetest pleasures!

Clean Contemporary Christian Western Romance
Click Here

Clean Historical Mail Order Bride Box Set Complete Series Click Here

DISCOVER THE BESTSELLERS BY BRENDA & KATIE

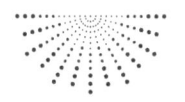

From the timeless to the newest chart-topping releases, our curated collection of **bestsellers all year round** ensures you never miss a literary masterpiece. These books have captured the hearts of readers worldwide, and we're confident they will captivate you too.

Top 10 Bestsellers of the Year

Clean Contemporary **Christian** *Western Romance.*

. . .

BILLIONAIRE COPPER CANYON COWBOY Romance series

Snowy Mountain Complete Series Books 1 - 9

Cartwright Wilderness Outfitters Complete Series

Seven Billionaire Cowboy Brothers at Christmas Wilmont Lodge Collection 1

Billionaire Cowboys Second Chance Romance at Sunset Ridge (6 books series)

The Billionaire Island Secret Romance Collection 1 Books 1 - 3

Charlie Delta Rescue Complete Series

A Home for Christmas Billionaire Cowboys (4 books series)

Seven Billionaire Cowboy Brothers at Christmas Wilmont Lodge Collection 2 Books 5 - 7

Recommended Reads others books Stories New from our library of love

Coming Home to Ryder's Ridge Mountain (6 books series)

We love hearing from you

Once you've read a book, we'd be grateful if you could leave a review. Your feedback not only helps us improve but also guides other readers in finding their next favorite story.

ABOUT THE AUTHORS

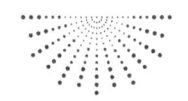

ARIZONA NATIVE BRENDA CLEMMONS HAS THE Wild West in her blood. While her ancestors, from a gold miner granddaddy to a small-town sheriff, helped lay the foundations of the western half of our country, Brenda's books take place in the modern day. No matter the century, the West remains an awe-inspiring, often dangerous place.

Brenda's heroes and heroines face all the challenges of the twenty-first century, set against a rugged backdrop that only adds to the excitement. Whether it's an intrepid helicopter search and rescue crew, big-hearted billionaire cowboys, or dedicated doctors who look after the health of citizens of small towns edged by ranches, at the core of each of Brenda's page-turning books is true love and steadfast faith.

KATIE WYATT IS 25% AMERICAN SIOUX Indian. Born and raised in Arizona, she has traveled and camped extensively through California, Arizona, Nevada, Mexico, and New Mexico. Looking at the incredible night sky and the giant Saguaro cacti, she has dreamed of what it would be like to live in the early pioneer times.

Spending time with a relative of the great Wyatt Earp, also named Wyatt Earp, Katie was mesmerized and inspired by the stories he told of bygone times. This historical interest in the old West became the inspiration for her Western romance novels.

Her books are a mixture of actual historical facts and events mixed with action and humor, challenges and adventures. The characters in Katie's clean romance novels draw from her own experiences and are so real that they almost jump off the pages. You feel like you're walking beside them through all the ups and downs of their lives. As the stories unfold, you'll find yourself both laughing and crying. The endings will never fail to leave you feeling warm inside.

Made in United States
Cleveland, OH
16 April 2025